"Kimberley Woodhouse has ⸺
Wars of nineteenth-century ⸺
ture and romance, science and suspense in spades. A fresh
setting and fascinating premise make this series sing!"

Laura Frantz, Christy Award-winning author
of *The Lacemaker*

"A powerful blend of faith and science in a riveting novel!
Woodhouse tackles a topic few other fiction writers have ex-
plored in her novel *Set in Stone* and peels back the layers with
her superb research and masterful storytelling. I adored going
on digs with a passionate, intelligent heroine and watching a
partnership form with an unlikely hero. I found myself both
savoring the story and eager to flip through the pages to find
out what would happen—a thrilling ride!"

Joanna Davidson Politano, author of *The Lost Melody*
and other historical fiction

Praise for Kimberley Woodhouse

"A propulsive launch with plenty of fuel for future adventures.
Readers will eagerly await the next in the series."

Publishers Weekly on *The Secrets Beneath*

"An outstanding western romance that will have readers looking forward to the next in the series."

Booklist on *The Heart's Choice*

"Kim has long been a favorite author of mine, and *The Secrets
Beneath* is no exception. This book is full of intrigue and adventure, twists and turns, and the kind of spiritual encouragement and romance Kim is known for. This is the start of

a new series, and I highly recommend you pick up a copy and enjoy the journey."

"This is a valuable author partnership merging Peterson's attention to historical detail with Woodhouse's cozy-mystery acumen. . . . Strong themes of justice and redemption shine through."

"*A Mark of Grace* is filled with heartache, love, and danger in a beautiful setting. I enjoyed revisiting the historic El Tovar Hotel through the pages of this spiritually satisfying and sweet romance."

SET *in* STONE

TREASURES *2* OF THE EARTH

SET *in* STONE

KIMBERLEY WOODHOUSE

BETHANYHOUSE
a division of Baker Publishing Group
Minneapolis, Minnesota

© 2024 by Kimberley Woodhouse

Published by Bethany House Publishers
Minneapolis, Minnesota
BethanyHouse.com

Bethany House Publishers is a division of
Baker Publishing Group, Grand Rapids, Michigan

Printed in the United States of America

Library of Congress Cataloging-in-Publication Data
Names: Woodhouse, Kimberley, author.
Title: Set in stone / Kimberley Woodhouse.
Description: Minneapolis, Minnesota : Bethany House, a division of Baker
    Publishing Group, 2024. | Series: Treasures of the earth ; 2
Identifiers: LCCN 2023040913 | ISBN 9780764241697 (paperback) | ISBN
    9780764242908 (casebound) | ISBN 9781493445332 (ebook)
Subjects: LCGFT: Christian fiction. | Novels.
Classification: LCC PS3623.O665 S48 2024 | DDC 813/.6—dc23/eng/20230912
LC record available at https://lccn.loc.gov/2023040913

Scripture quotations are from the King James Version of the Bible.

This is a work of historical reconstruction; the appearances of certain historical
figures are therefore inevitable. All other characters, however, are products of the
author's imagination, and any resemblance to actual persons, living or dead, is co-
incidental.

Baker Publishing Group publications use paper produced from sustainable forestry
practices and post-consumer waste whenever possible.

24 25 26 27 28 29 30   7 6 5 4 3 2 1

This book is lovingly dedicated to:

My dear friends,
Jeni and Gary Koch

Two people who have walked the road of life with Jeremy and me for a decade plus, and we love you dearly.

GARY—you're awesome. Plain and simple. I could write paragraphs about you but you'd probably get mad at me, so I will refrain. Your zest for reading thrills me and you always know how to make me laugh.

JENI—dear friend, fellow crafter, Bible study partner, prayer partner, and my research buddy. Thank you for sacrificing so much time to journey with me to Utah, Wyoming, Colorado, and allllllll the museums so I could write this series. Your willingness to step off the beaten path and trek with me into the middle of nowhere to find just the right spot to set a story shows how much you must love this crazy author.

Thank you both for sticking with me all these years. For praying. For loving on us. For reading. And most importantly, for being our friends.

DEAR READER

I gave the heroine in this story her first name in honor of my dear friend, prayer partner, and golfing buddy—Martha Ilgenfritz.

If you haven't read the first book in this series, *The Secrets Beneath*, that's all right (though you really should go pick it up—no pressure). But allow me to give you a little context and set the stage. Dinosaur National Monument is in the northwest corner of Colorado and the northeast corner of Utah. Earl Douglass—a paleontologist for the Carnegie Museum in Pittsburgh—found the first bones in 1909, which were the beginning of the dinosaur quarry which is now famous around the world. Earl was a fascinating man and dreamed of having a place where people could see the bones in the actual rock for all time. His dream became reality.

It's because of him that Dinosaur National Monument is there. And it's amazing.

The idea for a series about women in paleontology and dinosaurs came because I threw out a question to my readers on my Facebook page about things (topics, people, historical events) they would like to see next in my books. Laura Flint tossed out "The Bone Wars." Now, if you don't know anything about that, you'll learn about them through this series, but you can also look them up online. I'll give links in the Note from the Author at the end of the book. But through our chats, Laura connected me with Diane Douglass Iverson. Earl's granddaughter. Isn't that awesome?

Through this amazing friendship, I learned incredible things about Earl. That's why you'll see quotes from his personal journals throughout the book. I hope they inspire and intrigue you as well. Diane has graciously given us permission to use Earl's words and poems and has helped me immeasurably throughout my research and writing of this book.

I spent almost two weeks out in Colorado, Wyoming, and Utah doing research. Meeting with real-life paleontologists like Dr. Sue Ann Bilbey, going to museum after museum, and visiting site after site. When it came down to figuring out the timeline for my novels, I wanted to show the progression in paleontology over the years. Book one showed the beginning of the Great Dinosaur Rush era. Women were also fascinated with paleontology, but it wasn't seemly for a woman to dig in the dirt back then. Anna—the main character of *The Secrets Beneath*—spent her life sketching all the finds at her father's digs, jumping in to save his find when his health fails.

Set in Stone brings us to the height of the Bone Wars. We're going to journey with Martha Jankowski, who dreams of becoming a full-fledged paleontologist with her name on a display at a museum.

Thank you for joining me as we travel once again through history to the bone quarries.

Until next time,
Kimberley

"Go forth into nature and see what she has to show thee. Enter the silent wood and lose thyself in thoughts unthought before. Let fancy construct worlds unknown—fairy worlds of the mind. All this is wonderful, but the wonder is of thyself the mystery of the mind and that matter can arrange itself, know to perceive, to perceive other forms, other arrangements of matter and then to think beyond, to construct a new world of its own yet of fragments of the old."

~Earl Douglass—Saturday, January 28, 1888

one

"It is hard to establish a philosophy that is optimistic and yet will fit with the terrors of this world."

~Earl Douglass

"Martha! Step away from the ridge."

At Father's deep voice booming behind her, Martha startled and backed away from the edge of the mesa. Two strong arms wrapped around her small frame and swept her to safety. Father shifted her around to see him, his eyes dark and serious.

"You must listen to me, Martha. If I am to teach you to dig, there are rules to follow. We need to keep you and the workers safe. Understand?"

She nodded, her fingers picking at the light cotton collar of Father's work shirt. Tears threatened to fall, and she could feel her bottom lip trembling. "I'm sorry." The thought of falling into the great chasm below them was almost as bad as hearing the fear in her father's voice. Everything inside her shook.

"You're safe, not to worry." He nodded and set her down

13

next to him, holding her small hand in his. "Now. I have a surprise for you."

"A surprise?" All the turmoil stopped as she hopped from one foot to the other. "What is it? I want to see!" Father's surprises were the best.

He chuckled as he led her down a small packed-dirt path. "You will, my dear. Are you ready to see the bones we discovered?"

Martha nodded as visions of long tails, ferocious teeth, and giant feet filled her imagination. "Is it a *Mega . . . Miglo . . . Megalosaurus*"—she forced the big word out slowly—"like Mr. Owen talked about?"

"No. And to my knowledge, those have only been found in England." Father squeezed her hand, his brown eyes warmed by the sunlight. "We are not quite sure what we've found. But that is part of the fun. Digging for bones gives us the chance to learn about the animals that roamed the earth thousands of years ago."

They rounded a corner down into the valley, where the excavation was taking place. The sharp sound of metal on metal echoed off the rocks. Red dirt swirled in thick clouds over some men as they dumped large wheelbarrows of dirt into a pile. Several wagons sat in the center, covered with tarps.

"What are those wagons?"

He glanced over to where Martha pointed. "Ah. Those are our transport wagons. The smaller bones we find on any dig are carefully placed first in crates and then in those wagons. The bones are covered so the sun does not dry out or damage them. Once the crates are full, they are transported to the nearest train station, where they are then shipped to the museum that purchased them. However . . ." Father turned them away from the bustling men to a smaller, quieter area. "This is where I am working. And this is where your surprise is."

Martha clapped her hands, a wide smile on her face. Today

was her favorite day. Her father wasn't around much because he was often away on trips. But this dig had kept him close to home. To watch him dig and find bones in the ground was a treat far greater than hearing the stories when he came home. This was real—not just in her imagination.

She skipped along beside him, kicking up dust around her sturdy work boots. Another gift from Father. They were thicker and plainer than the shiny patent leather shoes Mother made her wear. But they were comfortable and didn't pinch her feet.

He slipped his jacket off and draped it on a nearby boulder. Then picked up a large wooden box with a big handle and put it on a small table. Martha peeked over the edge of the box as he pulled out several tools. A pointy triangle, a big hammer, a magnifying glass, a brush with stiff bristles, a skinny metal pole with a pointy end, and a flat metal rod with a round bottom were laid out on the small wooden table beside the boulder.

She pressed into his side. "Do you use all of these?"

"I do, every day. Let me tell you what they are." Father picked up the pointy pole and the metal rod with the flat edge. "These two tools are called chisels. They work in different ways. The flat edge can help break up rocks that are tucked along a bone without damaging it. The pointed chisel helps break up stones in areas that a flat chisel can't get into. You use them by tapping the hammer on the flat bottom of each tool. But you must be careful not to hit too hard or you risk damaging the bone." He set them down and picked up the brush. "This clears away dirt and debris so you can better see where you are working." He held the brush out to Martha. She took it and almost dropped it. It was heavier than it looked. The worn wooden handle was too big for her hands. She ran her fingers over the soft end of the stiff bristles, sending dust swirling around her fingers.

She sneezed.

Father smiled at her and took the brush from her, then picked up the magnifying glass. Holding it in front of his face, he crossed his eyes. She let out a loud giggle. His eyes were large and funny looking behind the glass. He handed it to her. "Now, let's see what fun we can have with this." He knelt in the dirt and motioned for her to join him. "Hold the glass over this hole here and tell me what you see."

Crouching down, she held the glass over the dirt and peered at the red clay. "Father, look!" She giggled. Tiny ants scurried over pebbles and disappeared into small holes. Bits of silver glinted from several rocks. She pulled the glass away and blinked. Everything she saw looked so small again.

"That magnifying glass helps me see little details in bones and rocks." He guided her hand back over the sparkling rocks. "You see that shiny substance?"

She nodded.

"That's called marcasite. It shows up in many rocks here at the dig. When someone finds it in big chunks, it can be worth a lot of money. Maybe today we will find a small chunk to save for good luck." He took the magnifying glass from her and stood. Oh, how she loved the sound of his voice. At home, it was his excitement as he told her the stories of his digs. But here? His love for the work colored every word he said. He was such a smart man—probably the smartest man to ever live. She smiled just thinking about it. One day, she wanted to be as smart as him and dig beside him. Wouldn't that be grand?

A moment later he was by her side again with a small cloth roll. A bit of twine wrapped around it in a simple bow. "Now. It's time for your surprise."

Martha took the roll from her father and pulled on one of the strings. The bow unraveled and she tugged it off the cloth, then unwrapped the roll on a boulder. Oh! There, tucked in small pockets, were the same kind of tools he had just shown her! But instead of being too big, they were just right for her hands. She pulled out the flat-headed chisel and clutched it in her hand. It wasn't heavy like Father's, but light and easy to hold. There was a small brush, hammer, pointed chisel, and . . .

Martha pulled on the dark brown handle sticking out of the last pocket. Her very own magnifying glass!

"Thank you!" she squealed. With careful movements she tucked the magnifying glass back in its pocket then threw her arms around his shoulders. "Thank you, thank you!"

His laughter rumbled in his chest. "You are welcome, my dear girl. You are a big six-year-old now. These tools aren't just for show. How would you like to help me dig a little today? We might even find a treasure to take home to your mother."

Martha nodded against his shoulder, basking in the warmth of his hug. "Let's try to find some marc . . . I don't remember the name."

"Marcasite."

"That's it. It's so pretty and shiny, I know Mother would love it."

He pulled back and brushed her dark hair away from her face. "You are right. She would love something pretty and shiny." He let her go and turned to the large rocks where treasures hid. "Well, Martha Jankowski, are you ready to work on your first dinosaur dig?"

She stood and straightened the canvas smock that covered her brown dress. "Yes, sir." She rolled her tools back up and held them close to her chest. Her heart pounded hard, and her smile grew so big that her cheeks pinched.

This really was her favorite day *ever*!

1872, Two Weeks Later • Outside Denver City, Colorado Territory

The light dimmed in the man's eyes as the pool of red around him grew.

Such a shame that he had to die. He'd been rather nice to look at. When his mouth was closed.

She tilted her head. Her gaze swept him from head to toe. The odd way his crumpled form was situated on the ground was rather . . . pathetic.

She stared for a while longer and then bowed her head. How long to wait? The scent of blood and death would soon draw wild animals and birds, which was just fine. They could finish the job. The man would disappear and be out of her life forever.

Still. Death deserved respect. She gave the man what he refused to give her the last few months of his life: a moment of silence. That was surely sufficient. It was more than he deserved. All his threats about exposing her plans to Marsh. His pitiful attempt to sabotage her.

What a fool to underestimate her passion and drive.

But then, they all did. Her father's associates. Her society friends. She was beloved for her beauty. A delicate ornament on some businessman's arm. They all acted like a woman couldn't be beautiful *and* clever.

The joke was on them.

With her left hand, she laid a four-button, white kid glove on his chest.

A hawk screamed, and she jumped. Pressing the same hand to her heart, she glanced at the sky. The sun slanted toward the Rocky Mountains.

Oh dear. She'd wasted too much time.

If she thought about taking his life, it made her head hurt. And he wasn't worth wasting a headache on. He didn't deserve . . . life.

With her back straight and her chin high, she turned on her heel and faced the magnificent mountains. Nothing but beauty and a fresh future ahead, one that would be in her complete control from now on. She inhaled a quick breath and allowed a smile to stretch across her face.

Now. Things could finally get back to the way they should be. After all, no one would even know he was gone. She had made sure of that.

But the weight in her right hand brought her attention down. The knife dripped blood onto the rocky soil. Her clothes were stained too. Reaching for the handle of her reticule with her clean hand, she forced herself to release her ironclad grip on the knife's leather handle. The weapon clattered to the ground.

Where was that rag? It had to be in there somewhere. After a few moments of digging with her untarnished hand, she pulled out the rag she'd torn from one of his old shirts. She swiped the cloth back and forth over the blood and dirt caking her right hand until no blood remained. Pressing the cloth between her clean and dirty palms, she rubbed until all reminders of the man—and what she'd done to him—were absent from her skin and the knife.

She tucked the rag-wrapped blade into her reticule and walked back over to her horse. In her saddlebags, she had a change of clothes. A glance around in all directions confirmed there wasn't another soul for miles. The tumbleweed-covered gulley was wide and desolate.

She changed into clean garments, then retrieved the matches from her bag. Gathering the soiled clothes and rag together, she tossed them on the parched ground. The match crackled as it ignited, and she threw it on the pile. She lit another one and threw it on the other side. In seconds, the flames licked up every corner of the pile and she watched it burn until a mound of black and gray ashes remained.

She took her canteen and poured a bit of water on them. They disintegrated into the dirt in a tiny sizzle and puff.

There.

It was done.

All was right with the world once again.

1872, THREE MONTHS LATER • DENVER CITY,
COLORADO TERRITORY

"What time is it, Nurse McGee?"

The older woman glanced at the large grandfather clock in the corner of the sitting room. "It is two in the afternoon, Miss Martha. Asking me the time won't make it go any faster."

Martha sighed and leaned back into the stiff back of the settee. Her legs swung back and forth, swirling the white ruffles of her dress up in the air. Waiting was boring. Dressing like a proper girl was boring. She missed the dirt and going to Father's dig site. Looking at pretty rocks and finding old bones was better than learning how to sit right.

"Enough of that, miss. If your mother saw you acting like this, she'd be upset for sure." Her nurse came over and smoothed Martha's dress back over her knees. With deft fingers she tightened the pale pink bows around the curly pigtails draped over Martha's shoulders. "Back straight. There's a good girl. Looking pretty like a fine miss. Won't that make your mother and father happy?"

Martha nodded. "What time are they coming?"

Nurse sat down next to her. "Two thirty. Only twenty more minutes. How about we read to pass the time?"

"No, thank you. Can I sit by the window and watch for them? I'll sit very still like a good girl and not kick my legs." She folded her hands under her chin. "Please?"

Nurse McGee studied her for a moment, green eyes narrowed as if she were searching for any trace of a lie in her face. Martha made her eyes wide and innocent.

"All right. You may. But the first sign of kicking and it's back in the chair. And when you hear the carriage, you come sit right back in this chair like your mother wants."

Martha jumped out of the chair and threw her arms

around Nurse's waist. "Thank you!" She skipped to the chair by the big picture window, ignoring the reprimanding cough. She hadn't promised not to skip. She sat in the chair, adjusting the ruffles over her knees, and folded her hands in her lap. The large trees in the front yard hid the activity of the street from view. But there were still plenty of things to see.

Two monarch butterflies danced in and out of the delicate purple blooms of wisteria just outside the window. A small hare bounded across the grass, pausing only to sniff a patch of white columbines. A squirrel darted up the maple tree—the one Mother insisted on planting so she could have a color other than yellow in the fall—and then disappeared into its large green leaves. Soon those leaves would turn the most beautiful shade of red. A color Martha adored.

The clopping of hooves drew her attention away from the animals in the front yard. Her parents' large black coach pulled up to the wrought iron gate. The coats of the black Clydesdale horses gleamed in the afternoon sun. Maybe if she was a good girl, and Mother was happy with her manners, Nurse would take her to the stables later to feed the horses carrots and sugar cubes.

She slid from the chair and raced back to the couch. "They're here! They're here!"

"Miss Martha! Lower your voice, child. They probably heard you all the way in Wyoming Territory," her nurse hissed, fussing over her dress and hair once more. "If Mrs. Jankowski saw you like that, I'd be fired for sure." With one final look, Nurse McGee nodded. She made her way to the small chair in the corner of the room and picked up her embroidery hoop.

Muffled voices filtered through the partially open drawing room door. Martha resisted the urge to peek. Mother was constantly telling her that ladies didn't listen in on the conversations of others. She was determined to be proper today. Make her parents proud. The door swung open, and she stood, her trembling fingers pressing into the folds of her dress.

Mother entered the room, the train of her dark blue traveling gown swishing over the carpet. She approached, and Martha stared.

Mother was smiling!

"Hello, my dear. How pretty you look today. That pink in your hair is lovely." She sat down on the couch and patted the cushion. "Your father will come to tea in a moment. Sit for now."

"Yes, ma'am." Martha swallowed. "You look lovely today as well." Her mother loved compliments. Martha gave her mother a small smile, careful not to show her teeth. A lady never showed her teeth. She sat on the edge of the couch, keeping her back straight. "Did you have a nice journey?"

Mother's smile grew, and she took Martha's hand. "These are very nice manners, my dear daughter. I am proud of you."

The words warmed Martha almost as much as Mother's hand holding hers. "Nurse has been helping me be proper every day since you left."

"I can see that. You have done well. Now"—Mother shifted and brought her face close to Martha's—"I have something to tell you that might be upsetting. But I need you to be a brave girl."

She nodded, the words making her insides quiver. Stiffening, she pinched her lips together and chanted in her mind *Be brave, be brave* over and over. Mother's breath smelled of mint, and Martha could see the small mark above Mother's lip that she tried to hide with powder.

Martha's heartbeat felt like a drum she once saw played in a parade. *Boom. Boom. Boom.* "I will try."

"Good. Now your father is home, but he has had an accident. A very bad one." Mother licked her lips and looked down at their joined hands. "He does not look the same, and you will have to be calm when you see him."

Father hurt? How? When?

Martha's questions died on her lips when another figure entered the room. A man walked in, his black suit slightly wrinkled. His black tie was askew, a small diamond holding it in place. His dark brown walking stick thumped the floor as he came toward her.

Her eyes grew wide. Her mouth went dry. "Father?"

This man lowering himself into the chair opposite her could not be her father. Three deep scars ran down the right side of his face, one of them tugging his mouth upward. It almost looked like he was smiling. Another scar ran from the side of his nose and cheek in a jagged pattern. It dipped down the left side of his jaw and disappeared behind his ear.

Tears pooled in her eyes. No. This could not be Father! He was handsome. His eyes were kind and warm, not distant and cross like this man's.

Martha shifted in her chair and looked up at Mother. Couldn't she see it wasn't the right man?

"Go greet your father."

Mother's tone was firm.

Martha knew better than to argue.

She stood and shuffled over to the chair. Her teeth pressed into the side of her cheek. The scars were even worse close up, but she would get a scolding if she was not polite. "Hello, Father."

His dark eyes focused on her, and Martha dropped her head, reluctant to meet his gaze. What would she see there?

"Hello, Martha."

His voice had the same deep rumble she remembered. Maybe it *was* him. Her shoulders relaxed a bit.

"How are you, Martha?"

"I am well. How are you? Did you have a pleasant journey?"

Martha asked the question Nurse had told her was appropriate to ask and glanced at her mother, who nodded and gestured for Martha to move closer.

She leaned against the arm of the chair, her fingers brushing the wool of Father's suit. The scent of dirt and pine needles clung to him. Father always smelled like that. It reminded her of digging for bones with him.

"The journey was long, but we have returned home." He toyed with the bulbous silver top of the walking stick. "I . . . I have a small present for you."

Martha looked up at him, trying to ignore the differences in his face. "You do? Are they tools for another dig?" She clasped her hands together under her chin.

Father's eyes narrowed to slits. "No. And there will be no more digs. Your mother and I have decided that you must focus your time on other pursuits."

No more digs? She stepped back and glanced at Mother then back to Father. The digs had been her special time with him. Why was he taking that away? "Why? I want to dig with you."

He gripped the walking stick in his fist and tapped the floor with it. "No. It is not ladylike. You must learn how to become a lady fitting your station. We will hear no argument, Martha. And you will not ask to dig with me ever again. Do you understand?"

Tears burned her eyes and one slid down her cheek. She swiped it away with the back of her hand and nodded.

"Good girl," he murmured. He stuck his hand in his pocket and fished out two sticks of candy. "I brought you back your favorite sassafras sticks and this." He put the sticks in her hand as well as a small round circle of gold. It was a coin. Small ridges lined both sides of the precious metal. *Three dollars* and the year 1870 were inscribed on one side. Martha flipped it over and found a woman with a funny crown and the words *United States of America* stamped on it. "This coin has given me lots of good luck in my life," Father said, his voice softer now. "And I want you to have it. I hope it will bring you as much luck as it brought me."

Martha clutched the candy and the coin close. "Thank you."

"Yes, well . . ." He coughed and patted her head. "That's a good girl."

Martha could feel tears in her eyes again. She was unsure what to do. He appeared to be dismissing her. Did she go back and sit with Mother? Or was she expected to talk with him some more? Her eyes darted back and forth between her parents, sweat making the candy in her hand sticky.

Suddenly, Nurse was beside her, a firm hand in the middle of her back. "Give your regards to your parents, miss. We will have tea in the nursery."

Martha gave her parents a small curtsy. "Thank you for the afternoon." Her voice was just above a whisper. Neither responded, and Nurse ushered her out of the drawing room and upstairs to the nursery.

A small tea tray with her favorite raspberry tarts and sandwiches was waiting on the table, but Martha wasn't hungry, not even for tarts. She dropped the sassafras sticks and coin on an empty saucer and ran to her bed, throwing herself into the soft safety of her pillow. The tears she held back downstairs now unleashed in full force.

What happened to her father? Why couldn't she dig with him anymore?

She sobbed into the fancy pillowcase. She didn't *want* to be a lady. She wanted to be in the mountains, getting bones out of rocks.

The feather mattress dipped as Nurse sat down next to her. "Come now, Miss Martha. It isn't as bad as all this fuss. Your parents are home. And they have grand plans for you. All will be well."

Martha pulled her face out of the pillow, a hiccup rattling

her ribs. "Did you see Father? What happened to him? Why does he look like that?"

Nurse sighed and patted her hand. "Those bone digs your father has done can be dangerous. All kinds of things can happen. Rockslides, floods, bandits." She pressed her lips together and looked at Martha with a sad smile. "But you know it doesn't matter what a person looks like on the outside. It's the inside that counts. Besides, he gave you this pretty coin. Right? He was thinking of you while he was away."

"It is a pretty coin." Martha sniffed, plucking it out of Nurse's hand. The ridges pressed into her palm as she traced the designs again. Father's lucky coin. How lucky could it be if his face had so many scars and he now walked with a stick and a limp? Her fingers closed over it, pressing it deeper into her skin. Maybe it was lucky because it kept him alive. And he'd given it to her.

Her stomach rumbled, and Nurse laughed. "There you go, Miss Martha. No more tears. Dry your eyes and let's have tea. There's a good girl." She patted the little girl's shoulder.

Martha walked to the table, the tantalizing smell of raspberry too hard to resist. Nurse McGee was right. Father had given her a lovely present. His own lucky coin. She would keep it close, always.

Everything was going to be fine.

~~~~~~~

1877 • Denver, Colorado

The sky was as dark as the strip of black velvet Mother sometimes wore around her neck. The stars twinkled against the darkness like the marcasite in rocks. Martha sighed, her cheek resting against her hand. It was almost bedtime, and Phoebe would be in soon to read with her and put her to bed. She loved her governess and their evening routine.

However, she missed her father.

He was the one who began the tradition of reading to her, but it had been years since he'd come to read her a story. If she closed her eyes, she could feel the rumble of his deep voice against her shoulder as he read *Alice's Adventures in Wonderland*. His silly high-pitched voice for the White Rabbit and the perfect snobbish and abrasive voice for the Queen of Hearts were vivid memories. Happy memories and silly tales.

There had been no made-up voices since his accident. The scars had not only taken away his smile, but his zest for life. Gone was the man who'd taught her about digging for fossils. The man who gave her small tools that fit her small hands. The man who loved to tell her stories.

But she didn't need a bedtime story anymore. She would be twelve next year. Mother said she was a young lady. Young ladies didn't read stories.

Martha agreed a little bit. She didn't like the little rhyming tales for children. However, reading was still one of her favorite things to do. And novels were her favorite. Thankfully, Phoebe loved to read almost as much as she did. They were halfway through *Little Women*, and Martha was eager to see where life would take Meg, Jo, Beth, and Amy.

Her bedroom door creaked open, and Phoebe's head popped around the corner. Her brown eyes creased at the corners with her smile. "What are you doing, dear? You should be in your nightgown."

Martha got up from the window seat and looked down at the wrinkles in her green dinner dress. It was a good thing Mother had already gone to her room. Martha would get another reprimand for being so disheveled. "I was just looking at the stars. They're very clear tonight."

Her governess crossed the room and slipped an arm around her shoulders. "I love looking at the stars too. Maybe, once we're ready for bed, we can have one more look." She wiggled her eyebrows, and Martha let out a giggle.

"Yes, please!"

Fifteen minutes later, Martha was snuggled on the cushions of her window seat. Phoebe was opposite her, the large black Bible she always read from at bedtime on her lap.

"The stars do look spectacular tonight. They remind me of a verse from the book of Psalms. 'He telleth the number of the stars; he calleth them all by their names.'" Phoebe glanced at her. "Isn't that fascinating to think about? God knows the name of every star."

That *was* fascinating. Martha traced a pattern on the windowpane, and sudden tears burned her eyes. She sniffed and glanced at her favorite person in all the world.

The older woman held a lace handkerchief out to her, eyebrows dipped low over her eyes. "What is it, sweet one?" Phoebe's voice was soft and low.

"I don't know!" The words burst out of her. "I miss my father. He doesn't come say good night to me anymore. Mother is so busy with her society friends that I never get to see her." She wiped at her eyes and blew her nose into the scrap of cloth. It smelled like lavender, Phoebe's favorite.

Phoebe shifted across the window seat to sit next to her and took her hand. "It's okay to miss your parents. They are very busy, but I'm sure they love you very much."

"Everything has changed so much since he came back all . . ." She choked back the words even as the tears fell. With another sniff, she looked down at her nightgown. Soft pink flowers dotted the light cotton garment. It had ruffles down the front, just like one she'd seen Mother wear. It was her favorite. "I'm sorry for crying, Phoebe. I know it's not ladylike."

Her governess squeezed her hand then let go. "Tears are nothing to apologize for, dear. Sometimes, when it's just you and the Lord, tears are a precious gift."

Martha chewed the inside of her cheek for a moment. "God doesn't think crying is for babies?"

"Of course He doesn't! Now, does this mean that we weep and scream and make a scene all the time? Certainly not. But—" Phoebe stood and picked up her Bible. She settled back in her chair and opened it, flipping the thin pages until she found her place. "Here is what God's Word says. Psalm fifty-six. 'Thou tellest my wanderings: put thou my tears into thy bottle: are they not in thy book?' God sees your tears, Martha. And He hears your cries."

Martha leaned back into the window seat and frowned. "I don't cry that much."

Phoebe chuckled. "That is true. But anytime you do cry, you can go to Jesus. Tell Him what hurts your heart. Share your fears. Ask Him to help you in your life. He is listening, and He wants you to know Him."

"Sometimes He feels as far away as my parents," she whispered, her chin trembling again. Her governess wrapped loving arms around her and squeezed her tight.

"My sweet girl, even when the Lord feels the farthest away, He is as close as the breath in your lungs. Remember what we read last week? In the book of John?"

Martha nodded, the soft fabric of Phoebe's dress soothing her cheek. "God loved the world so much He sent Jesus to die for us."

"And?"

"And if I seek Him and believe in Him, He will give me eternal life."

"That's right. Never forget, no matter what comes your way in life, Jesus loves you so very much." Phoebe pressed a kiss to Martha's head. "And I do too."

Martha soaked in the warmth of the words. The last of her tears slipped down her cheeks but she swiped them away. When Phoebe talked about God, it always made sense, like He was in the room with them. But . . .

Did God hear her like He heard Phoebe? She just wasn't sure.

"It's time for bed." Phoebe squeezed her once more then let go and stood. "Wash your face and get in bed. I'll set the window seat to rights."

Martha nodded and made her way to the washstand in the opposite corner of her room. She poured a bit of water in the basin and cupped her hands in the tiny pool. The water was lukewarm and soothed her puffy eyes. She plucked the towel from the hook on her wall and patted her face dry. Her limbs felt heavy as she climbed in bed and pulled the coverlet up to her chin. Snuggling into her pillow, she watched Phoebe move from lamp to lamp, dousing the flames until the lamps by the bedroom door and Martha's bed were the only lights flickering.

Her governess smoothed the damp tendrils of hair away from Martha's brow and smiled. "Will you be able to sleep tonight?"

She nodded, her eyelids already heavy. "Thank you for listening."

"Anytime." Phoebe turned the lamp down low and settled in the chair next to Martha's bed. She always stayed until Martha was deep in sleep. Sometimes Phoebe was in the same chair when Martha awoke the following morning.

No longer able to keep her eyes open, she listened to the soft rustle of pages.

Phoebe began to read. "The Lord is my light and my salvation; whom shall I fear?"

The words wrapped around her with a peace she didn't know was possible, and she succumbed to sleep.

1878 • DENVER

Martha rubbed the small coin in between her fingers as she paced her room. Where was Phoebe? She should be here by now. Martha needed to prepare for breakfast and appear at the table promptly, or there would be words from Mother.

Martha sighed. Mother's words had grown much harsher of late. Because she was supposed to understand how to be a lady by now.

She glanced at the clock again. It was not like Phoebe to be even a minute late. How could she be fifteen whole minutes delayed?

With a huff, Martha yanked her bedroom door open. She scurried down the long hallway, past the grand staircase that led down to the main hall. Turning left, she headed toward the attic stairs and pulled the door open. Martha took them two at a time. "Phoebe? Are you up here? Mother is going to be furious that I'm late this morning. What excuse should we gi—"

The word stuck in her throat as she entered Phoebe's small room.

Empty drawers hung open. All of Phoebe's little touches, the doily on the nightstand and the miniature of her and her mother, were gone. Martha's gaze darted around and focused in on Phoebe. The older woman stood at her bedside, folding a dress into her small suitcase. Tears slid down her face.

Martha ran to her, almost knocking the two of them to the floor with the force of her hug. "What is this, Phoebe? Where are you going? Why are you packing? Why is everything empty?"

Her governess pulled her arms out from Martha's stranglehold and gave her a short hug. "I have to leave, dear one."

Blood rushed from Martha's cheeks. Panic prickled the back of her neck. This couldn't be happening. "What? No. You can't leave." A sob choked her throat. "Why are you leaving me?"

"My mother is sick." Phoebe's voice cracked. "She needs me to care for her. I received the letter just this morning. She wrote to hasten my return home." Gently, she pried Martha's arms from her waist with a soft squeeze. "I am sorry you found

31

out this way. I planned to come see you once my packing was finished."

Everything inside her went numb. It was like the woman's voice was wrapped in cotton, so distant and fuzzy. "Your mother is sick? Is she dying?"

Phoebe winced at the boldness of the question.

Martha covered her mouth for a moment. "I'm so sorry. That was not polite for me to ask."

A deep sigh eased out of Phoebe, her face ashen. She turned and placed her hands on Martha's shoulders. "It was not polite, that is true. But I know it was from your heart. Your care for me and my family is evident. That means a great deal to me." She paused and clamped her lips together. They trembled. "I do not know if my mother is dying. Just that she is very ill. And I am quite worried about her." A noise from the stairs made Phoebe jump.

Fear undulated off Phoebe like the ripples after a stone was plunked in water. What was going on?

"Please, I don't have time to chat right now." Phoebe's gaze shot to the door, her voice firm and louder than before. "Let me pack, and I will come see you in a minute." She turned back to her bag and started pressing folded dresses into it.

Martha took a step back. Was Phoebe . . .dismissing her?

She trudged her way back downstairs to her room, tears clouding her vision. She threw herself on the bed and sobbed into the pillow. What was she to do? How could the one person Martha trusted and needed leave her? It wasn't fair. Couldn't Phoebe see that she was needed here? With her?

Even as the thoughts swirled, her face grew hot.

She was being selfish. She was not caring for Phoebe as Phoebe had cared for her. What had she called that rule? The Golden Rule? Martha sniffed and pressed her hands to her eyes. "Whatsoever ye would that men do to you, do ye even so to them." She sat up and hugged the soggy pillow to her chest. It wasn't fair, but Martha could see that her attitude was wrong. Despite her broken heart, she needed to support her only friend.

Her bedroom door creaked open. Martha glanced up then stood quick as she could. She placed the pillow in its proper place and tried to wipe all the tears from her eyes and face. "Hello, Mother."

Victoria Jankowski glided into the room with silent footsteps, her skirts barely making a sound as they brushed the plush carpet. Even after years of practice Martha hadn't mastered the same feat. It was as if even walking was to showcase her mother's elegance and wealth.

Mother frowned, studying Martha's ensemble. "You are still in your nightgown." It was a statement, not a question.

"I am, Mother. Phoebe was late and then I found her packing. She's leaving to see her sick mother and—"

"Yes, yes. I know. Are you unable to dress yourself?" Mother arched an eyebrow. "Perhaps it is good that woman is leaving, since your dependence upon her keeps you from even the simplest of tasks."

Martha's cheeks heated. She lowered her gaze to the carpet. "I am sorry. The news of Phoebe's departure upset my morning. I will dress and meet you for breakfast."

Two fingers slid under Martha's chin and tipped it upward. Martha knew better than to meet Mother's eyes, so she kept her gaze down.

"I had hoped that after breakfast, you would be suitable for morning calls. It is time to teach you the running of the household. But I cannot have you greeting guests with puffy eyes and a sad countenance." Mother dropped her hand and sighed. "You will not make a scene this morning. You will say your good-byes. After your governess leaves, you will report to me in the front drawing room. Instead of morning calls, we will review the setting for a proper tea service."

Martha kept her eyes focused on the cabbage roses swirling in her carpet as Mother moved toward the door.

"Do try not to disappoint me further this morning." Mother's words were smooth and soft, but the warning was clear.

With a click, the door closed.

Martha's knees buckled, and she plopped down on the bed. Tears stung the corners of her eyes, but she balled her fists and pressed them against her face until the temptation to weep passed. Bearing the brunt of Mother's constant disapproval was awful. Surely it would be easier if Mother would just strike her. Of course, Mother would never hurt her that way.

Besides, maybe Mother didn't know how deep her words cut at times. She was always so focused on two things: ensuring with Father that the Jankowski family business kept running and making Martha the perfect socialite. Because above all else, the family name *must* be upheld.

Martha stood and went over to her wardrobe, selecting a pretty, pale blue dress suitable for tea service. She slipped the dress on, its soft waves swirling around her legs. Soon she would be wearing full-length gowns. Maybe Phoebe could—

Martha shook her head. It was so natural for her thoughts and heart to turn to her governess.

Her friend.

What would she do now without Phoebe? Her friend always followed Mother's orders to teach and raise Martha with all the society accomplishments, but she did so with warmth and care. And she encouraged Martha as she tried to learn everything from the proper dinner setting to playing the pianoforte and harp. Indeed, Martha's talent at the pianoforte had blossomed under her governess's tutelage. It was the one area where Mother complimented her.

Now Phoebe was leaving.

Martha would be all alone.

Her bedroom door opened. She tensed, anticipating Mother

again. Instead, Phoebe bustled through the door, looking smart in a dark gray traveling dress and matching hat. Tears brimmed in her eyes as she approached Martha.

"I am so sorry for the sudden nature of my departure," Phoebe whispered, and Martha threw her arms around the woman's waist.

"I need to apologize." Martha sniffed. "I was so rude to you earlier. Please accept my heartfelt wishes for your mother's speedy recovery." Martha forced herself to give a slight smile to the woman who had meant so much to her. Even Mother would not fault that bit of social grace.

"Thank you, but I would much rather have your prayers." Phoebe squeezed her again then stepped back. She cupped Martha's tear-stained cheek in her gloved hand. "Do not forget all our chats, Martha. I know the situation with your parents is difficult, but the Lord is with you. You can call on Him. He loves you."

Her words were like salt in the wounds of Martha's heart. How she wished she had the same peace that encompassed her friend! "I will try not to forget. And I will pray for your mother. When do you think you will be back?" The question escaped on a whisper.

Phoebe dropped her hand, her frown deepening. "I will not be returning."

"What?"

"My mother is much too ill, and if she is dying, I have to be with her. Only the Lord knows how long she has."

The room tilted for a moment as Martha digested this news. Then it righted again, leaving her lightheaded. "I see."

She really was alone now.

"I will write to you every chance I get. Please know how hard this is for me, Martha. You know how much I care for you. You are like a little sister to me, and I will miss seeing you every day. Your inquisitive nature and thirst for learning are a delight. As is the tender heart you possess but hide away. As your mother teaches you the ways of society, don't lose those things. They are gifts and will serve you well in life, dear one." Phoebe hugged Martha one last time. "I will miss you."

She could scarcely return the affection. Her heart constricted, making it difficult to breathe. Phoebe patted her cheek then made her way out the door. In a daze, Martha followed her, remembering that Mother wanted her to properly see Phoebe on her way. She walked downstairs in time to see a footman pass Phoebe's bags to a hansom cab driver. Mother was by the door, looking every inch the perfect hostess.

Martha took her place by Mother's side. Phoebe looked at the two of them with a sad smile. She held her hand out to Mother, a bold move.

"Thank you for the years of employment in your house, Mrs. Jankowski. It was a pleasure to serve your family."

Mother's smile was thin. "We appreciate your service. I trust the letter of reference I gave you will be enough if you must find employment?"

Phoebe dropped her hand, her cheeks sporting two red splotches. "Yes, ma'am. Thank you."

Mother nodded. "You will not want to be late for your train. Say your good-byes, Martha."

Martha fought to exhibit the same cool, calm demeanor as her mother, but her best friend in the whole world was leaving. The *only* friend she had. Her confidante. Her guide. She swallowed the lump in her throat and hugged Phoebe tight one last time. "I pray your journey is safe."

Phoebe smiled. "Thank you, dear one. I pray we meet again someday."

Martha released her and nodded, a lone tear trailing down her cheek. "Me too."

"Martha!" Mother's voice cut through the marbled hallway. Her insides cringed as she straightened her shoulders and stepped back into the foyer. There would be no other good-byes.

The large oak door shut with a final click. Martha inhaled a sharp breath through her nose to stem her emotions. She would mourn later.

When she was alone.

She turned, steeling herself to meet her mother's expectations.

1884 • AT THE FOOT OF THE ROCKY MOUNTAINS, WEST OF DENVER, COLORADO

Martha stood at the trailhead, sweat slicking her palms. The spring sun was hot on her face, and her feet itched inside her work boots. But she'd have to ignore it. Nothing could stand in her way today.

A breeze teased tendrils of hair across her forehead. She promptly shoved them back under her bonnet and took a deep breath. She would not waste this opportunity. A large shadow blocked the sun, and Martha looked up. Mr. Johnson gave her a smile. He'd been the foreman for her father's dig years ago, and now he was the key to her getting the chance to follow in Father's footsteps.

Today, Martha would join her first dig. She *would*.

Wiping her hands on her work dress, she smiled back at the foreman. "Mother said you would be here today and let me work on your dig."

"Indeed, Miss Jankowski. It's an honor to meet you. I remember many stories about you from your father." His smile slid into a frown. "It's a shame he can't join us."

Martha nodded, without an adequate response to this giant of a man. It *was* a shame her father was no longer digging, but what were the proper manners in this situation? Especially after she'd connived her way here with her mother to allow it. Best to just continue on with confidence, right? "This is my companion, Miss Ducasse."

The older woman tipped her head, her face shadowed by the large parasol keeping the sun from her pale skin.

"It's a privilege to meet you, Miss Ducasse. And a pleasure to have Antoni Jankowski's daughter with us. Follow me, please. I will show you where we are working."

The trio made their way to a small quarry where only a handful of men were working. Martha surveyed the scene. Her stomach seemed filled with butterflies. But along with her excitement, doubts niggled at the back of her mind. Even though this dig was smaller than the one she remembered. Less activity, fewer men working. Even the quarry itself was tiny compared to the dig she'd attended with Father. Of course, everything was enormous at the age of six.

Now her eighteen-year-old eyes took in the reality of the dig site.

"We just found this spot a couple of weeks ago." Mr. Johnson led her to the large wagon bed in the center of the work area. "Several small animal skeletons have been pulled out in the northwest outcropping there. It's an excellent place to start digging and learning about the science of bones."

While it wasn't her first dig, it was the first one in a long time. She longed to soak in every second, every shovelful of dirt, every teeny-tiny fossil she could find no matter its significance. "I appreciate you allowing me on your dig, Mr. Johnson. My mother is most thankful for your kindness and prepared a luncheon for you and your men to be taken at your convenience." Martha laced her fingers together and swallowed hard against her dry throat. Mother wouldn't have found fault with that speech.

"That is very generous. Thank you. Now, I will show you where you can dig today and if you have any questions, please seek me out."

He led her to a flat space where small boulders protruded from the ground. A mound of red and brown dirt was piled on one side of a hole about three feet wide and six inches deep. Mr. Johnson crouched down and gestured for Martha to follow suit. She knelt, rocks pressing into her knees through the fabric of her dress.

"You see this long, curved line here?" He gestured to a small lip at the top of the hole. Martha's breath caught. The faint imprint of bones was still in the rock! "We found a snake skeleton here. And the vertebrae and hind leg of some sort of rabbit here. We think there might be more in this area. Would you be up to seeing what else can be found?"

She nodded and gestured for Lily Rose, her companion, to hand over her bag. Martha untied the thick string cinching it together and pulled out the roll of tools she'd purchased the minute her mother agreed to let her go back out on a dig site. "I will do my best to find something for you today."

Her words tumbled out in a rush, and Mr. Johnson laughed and sat back on his heels. "The chances of finding something are always slim, Miss Jankowski. But I can see you've got the fever for the job. Your father had that same look in his eyes when he started working. Always determined to find the next big skeleton. I know he always wanted to dig up a dinosaur." A sad smile tugged at the older man's lips. "Too bad that dream was never fulfilled."

Martha peered into the small hole then back at the foreman. Though she was young, and being on a dig with her companion and a long-lost family friend was not society's way, her fingers itched to get started. The heat of the sun, the tangy smell of dirt and pine dancing on the breeze, and the thrill of the search had her blood pounding in her ears. The chance to make a discovery here put those boring society dinner parties to shame.

Being here in the mountains, where the rocks had secrets

waiting to be unearthed, was the fulfillment of her dreams. She wouldn't take that for granted. She would make her parents proud.

And it made her feel close to Father in a way she hadn't felt in a long, long time. Especially since he'd become more and more of a recluse the past few years. For Mr. Johnson to compare her to him—at least who he'd once been—was an honor.

She plucked her small chisel, brush, and hammer out of her tool roll and sent him a smile. "Someday, Mr. Johnson, I will find a dinosaur. I know there's one in these foothills." She gazed at the mountain peaks in the distance. "And when I find it, it will go in a beautiful museum. My name will be on the plaque right next to it. 'Martha Jankowski, Paleontologist.'"

Lily Rose stepped closer and touched Martha's arm—a sure sign she was displeased with Martha's boldness. But Martha lifted her chin and ignored her companion.

"Those are some mighty big dreams, young lady." The foreman scratched his head, but he didn't laugh or give her a condescending expression, bless him.

"They are." Martha shifted so she could start tapping into some loose rock. "But what good is it having dreams if they aren't big?"

Mr. Johnson chuckled and stood. "That's a truth, Miss Martha. I'll leave you to it for now. And we will eat that luncheon in an hour."

Martha nodded and turned to her work, but not before she caught Lily Rose's raised eyebrows. What did it matter? Yes, her mother hired her companion to guide her in the ways of society as an adult, but that didn't mean Lily Rose could tell Martha what to do.

Without a word, she knelt in the hole. The fine, pointed chisel slotted into a small crack between two flat rocks. She tapped the top with four sharp raps. The rocks split and she dug them out. With rapid strokes, she brushed dirt and pebbles out of the way then sighed. Nothing. It wasn't surprising. Pale-ontology wasn't for the faint of heart. She'd have to be patient and able to press on despite coming up empty on a dig.

Luncheon came and went and still she dug. The holes in her small plot multiplied. So far the only interesting thing she'd uncovered was a small mound of marcasite and a cater-pillar. Martha used her fingers to dig out a few stuck pebbles then grabbed her brush. Once the debris was out of the new hole she'd made, she began tapping again. A large chunk of rock broke away from the outermost edge of the red dirt. She tapped again. . . .

Wait a minute.

That didn't sound like chisel hitting rock. Her heart thumped against her ribs.

She dug and swept away more rock and dirt. "My canteen," she muttered, her gaze darting around her worksite. "Where is my canteen?" She spotted it by her tool roll and stretched to grab it. Unscrewing the cap, she dribbled a little water in the hole and wiped the mud away carefully with a rag. There, poking out of the Colorado clay, was some sort of bone!

"Mr. Johnson!" Martha jumped to her feet. "I think I found something!"

The foreman approached and crouched down next to her, peering at the protrusion. He ran a bare finger along the ridge. "Certainly feels like a bone. Well done." He smiled at her. "One of my men can come and finish the job."

His statement doused the joy bubbling through Martha. If she pushed too hard, he might kick her off his dig, but she couldn't pass up the opportunity. "Could I dig just a little more? Make sure it's worth the attention of one of your work-ers?"

Mr. Johnson hesitated then nodded. "But if you get deeper and it looks like it is too big for you to remove, you call me."

"I will, I promise." Martha placed her hand over her heart.

She bent back over the protrusion and thought for a minute while Lily Rose sat on a boulder with her parasol and watched. The silent scrutiny spoke volumes.

No matter. Martha wasn't about to stop now. Her flat-edged chisel might help loosen some of the harder rock around whatever this thing was. For the next hour, she found a rhythm of working. Her fine chisel broke up the surface rock and dirt closest to the bone. She used the sharp-edged trowel to scoop out dirt and pry clumps of rocks out of the stubborn clay. The flat-edged chisel gave her enough leverage to loosen the object and break it free from its Rocky Mountain prison.

"Martha—"

She glanced at Lily Rose.

"How long would your mother want you to be out in the sun?"

Martha shifted her weight back onto her heels and glanced at her companion. Now was the time to be bold . . . authoritative. She was a Jankowski after all. "I promised Mr. Johnson a full day of work, and I intend to stand up to my agreement. Perhaps if you would prefer, I could find another companion."

The woman flinched but didn't break eye contact. "That won't be required. If you are up to the challenge and the heat, then so am I." She lifted her chin a bit.

Lily Rose Ducasse had been hired by Martha's mother as her companion when she was thirteen years of age. At first, it had been a nuisance—the whole companion thing—that Martha bucked against. But over time, she'd come to appreciate her mother's wisdom. Lily Rose's private instruction in etiquette had saved Martha more times than she could count.

Rarely did the two of them come to odds, but every once in a while, Martha felt it necessary to insist that her companion understand her place. Mother had taught Martha well in that area and while she was not as harsh as her parent, she didn't mind hanging the carrot over her companion's head. Losing employment at the Jankowski mansion would tarnish Miss Ducasse's reputation forever.

Ever since Phoebe left, Martha had hardened herself toward allowing anyone into her private thoughts and dreams.

Mother trained her. Martha hated it, but she did it and did it well. Appeasing her mother in all things high society helped Martha gain what she wanted in the long run.

Patience had become her best friend. Strategy, her greatest tool.

It had won her the chance to dig once again.

Soon, a small bone began to take shape. It was slender at one end with a sharp point jutting out of the middle and had a small bulb at the other end.

A tingling zipped through Martha, making her hands tremble. She took several deep breaths to calm her nerves. It looked like a few more well-placed taps would get the bone free. Just a few moments later, she tugged on the bone, and it came free.

Martha grabbed her rag and wiped it down, unable to contain a little cry of joy and inspecting it again. Sure enough, it was a leg bone. She scrambled to her feet and in a very unladylike manner ran across the small quarry. "Mr. Johnson! I've got it!"

"Well, let's see what we have here." He took the bone and ran his hands along it, then held it up, studying the ends. "Miss Martha, if I am not mistaken, you have found the leg bone of a crocodile. Quite remarkable that you were able to remove it in one day. Sometimes it takes much, much longer. You were taught well."

His praise lifted her spirits even higher. She stared at the bone in the man's hands and chewed her lip. "A crocodile? Aren't they saltwater inhabitants?"

"That's right. But we found a few like this when we dug in Morrison, Colorado, a few years back. Most people think bones like this would be found on the east or west coast of our country. I can't explain it, but at one point, this land must have flowed with several rivers with all kinds of critters living in their waters. I bet if we keep digging in that area, we'd find turtles, starfish, maybe even shark teeth." He placed the bone back in Martha's hands. "It's an important find today, Miss Martha. And you should be proud that you persevered and dug it out. I'll have my men expand their dig to your area tomorrow morning."

She studied the bone, its angles and planes. Well, it wasn't a dinosaur. But it was her first find. Hopefully, Mother would let her talk to Father about it tonight. Would he be pleased? Even proud?

"May . . . may I take this with me tonight? I'd like my father to see it."

"Of course. Bring it back tomorrow, and we will start again." Mr. Johnson glanced at the sky. The afternoon was fading into the deeper blue of evening. "You've done a fine job today, Miss Jankowski. And I look forward to having you return."

The grin on Martha's face was so wide it hurt her cheeks. "Thank you, sir. I will see you tomorrow." She went back to her site and gathered her tools in her bag. Lily Rose took the bag, but Martha wrapped the bone in her handkerchief and tucked it in her pocket. She couldn't wait to show Mother and Father. Sure, not everyone found a fossil their first day. But it had to be a good sign to not only find a bone, but to release it from its rocky clutches.

After a long hike back to the carriage, Martha climbed in and then leaned against the padded squabs. If only Phoebe was still with her. She would have loved examining every inch of Martha's discovery, talking about how amazing it was that God could have created such a creature. The thought made her eyes sting with tears. God had seemed so far away since her governess left. But maybe . . .

Could He have helped her today?

She pushed the thoughts away and pulled the bone out again and something plunked on the seat. Her fingers brushed the leather until she found the object. Father's lucky coin. Martha picked it up and rubbed it between her forefinger and thumb. Maybe this was why she'd been so fortunate her first day. Father had said it brought him loads of fortune on different digs.

"*A man's heart deviseth his way: but the* LORD *directeth his steps.*"

The words flashed like lightning in Martha's mind. It was a Bible verse Phoebe read to her many times in their discussions about how to live one's life dependent on God, not on luck. How could she know if she found this bone because the Lord directed her steps? Did that mean her father's coin had no meaning?

God had been out of her reach ever since Phoebe left . . . her father even longer. It would be nice to cling to one or the other right now. But instead, she felt alone.

Martha sighed and slipped the coin back in her pocket. Those thoughts were too heavy for such a happy day. For now, she would be content with her find. It was one small step in her plans. She meant what she said to Mr. Johnson today. She was determined to find a dinosaur. Mother didn't know it yet, but Martha had much bigger plans and dreams. Over time, she'd win her parents over.

Her name would appear on a museum plaque, honoring her contributions to science. And she wouldn't be a disappointment to the Jankowski name.

Martha unwrapped the crocodile bone and traced its lines with her fingertips, a small smile on her lips.

She was going to show everyone what she was capable of. Even if she had to do it all by herself.

The smile grew and she lifted her chin as the carriage

rumbled down the rough road back toward Denver. Loneliness had been her constant companion for too many years now. And it had molded her into who she was today.

Maybe being alone wasn't so bad.

It was just her and the bones set in stone.

two

"As far as success in my work is concerned, I could not ask for more. For years I have wanted to get nearly complete skeletons. I had found much that was scientifically interesting but felt I had not found such complete things as I wanted to and others were ahead of me in that respect and there is no skeleton in the museum set up that I have collected. Now I have suddenly most of the skeleton of a large dinosaur, apparently the most complete that has been found, and now there is the prospect of a little fellow which is probably new."

~Earl Douglass

Gripping her lucky coin in her gloved fist, Martha Jankowski stared up at the double doors of the museum and chewed on the inside of her cheek.

She could do this. What was there to be worried about?

Nerves hadn't unsettled her on her first day of university. They hadn't given her grief when she'd told her society friends

47

what she intended to spend her life pursuing. So why should they bother her now?

The sun warmed her face, and she smiled. Her dream of studying paleontology had come true. Every moment of learning fanned the desire to return to her home state and dig. To unearth the majesty of dinosaurs. The thrill of brushing back layers of rock and sand and finding bones—large or small— was like oxygen to her lungs. And worth the days, the weeks of finding nothing.

If she could brave the disappointment of cracked bones, empty quarries, and the ever-changing weather, surely she could face a museum director. At some point a woman would have the honor of being the first to display a full dinosaur skeleton. Why not her?

She was as worthy as any man to have her name on an exhibit in the museum. A nervous thrill shot through her. The latest bone uncovered in her quarry proved it.

Martha dropped the coin in her pocket and squared her shoulders. Enough dawdling. The museum doors wouldn't open by themselves. Lifting her chin, she stomped her way up the stairs and refused to look back. The museum director was waiting for her.

She tugged on the massive door with a bit more gusto than necessary and it opened in a swoosh of air. The interior of the building was dim compared to the bright sunshine on a cloudless day.

"Good morning, Miss Jankowski." Mr. Spalding greeted her as she stepped inside the lobby. "How lovely to see you today."

"Good morning." The words barely made it past the lump in her throat. She swallowed against the dryness that threatened to overtake her mouth. "Have you had an opportunity to look over my proposal?"

He held out an arm toward a door behind them. "Why don't we go into my office to discuss the particulars?"

Was that a positive or negative tone? And he hadn't answered her question. Not a great way to start out. With a nod, she followed him to his office.

He opened the door for her, and she entered.

"Please, have a seat." He pointed to the plush burgundy chair.

The door closed behind her with a resounding click. His slow, soft footfalls on the carpet made the seconds longer.

Oh, for heaven's sake. Why couldn't she simply sit and wait like a lady who didn't have a care in the world?

He walked around his desk. Touched a paper or two and finally took his seat. "Since this is of utmost secrecy, I'm hoping it is agreeable with you to meet in private?"

As if she cared about propriety at this moment. She was about to burst at the seams. But she kept her calm façade in place. "It is perfectly acceptable. Thank you."

"All right then"—he steepled his fingers and leaned back in his chair with a smile—"I'm excited to hear what you've found."

"I believe it is an intact *Apatosaurus* skeleton. Quite beautiful."

His eyebrows shot up. "That's splendid."

Encouraged by his clear excitement, she drew in a steadying breath and straightened her shoulders. "Yes, it is."

"Intact, you say? Are you certain?"

"From what we can tell at this time, it appears to be complete. Of course, we won't know for sure until we have every single bone out of the quarry." She had a hard time keeping her lips from curving into a smile. The more she worked at keeping a serious expression, the more difficult it became to not allow her leg to bounce up and down. Bother with sitting still. She plunked her reticule over her knees and willed every bit of her body to cooperate.

"Am I allowed to know the location?"

She shook her head in a much more violent manner than she should as a lady, but it was imperative she have control over her dig and get that point across. No matter how intimidating he might be.

"I'm sure you've heard about the recent spree of dig site sabotage." She leaned forward. "Bones were intentionally broken at a site in Cañon City last week. And one of my men said someone else covered a partially unearthed set of ribs with mud. The competition is too fierce. I'm sure you understand the necessity of discretion regarding my quarry. The Great Dinosaur Rush is on, and I don't wish for my findings to get trampled, destroyed, or stolen in the middle of it." The more she spoke, the more confident she felt. She could do this.

"Yes, yes." He dipped his chin. His lips formed a thin line, and he angled forward over his desk, leaning his elbows on the embossed desk pad. "Well then, back to your proposal."

"Yes, sir." She stiffened.

"I am pleased to offer you an exhibit here at the museum—with your name on it as requested—as soon as we have the complete skeleton in our possession, and it is verified." He paused. "There is a slight divergence from your proposal though. I must inform you that there is a deadline."

"Deadline?" She squeaked, then caught herself. Pulling a lacy handkerchief out of her handbag, she coughed behind it. "Apologies," she murmured. "Please continue."

"Yes, Miss Jankowski. I do express my regret for this, but it is necessary. The museum owner has insisted."

At least he appeared a tiny bit apologetic.

Straightening her spine, Martha arched an eyebrow, ignoring the panicked tightening of her chest. How she wished she had inherited her mother's cool and calm demeanor. Even after all these years of studying under her mother's tutelage, she found herself unable to be as composed under pressure.

But then, no one could compare with Mother. Nothing ever took her by surprise. "Perhaps I could speak to the owner?"

"No, miss." He released a long sigh. "You see, there's another team digging with the promise of an intact skeleton of a *Brontosaurus*—only time will tell if it is the same genus as yours. The owner here believes it is in their best interest for the museum to make it a competition for the two of you. Look at what the competition between Cope and Marsh has done for the field of paleontology." His grin was all too forced.

Anger flooded her chest. She surged to her feet, eyes narrowed. "And look at how much *damage* they have done! Need I remind you how many fossils have been lost because of their disgusting rivalry?" Her gloved knuckle rapped the hardwood desk, emphasizing her point.

"Now, now, Miss Jankowski. No need to upset yourself. We don't need to defame the prominent men of our field. I assure you, our owner has set forth some specific guidelines that will ensure nothing underhanded will take place. But the deadline remains. If you wish to have an exhibit here, those are the terms." His tone held less exuberance now and more stern scolding.

Martha pressed her lips together, stemming the rest of her argument. With a calming breath, she forced herself back to her seat. "I understand." She would not lose this opportunity. She offered her most polite smile and stretched out her hand. "I'd like to read over the guidelines."

He reached into his desk and pulled out a sheet of paper. "They are detailed here."

She scanned the document and let out a relieved sigh.

Rules for the competition:

1. No destruction of bones or fossils. The integrity of the dig sites must be upheld at all times.

2. No trespassing on the property of the other team's dig. However, the teams are responsible for their own security. Trespassing violations with evidence can be reported to the museum director.
3. No spying on the other team's dig.
4. No poaching members from each other's dig teams.
5. Teams cannot be larger than 100 men and hours cannot exceed fifteen work hours in a day.
6. Campaigns of disinformation or smears of integrity of the other team may not be made in the newspapers.
7. No attempts to bribe the museum director to accept anything other than an intact dinosaur skeleton.
8. There will be no make-up days due to weather. The end date of the competition, August twenty-sixth, is firm.
9. Upon the signing of the contract, the name of the entrant—should they win—will appear on the exhibit of the dinosaur skeleton alongside that of this museum in any given museum of the owner's choosing.
10. The winning team will receive $1,500, their picture in papers across America, and recognition of their work in the museum exhibit.
11. No attempt may be made to directly contact the owner.
12. Violation of any of these rules will result in the disqualification of the team in violation and a report to the authorities.

Well, the rules outlined a fair competition and consequences for any suspected sabotage. That was something. But a deadline? She bit the inside of her cheek, her mind racing. Rushing wasn't good in this line of work, which was tedious and could take a lot of time.

But the guidelines did say each team could have up to a hundred workers. That number was enormous compared to what she had.

She could hire more workers, but that meant more people would know about her location. Her findings. All the details about her dig site. She could hire security to protect the property. At least she legally owned the property, and the quarry was registered in her name alone. A generous gift from her parents when she turned twenty-one and told them of her discovery and desire to make a proposal to the museum.

Mother seemed supportive in her own distant way, and Father . . . well, Father went along with whatever Mother said. Martha, as their only child, wasn't denied much as long as she upheld Mother's one rule: bring credit to the Jankowski name.

That rule always hung over her head. All her growing up years, she'd never measured up to her mother's high-society standards. Her single place of comfort was digging in the dirt. Probably instilled in her by her father. Back when he had been one of those men out digging for dinosaur bones. Unlike Marsh, who was wealthy and hired men to do all the excavating in his fight for his name at the top of everything, Father enjoyed the actual digging.

Until he came home scarred and broken. Father never went out on another expedition. As much as she'd begged him to talk about it over the years, he refused. The light in his eyes disappeared. Mother was closed off as well. Discussion about that summer was prohibited. It was a wonder Martha had been able to convince her parents to allow her to follow in her father's footsteps.

Mr. Spalding cleared his throat, drawing her out of her thoughts.

She blinked and focused on the task at hand. "On first glance, everything seems to be in order. I appreciate the fact that the owner has put such foresight into this. Is it all right if I take this home to review?"

"Yes. But we need the contract signed by Monday morning."

"I see. That is acceptable." For the most part. She despised the thought that someone else was vying for the exhibit space. But there was nothing to do about it now. "I appreciate your time, Mr. Spalding." She stood.

He did as well and gave a polite bow. "It's an honor to work with you, Miss Jankowski. I look forward to seeing what you uncover." His smile was genuine enough.

She smiled back, turned on her heel, and headed out the door, her insides quaking. Every ounce of her mother's training kicked in and she held her head high as she walked down the sidewalk. Streetcars rolled by, the loud conversation of passengers floating on the spring breeze. The sun warmed Martha's face once again after the dim and dreary interior of the museum, restoring some of her energy. Being out in nature always did so. Society, with all its airs and rules, drained her. But occasionally attending the events requested by her mother was the price she had to pay for doing what she loved.

Her thoughts drifted back to her meeting with the museum director as she rounded the corner toward the stately Jankowski mansion. A competition hadn't factored into her plans, or funds. Asking her parents for help meant another list of soirees she would be required to attend in return. She slipped through the wrought iron gate, up the stairs, and through the front door, eager to make it to her bedroom. She needed time to think this through. Without knowing anything about the other dig and its team, how was she supposed to prepare for this?

"Martha."

She jumped and grasped the wooden banister to steady her footing. Spinning around, she spotted her mother emerging from the drawing room. Mother was a striking woman. Her light blonde hair haloed her fine-boned features. Her heart-shaped face framed pale blue eyes, a sharp nose, and rosebud lips that rarely smiled.

Mother crossed the plush carpet of the entryway, full skirts swishing around her feet.

"Hello, Mother."

Mother's keen eyes examined every inch of Martha's outfit, from the brim of her blue velvet hat to the tips of her black leather shoes covered in street dust. Martha tensed against the impending critique.

Instead, Mother's lashes shuttered her eyes as she offered the barest hint of a smile. "Come join me for afternoon refreshment. I would like to hear about your visit with the museum director."

Martha's eyebrows rose. "You . . . want to hear about that?" Was she dreaming? Mother's invitation enticed her like the smell of a dig.

"Of course. This is quite an adventure for you. And I want to ensure our investment is sound."

Just like that . . . the catch. Once again, it was all about money, about what their investment would bring to the Jankowski name. She should have known better. Martha lifted her chin. "It is sound, I promise." No quivering chin, no squeaky words.

"Fantastic." Mother led them to the sitting room.

The façade back in place, Martha followed. Ever the dutiful daughter.

In public, Mother often praised her work. Many of the richest men in Denver had been impressed by Martha's assistance in the findings of *Plesiosaurs, Sauropods,* and *Pterosaurs,* which made her parents proud. But it had been only that . . . assistance.

It had taken more than a year—including twelve dinners with the elite social crowd of Denver—to convince her parents that she had the skills and the know-how to branch out on her own. She could entertain scads of people with her knowledge of fossils one minute and enthrall them with her piano playing the next. Good thing she really did enjoy the conversations with her parents' friends and connections and loved playing the piano,

But what gave her the greatest joy was being at her dig site.

The Great Dinosaur Rush produced unprecedented focus to the field of paleontology. The past decade revealed finds beyond her wildest dreams. How awful that the two men who had brought acclaim and the world's eye to the discovery of dinosaur fossils also shamed themselves for all to see.

She wanted to be different. Wouldn't it be wonderful if she could find bones, display them, give lectures around the country, and get people excited about paleontology and geology? Instead of double-crossing other digs through bribery, spying, thievery, dishonesty, and rushing to publish in journals to outdo the competition—she would do things well. Respectfully. And demand such integrity from all of her teams.

What was she doing? Judging and condemning so swiftly. She wouldn't even have the opportunity with the museum right now if not for Othniel Marsh and Edward Cope bringing the fossilized bones of the great beasts to everyone's attention. But the way they went about accomplishing it had been quite horrid. Imagine going so far as destroying fossils so their opponent couldn't have access to them!

Still . . . without their driven pursuit, she probably wouldn't be able to do what she loved. How many decades would it have taken to get people to pay attention?

She shuddered to think about it.

No matter what horrors and disreputable activities the two did to one another, it helped her cause now. That was what mattered.

This competition would be civilized. Everyone would play fair. And it wouldn't matter one bit that she was a woman.

If Mary Anning could dig up fossils in Lyme Regis decades ago, then she could do the same thing here in America. She wasn't out to prove anything, she simply wanted to be allowed to dig and to be known for her accomplishments. Was that asking too much?

Even with the internal pep talk, the weight of the situation sagged her shoulders.

There wasn't a lot of time to complete her find. A deadline now loomed over her head.

It might take a bit more begging to her parents—this was sure to cost a great deal more—but in the end they'd allow her to do whatever she wanted. They always did.

The real question was . . . did she have a chance at winning?

***

Saturday, April 6, 1889 • Outside Denver

"Glad you've done this kind of work before. Can you start right away?" The thin-as-a-rail foreman sent Jacob Duncan a questioning look. A pencil tucked behind his ear and papers in his hand, he appeared a tad overwhelmed.

"Sure. Today? Monday? When do you need me?" His hands tingled with anticipation. After all these years of helping with fossil excavating digs, he was working on a *dinosaur* dig! This was the best news he'd had in the last few years.

He'd been saving his money so he could trek out here to Colorado with hopes of being hired on. After only three weeks, he'd done exactly that. God was good. Wait until he wrote home to his family.

"There's still plenty of hours to put in a full day today. Then on Monday, I'll assign you to a specific crew and area of the dig. We've been at it a few weeks, but there's a deadline of end of summer, so we will be working long hours."

"Yes, sir. I'm ready for whatever you need me to do." Jacob plopped his hat back on his head.

"Just remember, you signed the agreement to not talk about the dig or alert anyone to its location. This is imperative. Even if you see one of your fellow workers in town, the boss doesn't want you guys discussing a word about it."

"Yes, sir." Wait a second. "Um, sir, is it all right if I tell my family back home?"

The foreman squinted. "They don't live anywhere around here?"

"No, sir. They don't even live in Colorado."

"I can't see how that would be a problem. As long as you don't share any details."

"I won't, sir. I promise."

"Good. Put on a pair of gloves and follow me." The foreman turned and took a brisk pace up the trail behind him.

Jacob tugged on his gloves and followed. The trail was thin and narrow—like the foreman—through the scrubby brush and red-tinted dirt. As they climbed, the ground grew more of a gray color mixed with browns. Then it changed back again. It was fascinating topography and geology here. Nestled at the foot of the Rocky Mountain range outside of Denver, the rolling ridges were dotted with masses of red and white rock plates that stood up at forty-five-degree angles pointing toward the mountains behind them. As Jacob followed the foreman along the trail, he shivered. Though spring had come, the foothills remained at least ten degrees colder than town.

Jacob blew into his hands as he tried to memorize the path to his dig. It was impossible to take it all in. Each turn on the trail revealed a new discovery. Small, spiked bushes grew out of dusty red rocks. The majestic pine trees towered in clusters on the ridge looming above him. Clouds drifted through an otherwise clear blue sky. The Rocky Mountains, still topped with thick white snow, jutted into the heavens.

"I will lift up mine eyes to the hills, from whence cometh my help. My help cometh from the LORD, which made heaven and earth."

Jacob ran his hand along a jutting ridge of rock, feeling the truth of the Word of God. He knew many men of faith who went to school to become pastors and preach the gospel. Jacob respected and admired those men.

But the glory of God's creation spoke to him in a way he couldn't explain. The feeling of dirt in his hands, touching the things of God's creation, made the Word come alive. Being in a forest or at a dig, chipping away to find what was set in stone ages ago . . . Jacob knew the Lord ordained all of it. It fascinated him.

Later, he'd record in his journal everything he saw. Maybe sketch it out if he could. But he'd have plenty of time since he would most likely be making use of this trail each day. In a week, he'd have it memorized.

The foreman proved himself a man of few words as they trekked up the trail.

They crested a ridge and Jacob gaped as he took in the scene before him. A huge quarry rested between two ridges with dozens of men digging, chiseling, and brushing. The clinking of metal against rock echoed around him and mixed with the hum of men talking, shovels scooping up the earth, and his own footsteps.

He had to focus back on the trail as they traversed down toward the quarry. The foreman continued his pace, oblivious to the shifting gravel in his wake. Small rocks rolled beneath the soles of Jacob's boots. He threw his hand against the small ledge on his right, sweat breaking out on his brow. The incline was much sharper going down into the dig site. Falling on his face wouldn't make the best impression. Even worse, an injury could keep him from working and he was in desperate need of this job.

After another minute of scrambling down the trail, the fore-man stopped and pointed. "Over there. All the rock and debris that has been removed from the site needs to be transferred to a pit on the other side of the ridge. The men will show you where to go."

Jacob saw two men working with wheelbarrows.

"It's not like digging for bones, but this pile has grown a bit out of hand. With the scent of rain in the air, we don't want any of the work to be covered up with everything we've already painstakingly removed. For today, why don't you three work together and then Monday, everyone can get back to the dig."

"Yes, sir."

"Good. Head on over and get to work."

"Yes, sir." He nodded and watched the man walk down into the quarry with his papers as he removed the pencil from behind his ear.

The dig was amazing to behold. Men worked all over the quarry with bones protruding from the rocky layers. What an immense project!

Jacob didn't envy the foreman's job. Personally, he'd hate to be the one in charge. All the pressure was stress he didn't wish to carry.

But digging in the dirt? This was where he belonged. Each day working at this dig was a step toward increasing his pale-ontological studies. Each hour was the chance to learn how God created this part of the earth, layer upon layer. His mind swirled with the possibilities of what they might find as he walked over to help the men clearing the enormous pile of debris.

"Jacob Duncan." He introduced himself with a grin at the two men who'd stopped and stared. "I'm here to help you today."

"Great." The man closest to him with red hair relaxed a little. He held out a hand. "I'm Jim and this is Henry. Grab that wheelbarrow over there and load it up with as much as you can. The fewer trips the better if we're gonna finish today. We'll show you where to haul it."

"Got it." Jacob rolled up his shirtsleeves, grabbed a shovel, and tightened his work gloves. Gripping the handles of the wheelbarrow, he made his way to the debris pile. The shovel scraped against the rock and soil. Red dust swirled in the air with each scoop. Once the barrow was full, he swiped sweat from his eyes, took a deep breath, and heaved the barrow up and forward on the unsteady path. His forearms burned in his attempt to keep the heavy load balanced. The wheel skipped and skidded over the gravel, tipping dangerously to one side. But he was too slow. His feet slipped, sending his load into the air and back to the ground in a shower of rocks and dirt. Air rushed from his lungs as he slammed into the ground.

Jacob clenched his eyes shut and tried to focus on calming the racing of his heart. Jim and Henry's laughter echoed off the rocks. His face burned. They'd be no help in cleaning up his mess.

After a few moments, he sat up with a groan. Bits of rock and red clay covered his shoulders and chest. With one more push he stood and glanced at the sky. His eyebrows shot up. The usually cloudless Colorado skies, which had been blue and sunny, were now gray with the hint of rain. Clouds moved in over the Rocky Mountains rising out of the ridges to the west of them. And they weren't white and fluffy. No, these were darker. Angrier.

He sighed. If he had to guess, they wouldn't finish before the rain hit—especially with him spilling his first load—but he would do what he was told anyway.

And quick. Even if every muscle in his back, legs, and arms screamed at him.

Jacob righted the wheelbarrow and pulled his shovel from the pile of rubble. He began tossing the mess back into its wheeled container and tried to ignore the discouragement that threatened to creep into his heart.

He shifted his thoughts to Monday. If he could help them accomplish *this* task then Monday would prove to be an incredible day. A day he could dig.

That was something to look forward to. Even with the grueling job in front of him, Jacob smiled. His dreams of one day becoming a paleontologist *might* come true.

three

"Doubts have arisen in my mind concerning the Bible and fears as to the destiny of man. By earnestly praying to God and studying His Word more of these doubts are being removed. I mean to make a point of studying the Bible more this year."

~Earl Douglass

MONDAY, APRIL 8, 1889 • OUTSIDE DENVER

Jacob let out a puff of breath, spraying red dust into the air. His hip was wedged between two ledges of rock. Stones pressed into his ribs and sweat trickled down his collar. Still, it was the only way to get to the dark edges he'd spotted an hour before. It took a trained eye to be able to tell the difference between rock, dirt, and potential fossil.

He tugged off a glove with his teeth. Running a bare finger down the ridge, the texture was smooth compared to the jagged rock surrounding it. It had to be a bone. Some of the other workers found a few vertebrae not too far from where he was last week before he started. It didn't necessarily ensure that his find was connected to the dig. He rolled to his back and stretched. But it didn't mean it wasn't part of the skeleton either.

Dust caked the corners of his mouth. He grimaced, feeling sand in his teeth. Another job hazard. Time for a water break. Then he would come back and see if there was a better way to dig out whatever he'd stumbled upon.

"Duncan!"

He scrambled to stand as Joe, the foreman, made his way to his station.

The wiry man clapped Jacob's shoulder with surprising force and stared at the ledge he'd vacated. "Did you find something?"

"I think so." Jacob pulled a kerchief out of his back pocket. "There's an ivory-gray colored ridge. It feels like a bone, but I need a better angle to uncover more."

Joe nodded. "It'll have to wait. I need you to help with a rib removal in quadrant seven. I can send someone else over here to take a closer look."

Disappointment spiraled in Jacob's chest. He swallowed and nodded.

Joe caught his eye and chuckled. "Don't look like I just shot your dog, Duncan. A rib is no small discovery. And it's hefty. We need strength like yours to make sure it doesn't crack when it comes out of this confounded rock." He took off his hat and beat it against his leg. "Besides, the other guys need to get to know ya. Know your skills."

Jacob's face burned. He needed to be careful about his attitude. He was here to work and learn from those who had worked in this field much longer than him. *I'm sorry, Lord. Help me not to let my pride get in the way.* He picked up his rucksack that held his tools and slung it over his shoulder.

The foreman led him down a small path to a quadrant southeast of his workstation. Several men were positioned in front of the rib bone, tapping rock with chisels and hammers. Other men hauled buckets of dirt to a pile not unlike what he moved last week.

Jacob watched the scene in fascination. There was a rhythm to the work that was satisfying to watch. He looked at his foreman. "Where do you want me to work?" He held his breath, hoping not to have to move dirt again.

"You see Abe over there on the left?" Joe gestured to a slim man bent over the thick end of the bone.

Jacob nodded.

"You'll be helping him get that end out today and possibly tomorrow."

"Yes, sir." He grinned and made his way to Abe.

Setting down his rucksack, he pulled out the cloth roll holding his tools. "Hi, I'm Jacob Duncan. Joe told me to come over and give you a hand."

Abe glanced up. His face was streaked with red dust. "Abe Smith. You any good with a fine point chisel?"

Jacob unraveled the roll and pulled the tool from a pocket. "Where do you want me?"

"Back of the bone, opposite me," Abe said, a cough strangling his words. He grabbed a canteen and took a long chug of water. Then he dumped the rest of the water over his head, the water making small rivers in the dirt on his skin. "The end here is stuck. I've been working to get it out for the last hour, but it won't budge."

Jacob walked around the ridge sticking up from the earth. He pulled out a small brush and flat-headed hammer along with the chisel. Swiping rock debris away from the bone, he inserted the chisel into a small crack in the dirt. With a few taps, red clay broke away in chunks, revealing a bit more of the rib.

A giddy grin threatened to split his face. He pressed his lips together, determined not to look too green. But the thrill of finding and revealing something hidden for hundreds and hundreds of years never got old. And this was the biggest bone he'd seen, by far.

"You from here?" Abe's voice cut through his thoughts.

"What? Oh. No. I'm from Chicago. How about you?"

"Wyoming territory."

Jacob swept more fine dust off the bone. "Do you have family back home?"

"Just my ma." After a long moment of silence, the other man went on. "My pa died when I was young. Had a brother too but he died when he was just a little 'un."

Jacob's heart twisted. He thought of his big family back home. Even with six people crammed into a small two-room house, he couldn't imagine life without them. To lose family so young was incomprehensible. "I'm sorry to hear that, Abe. That had to be hard." He swallowed. His words sounded hollow to his own ears. *Lord, please help me show this man Your kindness and comfort.*

Abe shrugged and bent back down over the dirt. "Don't know no different. Just how it goes sometimes."

What could he say to someone who'd lost so much? He tapped and dug in the dirt, praying for his digging partner.

"I'm gonna get more water down at the creek. Do you need some more?"

"Thank you. That would be helpful." Jacob passed the canteen to the standing man. "Do you want me to go with you?"

Abe shook his head. "Just keep working on that rock over there. Whatever you're doin' is helping me on this side. I'll be back."

Jacob watched Abe walk down the path toward the small creek that ran along their worksite. His shoulders hunched tight, and his head stayed down. No one greeted him or acknowledged him.

Sighing, Jacob scooped more dirt and rocks out of the small hole he created. He tapped his chisel again, scattering the ants trying to climb the bone. Maybe he could make friends with Abe. And not just because Abe seemed lonely. But because he could use a friend too.

His canteen careened over the boulder behind him, sliding to a stop with a solid thud into another rock.

He jumped up and found Abe sitting back down on the other end of the rib. "You could have warned me." The words released on a chuckle.

Abe's shoulders shook with laughter. "But that's not fun. Come on, Duncan, relax. It was just a joke. You were lookin' so serious."

Jacob grunted and sat back down. He looked at his canteen and shook his head, a small smile forming. "You still could've said something," he grumbled. "We wouldn't want it to damage any of the fossils."

"It wasn't anywhere near them. Next time, I'll throw it at your head. No chance in damagin' it." Abe's laughter floated on the air and Jacob joined him. "Look at how close we are ta gettin' it out." His new partner pointed.

The tension seeped out of Jacob as he gazed at the length of the fossil. Abe could toss a canteen at him whenever he wanted. They were about to pull a fossilized bone out of the ground!

MONDAY, APRIL 8, 1889 • UNIVERSITY OF DENVER

Martha made her way into the lecture hall where hundreds of men had gathered. She scanned the crowd. Shoulder to shoulder, the guests, dressed in evening tailcoats and top hats, filled the room.

She wouldn't be able to see above any of them. With a frown, she stood on her tiptoes, craning her neck from side to side in hopes to see the stage. But suit-clad shoulders still blocked her view.

Her feet itched to stomp the planked floor, but she resisted. She was back in society. The scientific society to be precise. Any displays of impatience from a lady might be tolerated among the elite as coquettish behavior. But among men of reason, Martha had to keep her emotions in check. Oh, why hadn't she asked Lily Rose to accompany her?

Because once Martha reached sixteen years of age, Lily Rose had done her utmost to erase Martha's passion for learning. For digging. For dinosaurs. She hadn't succeeded, of course. But that was why Martha was alone tonight. Every once in a while, she liked to give Lily Rose a break. Especially when she wanted to attend a lecture or exhibition. And it saved Martha from listening to Lily Rose's negative comments about women studying science or religion. The woman had strong opinions about both. Especially when it came to women in what society presumed was a man's field. In addition to Martha's regular studies, the older French woman had taught Martha the intricate rules of society and had held her to high standards—even stricter than her mother's.

But lately her companion had become a dichotomy when it came to her personal opinions. When Martha had showed Lily Rose the contract for the competition, the woman had told her to make sure that Martha had a separate account for her own money to make sure no man could get his hand on the earnings of *her* accomplishments. Martha had laughed off the woman's advice, saying it wasn't a certainty she would win.

Now, the memory of the conversation made Martha frown. Perhaps she needed to check in with Lily Rose and make sure she was all right.

Surveying the room of men, Martha gripped her handbag close. It really would have been nice to have the other woman here. No matter her opinions. In hindsight, she should have known that tonight was not the time to leave Lily Rose at home. A twinge of discomfort settled for a moment—was she the *only* woman here?—but she lifted her chin, determined to work her way through the mass of men.

"Excuse me." It was impolite to raise her voice, however she could count on the pitch of it to contrast the depths of the men's tones. Men parted and made a slight path for her, removing their hats for a moment as they spoke their greetings.

"Pardon me." She continued a few steps forward. No reason to let someone taller get the best seat possible. It would probably take her an hour to move through the mass of men, but she had time.

As she wound her way through the back of the crowd toward the front of the auditorium, she counted three other women present. And she knew all three of them. Wives of some well-known reverends in the area. She shouldn't be surprised. It was a lecture on the Bible and science working hand in hand.

Many believed it was impossible to be a scientist and a person of faith at the same time. While she would claim she was one of the latter, she was also a scientist first and foremost. All her education, all her experience and work in the field, had been in the pursuit of science.

She longed for a connection between the two. Not that she was all that religious. Oh, she went to church on Sundays, like any well-born lady should. But something inside urged her forward in her search. This prodding—almost a gnawing— inside, drove her quest for knowledge. For the truth. Even though Mother's lips pinched together in a disapproving line every time Martha brought up the subject.

Probably because it brought reminders of Phoebe.

The bright woman had filled Martha's life with color, enthusiasm, and joy. Brought in as governess when she was still quite young, Phoebe was unlike anyone she'd ever known.

She had an insatiable appetite for learning—just like Martha—and loved books, art, museums, and anything that had to do with history. Archaeology and geology were two of her favorite subjects. Still, there was so much more to the governess. A simple gratitude to be alive seemed to flow out of her each and every day.

She also quoted the Bible better than anyone Martha had ever heard. Much better than the reverend at church. And when Phoebe prayed? It sounded like she was talking to God and He was right there in the room with them. When she spoke about the Bible, she was full of animation. There was a light in her that was bright and magnetic. She lived her faith in everything she did. Not just on Sundays. Her beliefs were . . . *real*. Much different from the façades that everyone in her social circle portrayed. Or in the scientific community for that matter.

More than anything in her life, Martha wanted that— something real. True.

When Phoebe left them, it broke Martha's heart. Try as she might, she never found anyone else like her. Then again, her experience was limited to her parents' social circle. And she was rarely allowed to the dinner parties and gatherings because she had still been a child. But she determined to live like Phoebe did. As time passed, Martha's memories faded to what seemed like dreams. She searched and grasped for something real like she'd seen in Phoebe, however, another person like her beloved governess wasn't to be found.

Thus her quest for knowledge. She pored over the vast number of books in their library at home and begged her parents for more. History had always been a boring subject to her before, but not anymore. When Lily Rose was hired as Martha's companion, she'd tried to change Martha's tutelage to only fine arts and fancy languages.

But Martha was stubborn and eventually, Lily Rose helped her study. Anything and everything she could get her hands on, until Martha was well-versed in French, Latin, mathematics, biology, chemistry, and music.

To understand man's history.

So she could understand the future.

But there was one subject Martha was never taught again. Religion. Nothing pertaining to God or the Bible. And Lily Rose never accompanied them to their church. She went to a different one.

At first, it had seemed odd. Martha even pressed her companion and tutor one day. The reply was stern and forceful. *No.*

Yet one simple fact kept Martha believing in God in her own small way. All of this couldn't have just . . . happened. No matter how many papers she read, it didn't make sense to her.

Honestly, it also comforted her to believe in a higher power. Like Phoebe had.

Oh! She'd bumped into a gentleman on her right. "Pardon me."

He dipped his chin at her, but his attention went right back to the conversation he'd been having. Gracious, how long would it take to get to the front?

Once she wriggled her way through the massive crowd and reached the front few rows, she breathed a bit easier and found an open seat in the third row. She should be able to hear the speakers from here. Several men stood and allowed her entrance into the row of seats.

A younger man dressed in a casual sack suit stood from the seat beside the empty one.

"Is this seat taken?" She smiled at him.

"No, miss." His hat in his hands was worn. The edges around his sleeves a bit frayed. But the bright light in his eyes was almost magnetic.

She sucked in a gasp. His eyes. There was something there . . . something just like Phoebe's.

The reminder brought a warm swirling to her insides. She instantly liked him and wanted to pepper him with questions. Who was he? Definitely not anyone she'd met at any other society occasions. "Thank you." She settled herself and snuck a glance at him from the corner of her eye.

The man beside her leaned forward a bit and studied her face. "Are you a student here?" His gaze was clear—not at all guarded like several gentlemen she'd known.

"No. I had been studying at Yale but am back home now. How about you?"

"Yale. Wow. That's quite impressive." His expression held a hint of awe. "I've had to put my studies on hold for a while. I'm simply here for the lecture." He grinned and held out a hand. "Jacob Duncan. It's a pleasure to make your acquaintance."

He was so genuine and honest looking it was impossible to keep her own full smile hidden. Who cared about etiquette at this juncture? It's not like Mother was here. "Martha Jankowski." She offered her own gloved hand in the way a lady should—knuckles up—but instead of him following the societal protocol, he shook it with a good bit of vigor.

Yes, she liked this fellow. A giggle burst out of her before she could stop it. Goodness, she sounded like a schoolgirl. "It's nice to meet you too, Mr. Duncan."

The evening hadn't been what he'd expected. Add to that he was exhausted from the day, which only added to his foul mood.

Rather than a lecture on the Bible backing up science or vice versa, so far, it had been more of an awkward, unplanned debate. He didn't like where things were headed. The poor man up on the stage seemed ready to hold his ground, but after a few men in the front row began to boo and heckle him, he stuttered his way through a few points.

Now it appeared he'd lost his train of thought. And his confidence.

Jacob shook his head. What was the world coming to? Why

couldn't someone have the freedom to share their thoughts and ideas? After another few minutes, one of the men claiming to be an expert jumped up on the stage and challenged the guest lecturer.

Had they all lost their minds?

The lecturer was now sweating and red, his shoulders slumped.

Jacob peered around him. Why wasn't anyone backing the man up? To his shock, the crowd thinned at that point. The crowd's earlier, excited chatter had shifted into tense, almost hostile silence from those who remained. Where that hostility was directed, Jacob wasn't sure.

It hadn't been that long since this university had been the Colorado Seminary. Surely there were still men of faith left here who could talk about its intersection with science with authority and persuasion.

From what he'd heard prior to the lecture, the crowd was full of them. Or so he'd thought. How swiftly the tides turned.

What a shame no one stood up to the naysayers. Even the clergymen left in the crowd were silent. Which struck him as quite odd.

If Jacob had more clout, or any kind of standing in society, he would have jumped to the man's defense.

"I see our point has been made." The man up front hopped down from the stage and the remaining attendees stood to go. He celebrated his victory with four other men. That was it. Four.

But they'd been loud and brash. Taunting anyone to disagree with them.

Jacob crossed his arms over his chest and waited. Once again, the loudest voices had gotten their way. He'd looked forward to an evening of education, encouragement, and intellectual discussion. Not watching an angry handful of men seeking to shut down another man because they disagreed with him. The animosity among the university crowd was surprising.

Conversations sprouted up around him as people milled about.

"Since I don't see us being able to make our way to the exit anytime soon, Mr. Duncan, might I inquire about your thoughts?" Miss Jankowski turned slightly in her seat, the skirt of her purple gown swishing against his shin. He shifted so he didn't crinkle the fine fabric. It probably cost a year's salary. But even so, it made her blue eyes stand out. There was something in their depths that drew him. Amusement? Interest? Definitely not disdain.

He'd been so caught up in his aggravation with what was happening up front that he'd momentarily forgotten about the interesting young woman beside him. Truly, the highlight of the evening before the lecture began. She wasn't forgotten anymore. Perhaps he could take a moment and get rid of his negative attitude. "What's on your mind?"

"I see you are displeased with the outcome of this evening."

"Aren't you?" Frustration bordering on a whine seeped into his voice. He definitely needed more sleep if an unfair debate could make him cranky. He cleared his throat and tried again. "That is to say, it wasn't exactly what I was anticipating."

She pursed her lips and looked up front and then to the dwindling mass of people. "I thought the same thing. I was hoping for some education this evening. In my field of work, I often struggle to articulate what seems so clear to me. That faith and science can, and do, work together. I hoped to learn how to express my beliefs in a more . . ." She paused and glanced at the empty stage, shoulders sagging. "A more courageous way, I suppose."

Field of work? Faith? Hm. "Oh? What is the work that you do?" Not many women *worked*. Especially not ones dressed like the cream of polite society. What a conundrum this woman was.

She held up a hand. "Let's not get into that right now." Looking around again—what was she concerned about?—she leaned an inch closer and lowered her voice. "Are you a man of faith?"

"I am." He cringed. "Not that my attitude a moment ago was a good example of it."

She opened her mouth and then snapped it shut. After several seconds, she started again. "Are you also a man of science? I mean, I assume so since you are here this evening."

"I am. I have been studying paleontology for the last seven years." He held up a finger. "I should clarify, I have been working on digs to help pay for my schooling. I'm not finished yet. With my education, that is. But then again, I feel like we should always keep learning. No matter our field or how long we've been at it."

Her lips tipped up. "Yes, I wholeheartedly agree." She fidgeted with the drawstring bag that matched her dress and then allowed it to fall to her lap. "Paleontology is fascinating. But I know many scientists in the field who are leaning more toward an older earth philosophy since the discovery of so many dinosaur fossils. There are many questions that now arise with the discovery of those great beasts. Several scientists say they don't believe they could have been on earth at the same time as man."

"And you? What do you think about that?" Dare he ask? But it was out there now.

"I'm not entirely sure what I think." She pressed her lips together for a moment. "But oh, I love dinosaurs." Her face lit up. "The study of them is of utmost importance. In addition, I have attended church my whole life and I believe the Bible to be the Good Book. While I have many questions about Darwin's species origins and greatly respect the scientists who are trying to figure it out, I do believe that all of this didn't . . . *happen* on its own."

Such exuberance! And knowledge. He should know not to judge anyone—for better or worse—by how they appeared on the outside. For all her finery, there was an undiluted joy when she spoke about dinosaurs and the world around them. She was even childlike in her expressions of faith. He fiddled with the button on his cuff. When had he last sounded that joyful about anything to anyone but his family?

"I'm sorry, Mr. Duncan," Miss Jankowski's voice broke through his thoughts. "Lily Rose—I'm sorry, my companion— reminds me with regularity that a conversation involves two people." Her head dipped closer, grabbing his attention. Her bright tone was at odds with the nervous twisting of her fingers around the ribbons of her handbag. Jacob mentally groaned. His mother would have his hide for leaving a beautiful young woman hanging in conversation.

"The apology is mine to make, Miss Jankowski. I was surprised by your confession, but I agree with you. I've been studying the papers of Georges Cuvier and find his work interesting. Have you read any of his writings?"

"I have heard of him, but not read his writings. I've had other priorities of late." Her eyes bored into his. "You are a fascinating man, Mr. Duncan." Glancing at the exit, she inhaled sharply. "Goodness." Rising to her feet, she looked toward the back door again. "Most of the crowd has left for the evening, and I must be on my way, but don't take that as a reflection on our chat. I would love to continue our discussion sometime. I promise I shall look up Mr. Cuvier to prepare for our next conversation."

He had come to his feet as well and turned his hat over and over in his hands. Next. She said *next*. Which meant she planned for them to speak again. That thought alone was enough to eliminate his foul mood from earlier. "I apologize for my ill attitude about the lecture earlier. It has been enlightening to speak with you. And I look forward to the chance to talk with you again."

"There is another lecture here next Monday that has piqued my interest. Perhaps we could meet here and discuss our ideas?" The tilt of her head put the small feather in her blonde curls at a jaunty angle, giving her a mischievous appearance. With a light cough, he suppressed the laugh in his throat. He didn't want her to mistake his amusement for mockery. It was quite the opposite.

What a bold young woman. He'd never met anyone like her. What could it hurt? He'd love to see her again, even if it meant sacrificing a little sleep. "I'd be honored."

"Whoever gets here first should save the other a seat. Don't you agree?" Her grin showed off a set of dimples.

He cleared his throat and smiled back. "I do. It sounds like we have a plan."

She curtsied and her purple hat dipped in his direction. "Until next Monday, Mr. Duncan."

"Until then." He watched her walk away. Such an odd encounter. But he was glad they'd met.

If she was willing to meet and discuss faith and science, he wouldn't say no. He wanted to continue his education as much as possible. Each opportunity to discuss ideas and theories with leaders in this field was the chance to learn and grow. He smiled. The chance to see Miss Jankowski again made this opportunity a little sweeter. Next week, he should make sure that he went to bed early Sunday night. It would be best if he didn't appear as a grouch two weeks in a row.

TUESDAY, APRIL 9, 1889 • OUTSIDE DENVER

When people stood in her path, she usually found a way around them.

But today was different. Today, she was furious. Today, *someone* hadn't followed directions. And that someone would have to pay. Looking behind her, she eyed the man squirming against his restraints on the ground. Stupid fool.

The gag over his mouth kept him from speaking but didn't quell his grunts and groans. The horrendous hullabaloo was enough to give her a headache.

"Shut up!" she tossed over her shoulder as she tied the long rope to her horse's pommel. "You had one simple job, and you couldn't even accomplish that."

He'd gotten too lazy. Too comfortable. And that couldn't be allowed.

After all these years, the people she surrounded herself with were loyal. Obedient. Willing to do whatever she asked, as though their lives depended on it.

Which they did.

And it didn't hurt that she compensated them well for their devotion.

Why this idiot decided to diverge from the plan was almost beyond her comprehension.

No matter. She lifted her chin. Every time she gazed into the mirror, she marveled at her gifts. She might not be young by the world's standards, not that anyone knew her actual lifespan in years. But anyone who looked at her saw her beauty. Her strength. Her resolve. Her independence.

She'd been complimented for them time and again.

Those words of affirmation would continue because people always saw what they wanted to see. And over the years she had perfected the art of pulling the wool over people's eyes.

Now if she could keep the occasional fool from messing up her carefully laid plans, everything would be perfect.

At least she'd found out before he threatened to unravel it all. She'd simply have to find another spy.

As much as she abhorred getting her hands dirty, sometimes

she had to take care of things herself. She allowed a smile. Sometimes she liked to.

She kicked her horse into a gallop and tugged her hat down low over her brow.

The rope behind her grew taut as it dragged the weight of the useless man. After a few miles, she called out, "Whoa."

Her trusted mare slowed and whinnied.

The woman jumped down, untied the man, and slipped his cowboy boot off his right foot. The rope had rubbed a light imprint into the leather. It wouldn't do to be sloppy. She hated sloppiness.

With careful movements, she extracted a single white glove from her bag and laid it on his chest. Then she wound up her rope. No sense in wasting good rope on a dead man. Once it was secure on her horse, she mounted it once again and headed back. Let the buzzards and coyotes have him. He wasn't going anywhere.

With a sigh, she stared at the snow-covered peaks in the distance.

Another distasteful—yet oddly satisfying—task was finished. With enough time to get cleaned up for dinner.

four

"Be awake for time is passing
And there's endless work to do
Thou shalt fail but never falter
Every day begins anew."

~Earl Douglass

WEDNESDAY, APRIL 10, 1889 · JANKOWSKI DIG SITE

Hands on her hips, Martha surveyed her site from the ridge above. Resting against the curve of a large boulder, she studied the massive skeleton emerging from the dust of the earth. For more than two years, she'd worked these rocks, this packed dirt. With a few trusted and experienced workers at the start. Now her team had ten men and would grow to accommodate the scale of the dig. It had cost her a great deal of money, but each man signed confidentiality contracts and pledged their loyalty. In the end, it would be well worth the investment. And hopefully help her win the competition.

Movement in the northeast quadrant caught her attention. A small group of men gathered around the right rib cage. Those bones would have to come out first. Though they were large, they were still delicate and would need the gentle touch of her most experienced crew. A few feet back from them, a larger group stood, ready with wheelbarrows and shovels to clear the rubble out of the way.

They were waiting for her. But the enormity of the moment was too much. She'd called for a break to gather her emotions and fled to this spot. Her sanctuary. The red dirt path was worn to a packed smoothness by countless hours of pacing. Tufts of sagebrush dotted the landscape. Purple and white columbine flowers brought bursts of color to the canvas of green and tan. The beauty of her home never ceased to inspire her. She did her best thinking up here, where the wind teased her hair, the sun warmed her skin, and the sky kissed the great jutting rocks and mesas shadowing the quarry.

But there was no need to think or pace now. Today was a joyful day. Everything was in place to begin the full excavation of the *Apatosaurus* skeleton. Her dreams were within her grasp. But above that, she could go back to her parents with her head held high. Their investment had not been in vain. She'd proved them wrong. Just like she'd told them she would. The memory was bittersweet as it replayed in her mind.

"Martha, my dear, this is outlandish." Her mother's eyebrows had arched high above her bright blue eyes. She brought her teacup to her lips then paused. "Though Denver is not quite the height of polite society as New York, you must know the irregularity of it will be talked about."

"Mother . . ." She made her tone as sweet as the sugar cube dissolving in her tea. It was the one that always worked with her parents. "The implications for what this magnificent of a find could do for paleontology are overwhelming. Not to mention the fact that placing the Jankowski name next to it in the museum would be a credit to you both. Father spent years of his life devoted to the search—and now I'm following in his footsteps." Martha set her teacup on the tray, working to school her features into a pleasant yet earnest expression. "Please . . . allow me to continue on the legacy. For our family."

Mother shared a glance with Father. Antoni Jankowski picked up a folded newspaper and tucked it beneath his arm. He stood and looked at Martha then back at Mother, his eyes cold and distant. "It's your decision, Victoria." He left the room, slamming the door behind him.

Mother didn't bat an eye. She sipped her tea, peering at Martha over the rim.

Martha refused to fidget. She could allow no evidence of her nerves—or of weakness.

Finally Mother spoke. "You make a fine argument, but we are also thinking of your reputation. We want what is best for you."

Martha's shoulders eased. A little thrill raced up her spine and she rejoiced a bit inside. Victory was almost hers. "This is the best for me. I'm a Jankowski. And I'm determined."

The crunch of boots on grass brought Martha back to the present.

The unmistakable scent of mint wafted through the air and she turned to greet Lily Rose. Her companion blew out her breath and leveled a look Martha's way as she took the last few steps to the top. "You should remember that this isn't an easy climb in women's footwear."

Martha stuck her own boot-clad foot out from under her skirts. "You could always give in and allow me to buy you a pair of these."

The woman grimaced. "I don't know why you insist on wearing men's boots—"

"You made my point a moment ago." Martha nudged her friend's foot with her own. "It's easier for me to climb around the dig site. I should get credit for not wearing trousers today."

Lily Rose rolled her eyes, but her smile took the sting out of the action. "Heavens, I would burn them all if I had the chance, but I know they assist you in your beloved work."

"You wouldn't dare do such a thing. Besides, I'd simply buy more." With a defiant lift of her chin, she winked. The two of them might not have the closest relationship, but there was something about spending so much time together that created an agreeable bond.

With a laugh, her companion lowered herself to a sitting position on a large boulder. "A fact I understand all too well."

Martha watched as the older woman adjusted her skirts with a natural grace. She glanced away, tucking her lip between her teeth. She would never be so graceful. No matter how hard she practiced. She picked a few random blades of grass from her skirt and ventured a question. "Are you getting tired of following me around and watching me dig in the dirt?" It still boggled Martha that her companion was unattached. With her blonde hair and beautiful complexion, Lily Rose was, by all society's standards, quite a beauty. It was a shame she hadn't found someone special.

"Never." Lily Rose twirled her parasol. "It was more tedious when you were younger and annoying in your childish ways."

They laughed together, Lily Rose's shoulder bumping hers with familiar fondness. "But you've become such a dear friend and I must admit I enjoy watching the bones come out of the earth. Perhaps not as much as you do, but I do find it interesting." She gazed out at the quarry then glanced back at Martha with a warmth in her eyes. "Besides, it's about time men were no longer at the top of every field. Women need recognition. I'm pleased as punch to assist you in your dreams. And there's the fact that I made a commitment to you and your parents. Until you get married, I'm bound by that—not that I mind."

Well. This was certainly a change from previous conversations. "I appreciate your support, Lily Rose. But you are not usually quite so . . . verbose in your praise of my work."

The older woman shifted on the boulder. "Do you think it's impossible for someone to change their mind?"

"Not at all." Martha smiled. "But this seems like a drastic shift."

Lily Rose looked over at her, a perfect dark blonde eyebrow arched high on her forehead. "You've been nagging me for years to see the value of your work. And now that I do, you want to argue with me about it?"

Martha let out a most unladylike snort. "A fair point. But I do wonder, Lily . . . don't you wish to find that perfect someone and settle down?"

Lily Rose shrugged. "Perhaps one day. You never know but that life can change in an instant. Perhaps my match is out there, and our paths are about to cross in a most unsuspecting way." A dreamy smile softened her features for a moment. Then she shook her head. "Nevertheless, I'm content enough right here."

Reaching out, Martha gripped the woman's arm. "Are you quite certain? I don't want you missing out on life because of me."

"Missing out?" Her longtime companion released an unladylike harrumph. "I would be missing out if I didn't get to see this dig to its completion. Now *that* would upset me."

For a moment they sat in comfortable silence.

While her companion had been a chaperone and in charge of her for the first few years they were together, it had been an easy transition to their new relationship once Martha turned seventeen. Journeying to Yale together, the two had come to understand one another throughout Martha's time at the university. After two years, they'd returned home as friends. Martha's parents paid Lily Rose a tidy sum to accompany Martha wherever she went. Mother insisted. Instead of giving instruction in behavior, manners, and which fork was used to eat a salad, now Lily Rose gave suggestions on attire and whom she should speak to and even more important—whom she should avoid. She also made sure that no one could ever suggest there was anything improper happening at the dig sites.

While no one necessarily told Martha what to do anymore—she had the freedom of a wealthy, intelligent socialite—it was nice to have Lily Rose in her corner for advice.

Not that they were extremely close. Yes, she was closer to Lily Rose than she was to her parents, but she and her companion weren't the kind of friends who shared intimate secrets and knew everything about one another. Martha had read about those kinds of friendships. Had even seen them on occasion but had never experienced it for herself other than Phoebe. A fact that pinched her heart. Was there something wrong with her that she hadn't been able to attract that kind of kinship? Or had she shut everyone else out after Phoebe left?

Was that kind of friendship a once-in-a-lifetime occurrence? Like fine jewels and only the dreams of storytellers?

Close relationships of any kind had puzzled Martha over the years. She'd never seen anything from her parents that showed they cared for each other more than anyone else. Goodness, they didn't even show *her* any great affection. Not since her father's accident.

But occasionally, after reading a good book, she found herself pondering . . . If love was so rare, why did the great authors and poets write about it? How did they know of it?

The clatter of a wheelbarrow coming down the path shook her out of the retrospective. If she wasn't careful, those thoughts could make her melancholy. And they didn't matter.

She had work to do, and the dinosaur wasn't about to dig itself up.

Standing back up, she took one more look down at the quarry. She'd paid a photographer a hefty sum to take a picture of the site when she was certain of what she'd uncovered. Then made him sign an agreement that he would speak of it to no one. One of the men on her crew was brilliant with sketches. Every day, she had him sketch their progress. Every step of the dig would be documented.

When she'd first written the proposal to the museum, she'd hoped to have the entire skeleton out of the ground by the end of *next* summer. That wasn't reasonable anymore—not with the deadline.

Bother. She'd wasted too much time on the ridge. "I better get back to it." She patted Lily Rose's shoulder and headed down the steep trail, thankful and determined to stay positive. They had several more hours of daylight today. That would help.

Footsteps behind her signaled that her companion was following. She always did.

As Martha rounded the curve back to the quarry site, she heard the men's voices. A bit more worked up than usual. She quickened her pace and ran right into her assistant. "What's going on, Mr. Parker?"

"One of the men came back a few minutes ago with word about the other dig."

She raised her eyebrows. "My instructions were specific. I didn't want anyone spying on the other group." Crossing her arms over her middle, she narrowed her gaze. All eyes in the quarry were now on her. "I don't want to know where it is. I don't want anything in our actions to give cause for anyone to cry foul."

"No one did any spying, miss." Wiry, young Josiah stepped forward. "The information came to me."

"How exactly did it *come* to you?" As much as she wanted to know whatever he'd found out, she had to make sure her crew understood the rules she'd laid out.

"I had to run home and change out my boots since I wore 'em clean through. My cousin raced over to tell me he was excited about his new job. Working at a dinosaur bone quarry. They hired fifty new men. He said they're under a deadline. Same as ours." Josiah wiped his sweaty face with his forearm. "But then he clamped his hand over his mouth and said something about how it was a secret and he wasn't supposed to say anything. I didn't respond, miss. I promise. That was when my stomach dropped down to my toes and I knew I had to tell ya."

She'd never known him to be anything but sincere. "Fifty men." Scanning the quarry and her small crew of ten men, she wanted to scream.

As much as she'd created the strict guidelines for her men and wanted to abide by them, she now had the intense need to know more. How far along were they at this rival dig . . . how big was their dinosaur . . . what genus was it—the director had said it was a *Brontosaurus*, but was it really? How many men did they have working total . . . ?

All the questions and thoughts swirled and she fought to keep them at bay. Fifty *more* men.

The lump in her throat grew. Fifty.

Against her ten.

She'd never make it.

SATURDAY, APRIL 13, 1889

"Hey, Duncan. Time for lunch."

Jacob pushed himself into a sitting position with a groan. For the last two hours, he'd been helping Abe dislodge three large bones related to the foot of their *Brontosaurus*. The outline of the foot bones was clear from the pointed claw-like toe to the larger joints that should lead up to the massive femurs. The toe bone alone was thicker than Jacob and almost as tall. It would take days, if not weeks, to excavate.

Fortunately, there were fifteen other men working on this portion of the dig. Usually, the men laughed and talked during their work. But today, there was an intensity sizzling in the air. The pressure to get these bones out of the rocks without breaking them was immense.

Jacob stood and brushed the rubble from his pants. He picked up his canteen and followed Abe to the meal tent. Thankfully the wind wasn't terrible today. He had enough dirt in his mouth from the dust and rubble in his quadrant. He was looking forward to eating food free of grit. Probably wishful thinking.

He filled his tin plate with baked beans, a couple slices of beef, and a biscuit. Abe found a section of table not crowded with the other workers. They sat and Abe dug into his lunch right away.

Jacob paused then bowed his head briefly, thanking the Lord for the food provided and asking for strength to keep digging. It was only noon, and he was already tired. Hopefully lunch would replenish his energy for what was sure to be a long afternoon of careful excavation. The blessing finished, he grabbed his fork and began to tuck away the hearty meal.

"Why do you do that?" Abe asked with a mouthful of food.

"Do what?"

"Bow your head over your food every time we eat." His friend stabbed a piece of meat and popped it in his mouth. His tone wasn't accusatory, merely curious.

"Oh." Jacob took a drink of water to clear his throat. "It's important to thank God for what's provided."

Abe chuckled and gestured at his plate with his fork. "You thank Him for this sorry excuse of a meal?"

Jacob smiled and pushed the beans around on his plate. "I

do. It may not be much, but it gives us the strength to keep doing our job. And it could be worse. I've been on digs where we've run out of food and had to forage." A shudder rippled across his shoulders. "There were days we didn't have anything to eat."

"How long you been diggin'?"

"Seven years. You?"

"'Bout the same." Abe scratched his jaw and dropped his spoon with a loud clatter on the tin plate. "Do you only pray over food?"

The jump in subjects jarred Jacob. He chewed his bite of biscuit for a moment before answering. "No. I talk to the Lord about a lot of things."

"Like what?"

He propped his elbows on the table and folded his hands together. "Anything really. My life out here in Colorado. How the dig is going. I ask the Lord to be with my family. I even pray for you."

Abe's shoulders stiffened. "You don't need to do that, Duncan. Don't know that the Almighty is interested in hearin' about the likes of me."

Jacob studied his new friend for a moment. Dark shadows hollowed out Abe's green eyes. His hair was wild from working in the wind. His shoulders curved inward in an almost permanent hunch. *Lord, please fill my mouth. Help me be a faithful witness.* "You're my friend. And I talk to Jesus about my friends. Besides"—he pinched off another bite of biscuit—"I can promise you the Lord takes an interest in you."

The slender man hunched even further over his empty plate. "You don't know what I've done, Duncan. The kind of life I've led. Trust me, God wants me to stay far away from Him." He stood and grabbed his plate. "I'll see you back at the site."

Jacob watched him walk away. Clearly the burdens Abe

carried were deeper than just losing his father and brother. Jacob sighed and tossed the hard edge of the biscuit on his empty plate. Standing up, he picked up his plate and cutlery to put them in the wash bucket.

A large man got up from the bench at the same time and jammed his shoulder into Jacob's, throwing him off balance. "We don't need your God talk around here," he growled.

Shock rippled through Jacob. "What?"

"Keep yer religion in yer church." The man's voice dipped low. "You don't want to find yerself in the bottom of a ravine." He shoved Jacob again and stalked out of the tent.

Jacob stood there. What should he do? He glanced around and noted several of the men glaring at him. He hadn't been shouting his faith from the top of the tent. Abe was the one asking questions. Still, he wasn't going to stay in the middle of the tent, making himself the target of their anger. He made quick work of his dishes and got out of the tent as fast as his legs would carry him.

His hands trembled, and his chest burned. If they expected him to stop praying for his meals or answering questions about his faith, they would be disappointed. Still, he needed to be wise. *"Be ye therefore wise as serpents, and harmless as doves."*

"Lord," he muttered under his breath as he followed the path back to his workstation. "Please lead me. Help me to learn what it means to be wise as a serpent and harmless as a dove." He came around the bend and spotted Abe digging around the *Brontosaurus* toe. Compassion filled his heart for his friend. He was broken in ways Jacob didn't fully understand. But he knew Jesus did. As he picked up his chisel and sat back down, Jacob continued to lift Abe to the Lord. And he asked for the courage to keep showing the younger man the love of Jesus, no matter what anyone else threatened to do to him.

Jacob almost fell onto his bed, he was so exhausted. The small room he rented in Denver allowed him to use the tub twice a week. He'd chosen tonight for one of his times since it was the end of the week and he'd rather go to church tomorrow *not* smelling like a horse that had been overworked. The effort of hauling the water up to his room had used up every ounce of remaining energy he had. But he climbed into the small bath and scrubbed away at the dirt that had taken up residence, hoping he'd be a bit rejuvenated and have the strength to tidy up things once he was done.

Another long day at the dig site had taxed every muscle in his body. More men were added daily, and the foreman put them in shifts and teams over specific areas. He said the boss had even offered them prizes for whichever team finished gathering all the bones from their area first.

While the money was a nice incentive, Jacob didn't like the way it made some of the men work in a haphazard manner. Safety should always come first for the men and the priceless fossils they worked with day in and day out.

There were now over seventy-five men chinking away at the stone quarry each day.

Not only did his body hurt when he came home, but his ears had begun to pound from all the noise.

Normally, his work at a dig site was lonely work. Oh, there were always a few others, but they were usually spread out over a large area chiseling away at the fossils. Working with Abe had been good. It was nice to have a partner. Someone to rely on.

Over the years, he'd been privileged to find an intact horse skeleton, a cat, and two dogs. Anytime they found a full or almost full skeleton, it was a prize. Usually, the bones were so scattered that it was difficult to find pieces that went together, so the rare finds with all the bones in close proximity were always celebrated. He'd had his name on a few of the finds and the funds from selling them to the museums helped with his schooling. But at this rate, he wouldn't be able to finish for a while. University was expensive and he worked to pay for a term and then worked another year or two to be able to afford the next term. All the while studying as much as he could.

It would be nice if all his experience in the field counted toward his education, but it seemed only wealthy students were handed that opportunity.

He shook his head. *Sorry to have such bitter thoughts, Lord. I should be thankful for all You've given me.*

He cringed. Twice now in the past week his exhaustion had led to a bad attitude. It wasn't that he'd never been a grouch before when he was tired, but as an adult, he'd done a pretty good job keeping his attitude positive and uplifting. Especially since he'd been challenged by his evangelist grandfather to always remember *Whom* he represented.

Even more of a reminder for him to take care of himself and get plenty of rest. The summer was sure to be a grueling one.

He leaned back against the edge of the tub. It wasn't the exhaustion getting to him. He'd allowed the thoughts of his peers to change his perception.

Many of the men he worked with came from nothing—poor backgrounds like him. Their prejudice toward people of wealth was overwhelming. It came up in practically every conversation.

Dunking his head to rinse out all the soap from his hair, he held his breath. When he came up, he shook his head—releasing the water and clearing his thoughts.

Prejudice of any kind wasn't honoring to God. *All right, Lord, please help me to guard my thoughts and mind while I'm at work.*

His shoulders relaxed and he sank into the water as deep

as he could, allowing his legs to hang over the edge of the tin tub.

Being shaped by one's environment was human nature. The people around, the opinions and words they said, the culture, the attitudes. All of it had an effect. He couldn't allow that to happen though. As a follower of Christ, he had a higher calling. To be transformed—not conformed to the world. And that was probably one of the greatest struggles man faced. It was easy to get caught up in the quest for money or accolades. Hadn't he experienced enough of that? He thought he'd learned his lesson, but like his grandfather said, it would be a continual battle until the day he died.

He'd simply have to do better.

He sat up. As he looked at the calendar on the wall, he smiled. In a couple days, he'd get to see Miss Jankowski again. The lecture on bugs was sure to be interesting, but the opportunity to discuss ideas with her again was even more so.

Over the course of the past week, he'd found himself thinking about her. Puzzling over her words and whatever mysterious work she had alluded to. It didn't hurt that she was a lovely woman with blonde hair and those intriguing dark blue eyes. Not that he had any aspirations of courting a woman so far out of his class, but he could appreciate the beauty God had given her.

The water chilled quickly, so he got out and dried himself off. There was still a letter from his family to read tonight. Which also meant he would need to stay awake long enough to respond.

Feeling a bit refreshed after taking care of the water and tub, Jacob sat on the single chair in front of a tiny table and opened the letter from his family.

Mom's beautiful script greeted him.

My Dearest Jacob,

Oh, how we have missed you these past months. I am writing on my own as the rest of the family is in bed, and I find myself praying for you and the work you are doing there.

My mother's heart has expressed concern over your chosen education the past few years. You know your father and I will support you in your choices, but I have to say that the burden I am feeling for you is great. It feels even greater the longer you are gone.

Reverend Moody was here a couple of weeks ago and he prayed for you. In all his wisdom, he tried to convince me that you were being a light in the darkness, but my fear has still grown. Is there any chance you would consider coming home?

Jacob's heart sank. It had been difficult to leave home because he loved his family—and because his desire to study paleontology had put a rift between his family and many members of their church. People who loved God but were fearful of the change in science since Darwin's book was published.

Reverend Moody had encouraged him to follow his calling, telling him that believers should never fear science because they knew the Author. He was confident that—in time—they would find the proof they needed. Nothing could shake the Word of God.

That had been enough for Jacob to head out on his quest. But now he wasn't so sure. Especially if his parents doubted him.

He finished the letter and laid the pages on the table. He swiped a hand down his face. Perhaps responding tonight wasn't the best idea. He needed to pray.

His family meant the world to him. And the influence of

his grandfather and Reverend Moody had been profound. *Am I doing the wrong thing, God?*

His desire to study archaeology and historical artifacts had turned to paleontology after he'd found his first fossilized bones. The intense longing to help the world understand God through science was profound. He had no idea how to accomplish it, but he still felt called.

But what if he was wrong?

five

"I am sitting on the brow of a hill where the breeze can cool me and blow away the insects. . . . The sky is a beautiful blue and it just struck me that there is no blue like that of the sky. It cannot be described only as sky blue. There are white clouds broken in many fragments and scattered beneath the blue. All the clouds are changing every minute."

~Earl Douglass

MONDAY, APRIL 15, 1889 • UNIVERSITY OF DENVER

Martha stifled a yawn. The lecturer was expounding on the value of the ladybug in gardens. The red and black spotted insects were particularly useful in keeping other insects from destroying fruits and vegetables. He'd made that point three times.

"Now I will briefly address the benefit of the arachnid." The older gentleman at the lectern pulled a sheet of paper out of a stack.

Martha shuddered. She wasn't all too fond of bugs of any kind when they were alive. They gave her the shivers.

The worst were spiders.

Not much scared her, but when the eight-legged things jumped or scurried across her path, she usually went out of her way to squash them under her boot. Nothing was more disturbing than something so small that could make her skin crawl and urge her to climb on a chair and scream.

Needless to say, she tuned out the speaker several times during his talk, turning her attention instead to the dig. It wouldn't bother her one whit to run across a fossilized spider. In fact, she'd probably cheer.

"To end this evening, 1 would like to talk about some interesting findings of late." The lecturer smiled. "It brings the worlds of entomology and paleontology together."

Martha's ears perked up. This evening had been a bit dry and lackluster, but maybe the man had saved the best for last. She sat up a little straighter and poked Lily Rose with her elbow. Her companion had fallen asleep. Again.

Not that she hadn't wanted to fall asleep herself.

"1 have it on good authority—from the man himself—that Mr. Hatcher has been pressed by Marsh to look for the tiny fossils of mammals that might have scurried beneath dinosaurs'—*Ceratopsians*'—feet." The man wiggled his eyebrows as his grin broadened and he leaned over the lectern. "He's found fossilized mammal teeth in ant hills of all places. Now isn't that exciting? It proves that our fields of science are all connected and if we wish to understand this incredible earth on which we live, we need to go to the smallest inhabitants—the bugs."

Applause rang out around them, and Martha joined in. Lily Rose, on her left, gave a polite clap or two, but Jacob, on her right, had come to his feet with a large portion of the audience.

When Martha arrived—quite early—with her companion, she'd made her way to the front row, taken her seat, and saved one for Mr. Duncan. After waiting half an hour, she'd feared he wouldn't make it, but he slipped into the row with two minutes to spare. Out of breath but grinning from ear to ear.

There hadn't been a chance for conversation—other than introductions—at the time and they'd settled in for the lecture.

Martha had wished to leave at least ten times during the past hour. Lily Rose's soft snores hadn't helped. Things changed with the lecturer's mention of John Bell Hatcher and made Martha glad she stayed until the end. Her enthusiasm bubbled up and she was eager to exchange ideas. Her mind was spinning.

The crowd's hum of conversation grew as people stood and milled about. Once again, she turned a bit in her seat. "Mr. Duncan, I'd love your thoughts on the evening."

He leaned forward and propped his elbows on his knees. An informal and relaxed posture. Something she wasn't accustomed to seeing, so she took the opportunity to study him. He angled his head back and forth as if weighing his thoughts.

"Well . . . to be honest, I'm not much of a bug enthusiast and found myself longing for my pillow. But I must admit I was quite intrigued with what he said at the end. That part would have been good to expound upon."

"I was thinking the same thing!" Shocked at her own outburst, she placed a hand over her lips. After a moment, she reclaimed her proper tone. "I am fascinated with what he said and would love to know more."

"Have you ever heard of this Hatcher fellow?" Mr. Duncan posed the question and stared at her. "If he was commissioned by Marsh, I'm sure all of his findings belong to the senior paleontologist. From what I've heard, Marsh isn't one to share the limelight."

She released a tiny huff. "You've heard correctly."

"I take it you're not a fan of Marsh? What about Cope?" He raised an eyebrow.

Tightening her lips, she paused for a moment so she wouldn't spew her intense feelings on the matter. A tiny pinch from Lily Rose reinforced her will. This was neither the time nor the place to unleash her full thoughts, but she couldn't stop her tongue from giving her opinion. "I'm not a fan of either one of them. Not one bit." She lifted her chin. "I hope this doesn't offend you, Mr. Duncan, but I do not appreciate how those two men have gone about their work. This horrible contention between them has brought shame on paleontology. I don't care how many people say it has brought the science to everyone's attention. It has accomplished more divisiveness and outright criminal activity than any good I believe it has brought. Paleontology"—she tapped her knee with her finger for emphasis—"deserves respect and honor. Not the hideous ridicule and disgrace their actions have summoned."

His eyes were wide as he stared at her.

So much for keeping her rant in check. Had she offended him?

"I appreciate the fact that you have obviously put a lot of thought into the subject. I'm not a fan of the men either." One side of his mouth lifted in a lopsided grin.

It put her at ease.

"If you come to spend much time with Miss Jankowski, you will find she has many thoughts on the subject," Lily Rose piped up from behind her.

Light laughter erupted from Martha, and she covered her mouth with her hand. "I apologize for my rant. I *do* have opinions."

Mr. Duncan leaned a bit past Martha and grinned at her companion. "I value both of your opinions. What do you think, Miss Ducasse?"

"I'm inclined to agree with Miss Jankowski, but don't mind me, I'm in need of some fresh air after that lecture."

Martha heard Lily Rose shift behind her, but she was on

the edge of her seat wanting to know more of Mr. Duncan's thoughts. "What do *you* think?"

"In all seriousness, I believe that their underhanded dealings aren't a good example to those who will follow in their footsteps." His eyes softened and he appeared thoughtful, studious. "It's why I'm hoping to continue working in the field and bring credit to it."

Why weren't more men honest and discerning like the one before her? "I appreciate the fact that you are a man of honor, Mr. Duncan. It will serve you well, I'm sure." Who was Jacob Duncan? He wore the same suit he'd worn last week, which reinforced the fact that he wasn't a man of means. That was fine. She didn't care about money or classes of people. Perhaps he didn't either and that's why he could be bold about what he believed to be right. He seemed comfortable spending time with her and discussing intellectual pursuits.

Maybe, like her, he hadn't had many interactions with those outside of his class. Mother had spoken to Martha on a few occasions about venturing out of one's class and always with negative tones. But without experiencing it herself, it never seemed to matter much. Martha had been sheltered. Perhaps Mr. Duncan had too. So what difference did it make?

Two people should be allowed to converse on a mutually agreeable subject. Regardless of social station.

"Thank you, Miss Jankowski. I appreciate your candor."

"To answer your previous question about Mr. Hatcher, I have studied his approach to mapping out the rock of a quarry on a grid and locating the bones and fossils to excavate before he starts to dig. It is a thoughtful and vigilant approach which I admire. But I hadn't heard of his findings in the anthills. That is interesting as well. Especially if there were any teeth of dinosaurs found."

Mr. Duncan looked behind him and stood. "It seems the hall

is emptying. Might I accompany you back to your conveyance and we could continue our chat?"

"That would be lovely." She stood and Lily Rose joined her.

"I'm intrigued by your knowledge of paleontology." He kept his hat in his hands as they walked up the aisle.

She bristled a bit at the statement. "Why? You don't believe a woman can be educated in the field?"

"Not at all." Her sharp tone seemed to roll right off him. "I'm simply intrigued and would like to know more. From what I can tell, you are more advanced in this subject than I am and like I said before, I wish to continue learning."

For half a second, she felt bad for how she had responded. But the way he looked at her—without any judgment—encouraged her to shake it off. Mr. Duncan was proving to be her favorite new acquaintance. A new idea formed. "Would you be interested in a job, Mr. Duncan?"

"That is awfully generous of you, Miss Jankowski, but I recently started a new job."

"Oh, I see." She took slow steps out of the building and toward her carriage. "This is ours." She pointed.

"Now, if you were offering me a job on a dinosaur dig, I might be tempted to quit and take you up on that." He laughed and opened the door for her.

Watching him for another moment, she debated whether she should tell him, but movement behind him drew her attention. She darted her gaze over Mr. Duncan's shoulder and spotted a young boy running toward them. The boy worked at her parents' home.

She stepped forward to meet him. "Isaac . . . is everything all right?"

"You mother asked me to fetch you, Miss Jankowski. Your father fell down the stairs. He's hurt pretty bad."

Panic prickled her skin. "Father fell? How? What?" Her mind was blank. "How badly is he hurt?"

Isaac's gaze dropped to the ground. "All Mrs. Jankowski said was you needed to be home fast."

Lily Rose was at her side in an instant. "Isaac, run back and tell Mrs. Jankowski that Martha is on her way."

The young boy nodded and took off running.

"Come on, Martha." Lily Rose's voice was firm. The older woman's arm slipped around her waist, drawing her close. "The carriage is ready."

Martha swallowed then glanced over her shoulder. Mr. Duncan stood to the side, hat in his hands. "Mr. Duncan . . ."

"Will be fine. In you go." Lily Rose helped her into the carriage and said something to their driver, Walter.

The carriage ride was a haze. Familiar streets looked like blurred paintings as the horses raced toward her home.

Lily Rose's hand covered hers. "I'm sure your father will be all right."

Tears gathered in Martha's eyes. "But what if he's not. What if he's—"

The carriage jerked to a stop, slamming Martha against the side. Walter opened the door. "Apologies, miss. I—"

"Thank you, Walter." She waved him off and scrambled out of the carriage. She picked up her skirts and raced up the stairs. The front door was open, and a group of servants clustered in the foyer.

"Mother!" Martha pushed through the servants to the front of the group. Her mother leaned on the banister, her eyes trained on the scene before her. Martha grabbed her hand. "It's all right. I'm here, Mother. How is Father?" The words tumbled from her as she struggled to catch her breath.

Mother didn't respond. She continued to stare at the ground.

Martha turned and drew back with a gasp. Her father was sprawled on the ground, one leg twisted beneath him. Blood oozed from a wound on the left side of his head, his dark hair matted to his skull. The right side of his head was covered with a thick bandage, but Martha could see blood seeping through its layers.

The doctor was bent over him, his ear to his chest. Their butler was next to him, waiting for instruction.

Martha's stomach roiled. Her legs shook violently. She gripped her mother's arm with trembling hands. "Mother, how did this happen?" Tears dripped over her nose. "Is Father dead? Mother!" She squeezed Mother's arm tightly, trying to get a response.

The doctor stood and turned to the two Jankowski woman. He wiped his thin fingers with a bandage and Martha closed her eyes. Her father's blood was all over his hands.

"Mrs. Jankowski, 1 am afraid it is not good news. Mr. Jankowski has sustained significant trauma to his head. Now, wounds to the skull do tend to bleed significantly, but that is not what is concerning." The doctor paused, and Martha opened her eyes. She swallowed and glanced at her mother, who was still staring at Father.

The doctor shifted his gaze from Mother to Martha. His glasses made his eyes look too large for his round face. "Miss Jankowski, 1 *am* sorry, but your father has lost consciousness and through my ministrations did not regain it. Your butler has offered the services of four strong footmen to move Mr. Jankowski to bed. There 1 will set his broken leg."

"Will he wake up?" Martha asked. Prayed. Hoped.

The doctor responded after a moment. "1 don't know, but 1 will do all in my power to see that he does. We will move him now. 1 will let you know when it is appropriate to see him."

The shuffling of the men and the groans that emanated from her father did nothing to move her mother. "Mother." She tugged at her sleeve. *"Mother!"*

Never had she seen the older woman speechless. Or unmoving. It unnerved Martha.

But then Mother's lips moved.

The noise around them kept Martha from understanding. "What? I didn't hear that."

"I . . . I didn't mean to . . . I tried to grab him when he tripped."

~⌒~

Wednesday, April 17, 1889 • Outside Denver

It had been two days since Jacob had seen Miss Jankowski and she had been on his mind almost constantly. He'd replayed their conversation in his mind too many times to count. She was fascinating. Intelligent. Beautiful. But he pushed those thoughts away for the moment. How badly was her father hurt? Had he lived? Was *she* all right?

With no way to contact her other than their next scheduled lecture meeting, *if* she showed up, he found his mind whirring with different scenarios about what could be happening.

He wasn't one to think the worst. Not in normal circumstances. But his mind wouldn't quit thinking about the fact that he might not see her again if her father succumbed to his injuries and she went into mourning. The idea was horrible on so many levels.

He didn't know where she lived and wouldn't presume that he would be accepted there anyway. She was far and above out of his class. Her parents didn't know him. He had no way of an introduction. Except maybe . . . through Martha's companion? Her name was Lily Rose . . . something. It started with a . . . D? With his attention on Miss Jankowski, he couldn't remember.

Then there was the job offer. It had been quite a shock when she'd tossed it out. And he'd wondered if she had been teasing him. But one look in her eyes had told him she was serious.

They didn't have a chance to speak of what the job was because the young boy had caught them as she was leaving.

Something else that had his imagination working in overdrive.

Especially while he was at work. The quarry was a hive of activity and noise. The pressure to produce increased daily it seemed.

He'd never heard of finishing an entire dig of this magnitude in one summer. But the man in charge—Russell Lancaster—was adamant about it and the backer had the money to make it happen apparently. There were so many men working that sometimes they were almost on top of each other. Not a good way to work with fossils.

But the pay was good and he'd keep his mouth shut. He could honor the Lord by doing a job well done and being a good example to the other men.

A bell clanged for the first shift's lunch break.

Sweat dripped from his nose as Jacob finished the small area where he was chiseling and then blew away the dust with a controlled breath. He had finished this side of the bone. Perhaps he could finish the other between today and tomorrow.

He stood and stretched and placed his tools in his box. Then he headed over to the tent for lunch.

The flaps were tied back on all sides because of the heat. They'd learned in the first few days that with so many men, the tent grew foul in a matter of seconds. The wind was a constant problem, whipping down the slopes of the Rocky Mountains with brutal ferocity. But a little dust and debris in their food was the tradeoff for fresh air.

Fresh air won by a unanimous vote.

Colorado weather was . . . weird. They'd had days that were hot out on the rock with the sun blazing down. And then others with the threat of snow and he had to wear a jacket.

He grabbed his lunch and took a seat on a long bench. Their foreman was seated across from him. The man everyone simply called Joe or sir nodded in Jacob's direction, his mouth full of food. As they chowed down, Joe was the first to finish. With a finger pointed at him, he spoke. "How's it going, Duncan?"

"Good, sir. By the end of tomorrow, I hope to have the metatarsal uncovered enough to work beneath it."

"Good. Good." The man nodded and grinned. "At this rate, we should be able to win this competition with ease. That means bonuses for everyone."

Men around him cheered.

Joe stood. "From what I've heard, the other team is small and poorly run." He guffawed. "Their foreman is a *woman*, if you can even believe it."

Derogatory comments about women echoed around him.

He cringed and opened his mouth to speak, but someone else beat him to it.

"A woman ain't got no business in this field." The man next to Jacob spit tobacco juice onto the ground. "Someone needs to tell her to give up now."

More laughter and jeers rose up from the crowd in the tent.

Jacob took a sip of water and it went down the wrong way. He began to sputter and cough.

The foreman winked. "She's probably some weak-minded socialite who wants to use up her inheritance to prove herself." He shrugged. "Janker—Jankow—some foreign-sounding name. It doesn't matter. We will win, boys! And win big!"

The celebratory noise was too much for him to shout over. Heat crept up his neck. Not only were they insulting women in general, but the foreman of the other dig. Whose name sounded all too familiar. Could it be that Martha Jankowski was working on a dinosaur dig of her own?

One guy's shout rose above the din. "We should find this other dig and demolish it."

"Yeah!" several others affirmed.

"Now hold on, fellas." Joe held up his hands. "The owner

of the museum has given strict instructions that no foul play can occur."

"But that doesn't mean that we can't spy on them, right?" The tobacco-spitting man beside Jacob sneered. "Maybe scare them a little?"

Jacob's coughing continued and he stood, but no one took notice. They were too wound up. Hands fisted at his side, Jacob watched the crowd of men. It was impossible to get word to Miss Jankowski right now.

Was that even legal for him to do? If he exposed his own team cheating . . . would that violate his contract?

It didn't matter what happened with the contract. He'd lose his job, but it was the right thing to do. He knew it.

He walked back to his little area of the dig. Picking up his brush and chisel, he squatted in front of the large hole he'd been digging in for days. Less than ten feet from where the short, slender tibia was being dug up. He'd hoped the longer and bigger fibula was in this spot too. Had longed to work on it himself.

But his thoughts warred inside him. He'd signed an agreement that he wouldn't talk about his dig or where it was. Surely the other men had as well. Not that he could imagine any of them being decent enough to abide by it.

Was that a requirement the owner of the museum had instated? Maybe Martha had done the same thing at her site.

If not . . . he had to warn her.

But how?

North of Denver

"Like I said in our previous conversation, the highest bidder wins the skeleton." She spoke into the telephone. The antiquated man on the other end expected *her* to come to him. Fool. He'd been calling every day since.

107

He coughed several times, making him sound even older and more decrepit. "I don't wish to play games. You know I want it. Now what will it take for us to come to an agreement?"

"What it will take is for you to be the highest bidder. Rules are rules. No exceptions. Right now, your bid is . . . *underwhelming.*"

He sputtered but she hung up her end of the line. As much as the convenience of the telephone had enhanced her life, it was also a nuisance. When the man was serious enough, he would come to her.

Good thing telephones were expensive. It would be chaos if any vagrant on the street had access to them.

Imagining the whole of Denver with telephones and the cacophony that would bring made her shiver. Foolishness, that's what it was. Common people needed to stay in their place. Which was out of her way. Plain and simple.

She took slow steps over to the window and peered out. The next bidder would arrive at any moment. Smoothing her hair back, she watched the elaborate carriage make its way up the long drive to her gate.

Right on time.

She turned and rang the bell for her men to join her.

Without a word, Simon and Charles entered the room and took up residence on either side of her desk where she did business negotiations. No one had dared to cross her with her hulking bodyguards present.

All these years, the use of this remote estate had given her the cover she needed. It had been her place of escape and sanctuary as well.

Returning to regular life in the city was tedious. But she didn't mind the duplicity. In fact, it made life a bit more exciting. Even fun.

She took her seat behind the massive mahogany desk and folded her hands on top.

The door opened and Gerard bowed. "Ma'am. A Mr. Ferdinand is here to see you."

"Show him in." A slight grin lifted her lips.

The bidder was smaller in stature than her last visitor but lifted his chin high in the air as he entered the room. "I simply must have the specimen." He stomped toward her, his tiny boots sounding almost like a child's.

"I'm glad to hear it. But you understand there are others vying for it as well."

"I shall outbid them all." The chin lifted even higher. Too much further and his nose would be pointed toward the ceiling.

"This is the current highest bid." She slid a piece of paper across the desktop.

He inched closer and eyed her two large bodyguards.

Simon stepped forward, a barely audible clearing of his throat sounding underneath his breath.

The bidder took the cue, grabbed the paper, and stepped back. His eyebrows shot up when he unfolded it. Chin up, he blinked a few times. "I'll double it."

"How shrewd of you, Mr. Ferdinand." Pointing to the pen and ink on the other side of the desk, she lifted one eyebrow toward him. "I'll need that in writing."

Let the games begin.

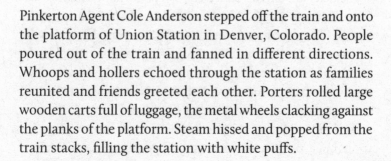

Pinkerton Agent Cole Anderson stepped off the train and onto the platform of Union Station in Denver, Colorado. People poured out of the train and fanned in different directions. Whoops and hollers echoed through the station as families reunited and friends greeted each other. Porters rolled large wooden carts full of luggage, the metal wheels clacking against the planks of the platform. Steam hissed and popped from the train stacks, filling the station with white puffs.

Smashing his cap on his head, Cole took a deep breath and pushed through the throng. His leather traveling bag thumped painfully against his knee. Young boys called to everyone passing by, offering to carry bags for a small fee. He scoffed. Small fee. By the time they reached the hotel, they would charge three times the beginning quote. He glanced at the boys again. Their dirty faces and tattered clothing evidenced their low social status. His frown lessened a bit. Couldn't begrudge them trying to make a living.

But Albert Hart, his boss, would have his hide for every frivolous expense. It didn't matter that the father of the victim whose murder he was investigating had paid quadruple the amount charged by the agency for such cases. The purse strings were still tight. The allotment for this trip wasn't the stingiest his boss had been. However, if the investigation went long, he might have to get creative with resources. Hopefully it wouldn't come to that. He would figure out what happened to Edwin Gilbert, let the boy's father know, and be home in Colorado Springs before the weekend. He'd promised his wife, Anna, he would try.

Cole sidestepped a small dog yapping and nipping at the ankles of travelers and stepped through the heavy wooden doors. Fresh air and sunshine greeted him. A welcome change from the dank smell of his second-class train car. He scanned the area and shot his free hand out in a wave.

A black hansom cab pulled close, and Cole opened the door. "The Tremont House," he instructed and settled against the squabs. The fabric was worn, but the cab was clean. Cole let out a slow breath. Traveling was getting rougher the older he got. In his younger years as an agent, he would ride for days, camp, then ride some more with ease. Now in his late forties, Cole was beginning to feel every bump and lump.

"Tremont House, sir," the cabbie called, interrupting his thoughts. Cole disembarked and flipped a coin to the driver.

He made his way up the short gravel walkway and through the door of the familiar boardinghouse. Tremont House had once been a glorious hotel for the wealthy and famous in Denver. But expansion in the city, as well as the opening of hotels like the opulent Windsor Hotel downtown, had taken business away. But it still held remnants of its former glory. Worn red velvet carpeted the stairs. Gilded framed paintings lined the lobby. And a crystal chandelier still lit up the dining room.

"What can we do for you?" A middle-aged woman from behind the dark wood desk studied him.

"One room for four nights, with the possibility of extending into the following week. Is it still a dollar a night?" Cole gave her a grin.

She nodded and he placed the appropriate number of coins in her outstretched hand. The woman dropped them into a small leather pouch tied to her waist. "Room seven, just down the hall to your left." She plunked a skeleton key on the desk. "Dinner is at six thirty. One bath a week, any more than that is fifty cents extra. No lady friends, this is a respectable establishment. No drunken behavior or you'll be kicked out. This is a temperance establishment as well."

He nodded. "Sounds fair. Thank you."

The woman gave him a smile that looked more like a grimace and turned back to the large wall of mail slots behind her.

Cole made his way down the hallway to room seven. The room was small, with a bed and a side table. A small gas light was over the table. The bedding was clean, if not a little threadbare. It didn't matter much to him. It wasn't like this was going to be home forever. He made short work of unpacking his clothing and shaving kit. The last item he pulled out was a small satchel of papers.

Everything related to his case was in this satchel. He tucked it under his arm and grabbed his hat, placing it on his head.

Lunch was necessary if he was going to formulate a plan for finding out the truth about young Mr. Edwin Gilbert.

A half an hour later, Cole finished off the last of his apple pie and coffee. With the table now clear of plates and cutlery, he unpacked the small satchel.

This was the type of case usually given to newer agents. The young man in question had a reputation for gambling, stealing, and gun fighting. The initial report from the Denver police was that while intoxicated, he fell from his horse and broke his neck. The notes from the doctor who examined his body detailed bruises and cuts consistent with being dragged by his horse for a short distance. And the investigating officer made note of the smell of whiskey on the body.

Cole frowned. That was where the case became strange.

Mr. Louis Gilbert contacted the Pinkerton Agency because he was certain his son was murdered. He ranted and raved about the incompetency of the Denver police. His son, he claimed, had never had a drink of liquor since his mother died three years ago. A deathbed promise. And one Mr. Gilbert was adamant his son kept. It was hard to imagine someone involved in various illegal enterprises, such as those young Edwin dabbled in, abstained from liquor. But stranger things had happened.

Especially in the Wild West.

He looked at the papers strewn across the table. There was a clue in here somewhere. Something that would give him the next step to take. Right now, all he had was a wealthy client with a dead son who was convinced murder was the cause of death. Hart handpicked Cole and tasked him with the impossible. Either prove the Denver police might have missed a murder and the murderer was still at large or break a father's heart.

Neither proposition was palatable.

But that was the job.

It was also the major reason he was at the Tremont House, the last known address for Edwin. He looked at the miniature the senior Mr. Gilbert gave him the night before he left. A solemn trio stared back at him. Edwin stood behind his parents, hair slicked back, eyes eerily pale in black and white. The photo was the last of the three of them, the mother dying just two months later.

Cole tapped the picture against his palm, a detail niggling in the back of his mind. A young man who surrendered to every vice except drinking. He scoffed. Impossible. Unless . . .

The guidelines given to him upon check-in came rushing back. What had that woman said? Tremont House was a temperance hotel. A thrill shot through him. Maybe she knew something—anything—that could help him.

He gathered his papers and put them back in the satchel but kept the miniature out. He shoved his hat on his head and made his way back to the front desk. The woman was still at her post.

"Hello again. I have a few questions about someone who stayed here a few months ago. Would you be able to help me?"

She narrowed her eyes and crossed her arms. "We don't give out information on patrons, sir."

Cole nodded, studying her. Her graying black hair was tucked neatly into a pile on her head. Her clothes were clean and pressed, not new, but well cared for. The mail was put away and the desk was tidy. This was a woman who cared about her job. That much was clear. "I'm with the Pinkertons. I'm not asking for anything personal. But his father is concerned. He has some doubts as to how his son died. Any information you would be willing to share would be most helpful, miss . . . ?"

An eyebrow arched on her forehead. "*Mrs.* Young." There was no censure in her response. A good sign she might help. "What was this young man's name?"

"Edwin Gilbert."

Mrs. Young's eyes welled with tears. "Oh, that poor boy. He was a decent sort. A charmer, but not a schemer. I was shocked when the police came by and said he died." She pulled a small handkerchief out of her cuff and dabbed her eyes.

What luck! She'd actually known him. "Just to be sure we are talking about the same young man . . . Can you confirm that this is the gentleman in question?" He handed her the picture.

"Yes, that's him." She smiled. "He wasn't lying when he said he took after his mother's side of the family."

Interesting. "Did you know him well?"

"Just small talk. But he always had a bit of the melancholia. Said he never quite got over his mother's passing." She handed him the miniature, brows drawn together. "I thought he fell off his horse and broke his neck."

"That is the report. They suspect he was drunk."

Mrs. Young drew back and fisted her hands on her hips. "That boy? No. No, sir. He had trouble in plenty of areas. Lord knows he did. But in all the months he lived here, there was never the smell of drink on him." She wagged a finger in Cole's direction. "I looked the other way on some things for that boy, but he knew drinking wouldn't be one of them."

"Did he tell you why he didn't drink?"

"He said he promised his mother he would be sober the rest of his life. Apparently, his grandfather died because of the stuff." She shook her head. "Yes, Edwin had many vices. But liquor was not one."

Cole looked at the miniature and back at Mrs. Young. "Thank you for your help, ma'am. I do appreciate it. And if you don't mind my saying so, it sounds like you filled a motherly void for him."

Mrs. Young nodded and wiped her eyes again. "He reminded me of my own boy. He's off on some great adventure in Europe and won't be back for some time. It was nice to look after someone again."

Cole tipped his hat. "You've been a great help, Mrs. Young. I shall return later this evening."

The older woman waved him off and Cole turned toward the doors of the hotel. There were times that confirmation of someone's story was almost as good as a lead. This was one of those times. He left the hotel and hailed a cab. The next stop in his investigation was the Denver Police Department.

Then he would find whoever murdered Edwin Gilbert.

six

"I was born among the hills, but I've always wanted to get up higher. I climbed all the highest hills but wanted to go still higher, to touch the clouds, to get above them."

~Earl Douglass

FRIDAY, APRIL 19, 1889 • OUTSIDE DENVER

Chiseling around the hoped-for fibula fossil, Jacob wrestled with what to do. He'd made a commitment to this dig and signed a contract. But he also wanted to report what he'd overheard so the other team didn't get hurt—mainly Martha.

And then . . . he really needed this job. Needed the money. What if he wouldn't get another opportunity like this?

Shaking his head at his own thoughts, he couldn't believe he'd even consider keeping the job for the money and experience. What was wrong with him?

The last couple days at the dig had been miserable. As much as Jacob tried to keep his head down, he overheard more and more chatter about the other team. Joe even seemed to encourage it since it bonded the men together, but Jacob despised every second of it. Every time someone said something blasting the other team, all he could picture was Martha Jankowski's face.

Three different times a discussion had erupted around him, and he'd spoken up about being respectable and abiding by the rules. How it was disgraceful for the men to be speaking of a woman in that way.

In response, he'd received stares, words of contempt, and a lot of derision.

For now, the foreman kept them working such long hours that no one had a chance to get away from the site. How long would it last?

Long hours in the sun today had drained him. That and the fact that he hadn't slept well last night. Between worrying about how to handle the situation here and concern for Miss Jankowski and her father, he'd kept himself awake until he went to the Lord in prayer about everything.

He'd tossed and turned for a few hours in fitful sleep after that.

The growing urgency to warn his new friend threatened to overwhelm him. And the nudge in his heart about his current job wouldn't leave him alone.

How could he stay on when the other men were being so dishonorable? His dream of participating in a dinosaur dig had come true—but at what cost?

At this rate, would he even be named in anything? He doubted it. Doubted that there would be any credit to anyone other than the man who owned the quarry.

So why was he here?

He could argue that it was for the experience and the education for his field. But it didn't hold much weight when measured against everything else. Reverend Moody's words to his parents were that Jacob was being a light. More than anything, that was what he wanted. But was he actually being that light? Was anyone listening?

Setting his tools down with one hand, he swiped at the sweat on his neck with the other. Time to refill his canteen. This dusty, dry work wreaked havoc on his throat.

Jacob stood up and went to fetch some water. He rounded a bend in the uphill trail and spotted Joe ahead of him, speaking with three new men he'd hired that morning.

"I need you to find the location of the other dig. Don't touch anything. Don't let anyone see ya. But once we know where it is, we can keep tabs on 'em. Got it?" The foreman's words were low, but their voices carried thanks to the echo and funneling effect.

Their words made the sweat on Jacob's neck run cold. Stopping in the middle of the trail wasn't an option—they'd know for sure that he'd overheard—so he continued on as if nothing had happened.

"We could always cause a disruption."

He couldn't help it. He stared at them.

The tallest of the three elbowed his buddies. "Ya know, to ensure we stay ahead."

"Not yet." Joe shook his head. "We've got to plan things so no one finds out it was us. Can't have the boss lose because we didn't follow the guidelines." The foreman turned to Jacob and their eyes locked.

"Afternoon." He nodded his head at the men as he reached them and walked on past.

"Afternoon, Jacob." Joe's voice. "I hear you've retrieved twice as many bones as any of the other men since you started." The man's voice was all too . . . chipper.

Jacob stopped and turned. Sent them a forced smile. "Just doing my job, sir. I need to get some water so I can get back to work." His throat was tight. Here was the chance to confront them. Tell them he'd heard everything. Remind them about their promise to be fair. Truthful. Instead, he kept walking.

"I don't like him." One of the men's words floated over to him. "He's religious. Caught him praying over his lunch."

Sick to his stomach, Jacob pressed up the trail. But it wasn't only because of what those men were planning. He'd ignored his conscience. Ignored the Lord. Where was his faith? His sense of right and wrong? This should have been over days ago. He should have done something about it. Reported it. And yet . . . he'd let it go. Selfishly wanting to continue on the dig.

Now? Their foreman was sending three men to spy on the other dig site.

The thought of them going to such lengths was disgusting. Hadn't paleontology gotten a bad enough name when people found out what Cope and Marsh had done to each other? What they were *still* doing to each other? It had made them the laughingstock of the scientific community. This cutthroat business of stabbing each other in the back and destroying other people's work was downright abominable.

He had to do something about it. Good people could make a name for their field of science by doing things with integrity.

Who could he go to? Perhaps the museum director. But would he stop these guys from doing anything horrible to Martha's team? Panic clawed at his chest. He found a large rock to lean against and tried to calm the racing of his heart.

The best thing for Jacob right now was to quit. To continue in a job like this when things weren't on the up and up went against everything he stood for. He missed the opportunity to speak up just then. He wouldn't do it again.

He couldn't put Martha's team at risk. He'd simply wait a few days and then quit. That would give him a little time to find another job and figure out an honest reason for quitting when he'd signed a contract.

The mess that he found himself in was overwhelming.

One fact remained. He had to do the right thing. But for the first time in his life, he was afraid.

He rubbed his face. How many times in Chicago had he spoken up about injustice? Confronted bullies who picked on his younger siblings. Stood for biblical truth when talking with classmates about science and faith.

Now he was alone. His support system was hundreds of miles away. And where was his faith in God? Where was that backbone that he'd been praised for by his family and friends?

He was a coward. It burned to admit it.

Lord, you know how scared I am. Why is it that the right thing is the hardest thing to do when I'm alone? I need Your strength. I didn't speak up when I should have. I choked on my words. Please forgive me. I really do think I should quit. But I don't have another job, and You know how much my family needs the money I make here.

Jacob looked up and watched the clouds tumble through the sky. The Lord held every cloud in His hand. Surely, He held Jacob in those same hands. Peace began to inch its way into his heart. *Thank you, Lord, for the reminder that You know every one of my days. Please give me the courage to quit this job. And help me to find a new one in the meantime. I trust You, Jesus.*

He stood and let out a breath. He felt alone without his father or mother to talk to, but the truth was he wasn't alone. God was with him. He would not be afraid.

~~

SATURDAY, APRIL 20, 1889 • JANKOWSKI MANSION, DENVER

The words on the page in front of Martha blurred. How many times could she attempt to read the same page before she gave up?

She closed the book and stared at her father. Bruises covered his face and arms. The doctor said that his back and legs were covered as well.

The grand staircase in their foyer spanned two stories. Apparently, he'd tripped on the top step and tumbled his way down the twenty-five steps.

Mother's words haunted her. Had she seen the whole thing, tried to save him, and been traumatized by it?

Martha couldn't imagine what it had been like.

Though in shock and speechless, her mother showed more emotion than she ever had before. There was hope that she cared more than her prim and proper manners allowed her to convey.

Martha shook her head. It was amazing her father was still alive. Thank goodness for the plush carpeting Mother had insisted on last year when the carpets had been replaced. It must have saved his life.

Each day, she'd come in here to sit by his side and each day, the same thoughts tumbled through her mind. Her mother and father had never been overly affectionate. Toward each other or anyone else for that matter. So it wasn't surprising that Mother didn't come by the sickroom often. She'd hired a nurse to attend to him twenty-four hours a day and would chat with Martha over dinner about her father's condition.

But deep down, Martha was convinced that her mother was struggling. She'd seen a shimmer in her eyes more than once. Even though she'd tried to keep it hidden. Perhaps it wasn't proper etiquette for a lady of her position to show how she felt, but they were alone much of the time.

Even so, Mother's manners were impeccable. One of the things that consoled Martha over the years was understanding that her parents were the same in front of her as they were in front of anyone else. So it wasn't like they were fake or putting on a show. This was simply who they were. All the time.

The door creaked open and she gazed up.

Lily Rose stood by the door. "I just returned from the quarry. The work is proceeding nicely."

Martha waved her into the room. "Thank you for going out there, I know it's not your favorite thing to do without me." Her glance went back to her father. "He looks peaceful, doesn't he? I'd hate for him to be in turmoil and pain."

Her companion looked down at Father, her hands clasped in front of her waist. "I'm sure the powders from the doctor help to keep him from feeling too much. That must be why he's sleeping so much. To allow his body to heal."

Nodding, she studied her father's face. "I hope that's true. The thought of him suffering makes me want to curl up into a ball and cry."

Nurse Krueger's voice washed over her from the corner of the room where she kept vigilant watch. "It's true, miss. His body is resting so he can heal. His face doesn't show that he's in any pain."

She'd have to be satisfied with that. The nurse understood things far better than she did. "Thank you, Nurse."

Lily Rose stepped closer. "Martha"—her voice was soft—"I believe your father would want you back out at your dig site. There's not anything you can do for him here."

"I know." Always the voice of reason. If anyone understood her passion for what she did, it was her companion. And her support of late had been a real source of comfort. But . . . leaving her father while he was bedridden?

That seemed . . . selfish and wrong.

"But you feel guilty for abandoning his side. I see it on your face. Why? It wasn't your fault he fell down the stairs. Your parents are getting older. We don't live forever, you know."

There was a coldness to Lily Rose's words that shivered down Martha's spine. The older woman might be right, but it felt so uncaring.

Still, Martha couldn't deny the warring emotions inside. Wanting to be back out on her dig—so much was at stake. Yet she also felt like she needed to be here. "I feel guilty that I haven't spoken to him much lately. I've been so busy, that . . . well . . ."

"Your father wouldn't want you wallowing about that, and you know it. You've spent more time at his side the past several days than you have in years, but that's not your fault." She squeezed Martha's shoulder. "Your parents have their life, and you have yours. You're blessed that they have given you the freedom that they have. They love you. You love them. But it's time to get back out there. You've worked two long years out at the quarry. It's too much to allow it to go by the wayside now and let the other team win." Lily Rose raised her brows and sent her a challenging look. "I don't have to remind you about the deadline."

"No. You don't." Selfishly, she wanted to do exactly as her companion suggested. Father *would* want her to be out there and get the exhibit with the Jankowski name on it. But if her father passed and she was out at the quarry, how would she feel? What would Mother say? Would people think she was a bad daughter? "I appreciate your encouragement, I do. But I need some time to think on it."

Her companion let out a little huff, a sure sign she wasn't pleased, but she nodded. "I'll be downstairs if you need me."

"Thank you." She didn't even look up. Kept her eyes on Father.

Last week at church, she'd seen a little girl with her father. They'd held hands as they walked into the great big building and shared sweet laughter and private looks with each other. During the service, the child had climbed up into the man's lap and laid her head on his shoulder. He hadn't admonished her that it wasn't proper. Hadn't pushed her away. Instead, he'd patted her back and rocked ever so slightly from side to side until she fell asleep.

It had been a wonder to Martha. She'd never seen such a thing in public like that. Oh, she'd read about it in books, but those were stories. This had been real. Right in front of her eyes.

Martha's mother had shaken her head at the display of affection and even commented on it over Sunday dinner. Apparently, the family was new in town. From Atlanta. And even though they were quite wealthy, it didn't keep her mother from frowning on their behavior.

All these years, she'd longed for a closer relationship with her parents . . . or someone. . . .

Anyone.

She vaguely remembered waiting at the front window for her father when she was little. For an hour or more each day. Most of the time, he never came. Mother or Nurse McGee would drag her from the window and insist she do something else.

On the rare occasion when he did return, she had trouble recognizing him because so much time had passed. The spring she turned six was filled with her favorite memories of Father. He'd taught her to dig. They spent time playing outside and reading stories at bedtime.

Then he'd gone on another dig. Three months later, he returned a completely different man.

His wounded body made him limp, and scars marred his face.

But it was deeper than that. At six years old, she'd had trouble connecting with him again.

The absence of her father for three months was an eternity for a little girl. His face no longer held the charm and appeal of a papa. He'd become distant. Sorrowful. And just a father.

Oh, he was still a handsome man.

And over time when she was little, she'd recognized him for who he was. There were plenty of daguerreotypes around their home to remind her of what he'd looked like before the scars. But they never spent time together anymore. No more stories. No more surprises. No more digging. Her sessions sitting and waiting beside the window no longer happened.

After a few years, those daguerreotypes were replaced with the one photograph Father had allowed since the accident. Martha had been sixteen, and Mother had insisted on an updated family photograph before she went to Yale. Martha could barely look at the photo, even now.

So yes, she felt guilty. Not that she thought she could fix the relationship. But if he understood she'd taken the time to be present during his recovery, perhaps that would show him she cared about him. Perhaps this accident could bring about a different relationship.

If he lived.

The qualification pounded in her mind.

She shook her head against the pessimism. Jankowskis pushed through. Faced the world with grit and optimism.

Creating a new and different relationship with her father was a pleasant thought, but Lily Rose was correct. It was time she got back out to the dig. Her father might be laid up for a long time. The summer would pass by, along with the opportunity to dig out her dinosaur.

She didn't even want to consider the fact that her father might never awaken. That was trouble for another day.

Martha stood up, leaned over Father, and kissed him on the forehead. She smiled. "I love you. I'm praying for your recovery. And I also want to make you proud. I *will* get that *Apatosaurus* out of the ground." Reaching into her pocket, she touched her lucky coin. *His* coin. There had to be a way to make her parents proud.

"His right boot was missing, and the horse was long gone."

Cole jotted the detail in his notebook and nodded. "Continue."

The slimmer officer, a middle-aged man named Nichols, shifted in his seat. "His coat smelled like whiskey. And with the path where his body clearly had been dragged . . ." He trailed off and shrugged. "It looked like what it was. He tottered off his horse and was dragged to death."

Cole set his pen down and folded his hands. He looked at Nichols. "Did you ever find the missing boot?"

The officer leaned back, hooking his thumbs in his uniform pockets. "Nope. Figured it'd been stuck in the stirrup."

The Pinkerton detective wrote that down, placing a question mark by the detail. That seemed too neat. He glanced at the other deputy named Price. "How about you, Deputy? Did you notice anything else in particular?"

"Not that I can recall, sir." Price slipped a thick finger between his collar and neck, tugging the stiff collar away from his skin. Cole narrowed his eyes. Was he sweating?

Nichols tried to subtly kick his partner, but Cole caught it. He leaned back in his chair, arms folded across his chest. Something was off. Someone was hiding something. "Now, gentlemen, I have eyewitness accounts from his landlady and four others that the man never took in a drop of liquor. Don't you find the smell of whiskey on his body odd?"

Price shrugged. "Everyone can have an off day, sir."

"That is true. Very true." Cole glanced between the two men, letting the silence linger in the room. "I would hate to return to Colorado Springs and tell this man's father that the Denver police chief's office refused to dig any further into a suspicious death. I'm sure he will not take kindly to that."

Price looked at Nichols then at the floor. Nichols leaned forward, glaring at Cole. "We did our job, Agent Anderson. If the father is upset by that, he is more than welcome to lodge a complaint with the police chief. Come on, Price. We're done here." He clapped his partner on the back and stood.

Cole glanced at Price. Sweat beaded across his forehead.

"Price!" Nichols barked. "Let's go."

Deputy Price looked at Nichols and shook his head. "I'll be out in a minute."

Red-faced, Nichols glared at the two men and left, slamming the door behind him.

"Don't mind him, Agent Anderson. He doesn't like to be wrong. He's got a good record and the thought that he might have missed something is offensive."

"Understandable." Cole nodded, though he suspected it went deeper than offended pride. "Did you have something to add to my investigation?"

"I do." Price wiped his forehead with his palm and sighed. "I didn't put this in my report because, quite frankly, sir, I didn't know what to do with it."

Cole scribbled notes in his book and gestured for Price to continue.

"When I was examining the body for any evidence, I went through all his pockets. His coat was clean. But on his vest . . ." He swallowed and wiped his face again. His brown hair was plastered to his head. "There was a lady's glove over his heart."

A . . . glove. That was it? The deputy was sweating over a lady's accessory. "Maybe it was from a lover or a sweetheart." Cole closed his notebook.

"Perhaps. It was made of fine kid leather, real quality. It smelled like roses. But while the rest of the man was covered in dirt and blood, the glove wasn't. It was pristine. Stark white against all that red dirt. And it just lay there. Right over his heart."

The agent leaned forward, the back of his neck prickling. "It was clean?"

"Yes. It scared me, but I couldn't tell you why. It just didn't look natural. I kept it on the body so the doctor could look at it. I also made a note to bring it up to the chief, but when I got back to the office, the case was declared an accident and closed. The doctor assigned to look at the body was only to do a surface examination. And that was the last I heard of it, until you showed up today."

Agent Anderson wrote down a few more notes, then capped his fountain pen. "Did you keep the glove? Is it in evidence?"

Price shrugged. "The doctor might know. He handled all Mr. Gilbert's personal effects."

Cole bit back a groan. No matter how scared this officer had been, why had he been reticent to catalog relevant evidence? He shoved his papers into his satchel then held out his hand to Price. "I appreciate your help today, Deputy Price. And for sharing these details."

"Do you think he was murdered, sir?" Price shook Cole's hand.

Cole picked a nonexistent piece of lint off his hat. How to answer? Especially when he was sure the two officers were hiding something. Best to tread carefully. "Hard to say. There is evidence that points to the conclusion your department came to. And evidence to the contrary. I hope to come to a solid conclusion in the next day or two."

The officer tugged his helmet on, the Denver police emblem gleaming in the afternoon light streaming through the window. With a brief nod in Cole's direction, he vacated the small interview room.

Cole stood in silence for a moment, his thoughts scattered in a dozen different ways. Cagey police officers. The glove of a mysterious lady.

Where had he heard that before?

No matter how hard he tried, he couldn't shake the feeling that it was important.

Another case, maybe?

A long time ago . . .

Of course.

A man stabbed and left to the wildlife. With a white glove on his chest.

Cole sucked in a breath.

If his instincts were correct, this was a much bigger case than just Edwin Gilbert's death.

seven

"I want to be inspired to rise above these little mean things like jealousy and resentment."

~Earl Douglass

Oh, the joys of living amongst imbeciles.

Choosing her next prey should be easy enough. Especially from this crowd.

Watching the parishioners from her seat near the center, she kept her ears attuned to the chatter around her.

Whatever possessed people to believe in a higher being on Sundays and then act like heathens the rest of the week? Why not skip the performance and do what they wanted to do?

It's not like they were nice to one another outside of this building. They weren't even all that nice *inside* the building. But they put forth an effort to *seem* nice.

As if to prove her point, the women behind her were talking about the reverend's wife and how horrid she looked in the

130

color she'd chosen to wear that morning. Of note was the almost delight in their tones as they gossiped. Two men in front of her spoke about the disgrace of one of their fellow bankers who'd been discovered at a brothel. The glint in their eyes told her all she needed to know about their own indiscretions.

The group across the aisle were talking about how shallow the Sunday School lesson had been and why couldn't their church hire decent help these days.

As if they understood their Bibles all that well. She knew what they did outside of this place.

If she wasn't keeping up her own façade, she'd laugh at them right now. But this congregation had been useful to her over the years.

The best information was found here among the elite. In their place of so-called worship.

THURSDAY, APRIL 25, 1889 • OUTSIDE DENVER

My Dearest Jacob,

We have loved receiving your letters and hearing that you are happy with your new job. Your father and I have prayed over you every evening and your siblings too. They each send their love and want me to tell you that you are missed.

This letter will be brief, but I need to share some quick things with you.

First, your cousin John has taken a mining job up in the mountains around Leadville. I'm not sure how far that is from you, but I thought it would be good to let you know in case the two of you can see one another. Your aunt Mary gave him your address at the boardinghouse in Denver.

Second, your father and I traveled to visit with Pastor Moody again. My fear and doubt had caused a great deal of anxiety and your father, wonderful man that he is, knew the only way to help me was to get wisdom from a man of God.

We spent two days with Pastor Moody, and after much study of Scripture and prayer, I was able to release my anxiety to the Lord. He was correct—it doesn't matter where God places you, it only matters that you use what you have to shine His light. He is certain that you can reach people with your good example and your testimony.

My fears were not from the Lord. And holding tightly to them wasn't helping anyone. You are in your Heavenly Father's hands, and I pray that He uses you in your beloved science.

I wanted to keep you in a sheltered, protective little space. But Pastor Moody reminded me that it isn't the believers who need the truth. It's those who haven't heard yet. He gave us a copy of his book, To the Work! To the Work!, *and it brought a lot of conviction to my heart. There's a chapter titled "Faith and Courage," which spoke to me as if he wrote it for me. At the beginning of the chapter he writes, "The key note of all our work for God should be Faith. In all my life I have never seen men or women disappointed in receiving answers to their prayers, if those persons were full of faith." Oh, Jacob, those words brought me to tears. My faith has been weak. But no more. "Unbelief is as much an enemy to the Christian as it is to the unconverted." I must admit to you that I got down on my knees and confessed my unbelief.*

Sometimes it is hard for a mother to release her child into the world. That is no excuse for me, but I had been holding on, wishing to control things. As the oldest of my children, you are teaching me a great deal.

I encourage you in your work, my son. Do it all for the glory of God and shine your light.

I love you,
Mom

Jacob refolded the letter and shoved it in his pocket. He'd read the letter last night, this morning before heading to the dig site, and now again as he took a quick break to fetch water.

He hadn't told his parents about the discouragement he was feeling about his job. Hadn't wanted them to worry.

But this letter from his mom had lifted his spirits and given him new purpose. He headed back to his area amidst all the noise and sat back on his heels. Staring at the rock layer in front of him, he examined his next move. The sun burned into his neck, sweat slipping under his collar, soaking his back. There was no summer breeze cooling his face today.

Grabbing his handkerchief, he wiped his face then gripped his brush. A few more swipes with it and then a couple chisels of hard rock gave way to a smooth, curved bone. His heart pounded against his ribs. His fingers trembled as they slid over the surface of the large bone, checking for cracks and chips. So far, so good. The bone curved against the red rock, slim by his left hand and widening before it disappeared beneath the rock. It looked like another rib bone. If the whole bone was intact, it would be his greatest find! But he wouldn't know for certain until more rock was chiseled away. It would take all afternoon and the next day if he ran out of light.

It was enough to get him through his self-imposed deadline and quit the job.

Even all the ugly things he'd overheard the past few days couldn't keep him from enjoying the work.

For a second, he felt guilty. He wasn't going to stay. All week, he'd been waiting for the opening—the right time—to put in his resignation.

Fear had kept him from doing it. Fear that Joe would suspect he'd overheard the conversation and that was why he was quitting. Fear that he wouldn't be able to find another job. Fear that they would say he was bound by the contract.

What would he do then? The only thing that had kept him

going was his faith and the job. The bones. He might have questioned his chosen profession before, but not anymore. This was what he was supposed to do. It would take time to figure out the balance, but he was determined.

If everything else could just go away, he'd be fine sitting here in the quarry and chiseling away at bones for the rest of his life.

But that wasn't the case. Men were conspiring to go against the rules. To spy. To sabotage. How far they would take it, he couldn't know, but instincts told him man would do anything for money. And money was at play here. The fossils were worth a fortune.

"Duncan." Joe's voice echoed down to him from above.

Jacob looked up. "Yes, sir?"

The foreman waved at him to come.

Maybe God was opening the door for Jacob to take care of things here and now. He took a deep breath, gathered his tools, then headed up the side of the quarry. At the top, his supervisor walked toward the tent where he had set up his table and papers.

Jacob followed.

Once they were at the tent, the foreman turned to him, hands on his hips. "There's no easy way to say this, Duncan. Especially since you're one of my best workers."

Oh, this didn't sound good. He held his breath.

"But the boss wants you fired. Today. I'm sorry. Gather your things, and you'll be given an extra week's pay. That's the best I can do."

For several seconds, all Jacob could do was blink. His ears pounded. "Sir? I . . . I don't understand."

The man shrugged but wouldn't meet his gaze. "I don't either. But the decision is final. Your contract for the summer has been voided."

"Have I done something wrong?" His lunch was no longer happy in his stomach. The churning started and his heart sank.

Did they know he'd overheard their plans? Or was it something else? One of the men complained about him talking about God. Could that be it? He opened his mouth, but his foreman raised a hand and stopped him.

"I can't say anything else. I'm sorry. You've been a good worker, Duncan." The man gripped Jacob's shoulder and then headed out of the tent.

"I guess that's that." He slapped his hat against his thigh as he watched the man walk away. He leaned against the table, deflating in the hot summer air. He'd never been fired before. Never. For a moment, he couldn't pull in a full breath.

God, You're in control and not surprised by these circumstances, even though I am. In my arrogance, I wanted to be the one to quit. He paused and thought about his time with the Lord a few days ago. That same peace filled his heart. His shoulders relaxed and his stomach settled down.

He'd been fired. It stung, sure. But hadn't he asked the Lord to lead him? To show him what to do next?

Jacob slid his hat back on, feeling a little lighter. God had answered his prayer. *You know best, and I need to rest in that.* Pastor Moody's prayer for him echoed in his mind. *And Lord, help me to be a light for You. Help me to remember that I must seek to find You in every circumstance.*

Staring out at the dig site one last time, Jacob resolved to do just that. Without saying a word to any of the other men, he tidied his work station, making sure to return the dig site's tools to the tool shed. He carefully wrapped the long rib bone that had been the highlight of working here. Dwarfing him in length, he hauled it up to Joe. "I'm thankful I was able to get this out intact." He tipped his hat at the man then headed to the trail that led him away from the dig site and back to where the wagons brought the men back to town.

At this time of day, there was little chance the wagons would be there.

When he reached the trailhead, he glanced around with a groan. Not a wagon or horse in sight.

It was a long walk back to Denver.

Jacob replayed the day's events in his mind. What could he learn about the Lord from what happened today? What did he need to learn about himself? Things he could have done better. His thoughts turned to the men whose complaints were of him talking too much about his faith.

All of the other men conversed while they were working. And the stories were not the cleanest. So Jacob had joined in with his thoughts and convictions. Could that be it? Maybe the men thought he was judging them . . . condemning them for their lewd behavior.

Which, okay, maybe he had been. He hadn't wanted to listen to the garbage the men spewed. But he could have handled it in a different way.

Lord, I don't know what to do. In my zeal to be a light for You, did I push those men further away? I'm sorry. Forgive me. Show me what steps I need to take next.

The encouragement he'd felt earlier from his mother's letter meant more to him now than it had this morning. It was humbling to see his mistakes. How he could have done things differently. How long had he acted like he knew everything? The blindness to his pride had cost him in many ways.

But the Lord had still been faithful. Given him an answer to the job problem. Even if it was painful. Jacob sighed. The past was the past, but he was determined to learn. To grow. It was evident he needed more time in the Word and with Jesus.

If he wanted to get back before dark, he'd better hurry. He shoved his hands into his pockets for the long trek home and picked up the pace.

He'd have to read the letter from home again for encouragement. Reaching into his pocket, he frowned.

Where had his mother's letter gone?

"I'm so glad to hear that Lily Rose convinced you to go back to your work, but I'm sorry to hear of your father's fall." The soft way Jacob looked at her tipped the world on its end. Martha barely knew the man and yet the look in his eyes made her feel at home. Comfortable.

"Thank you. We are praying for his recovery, but I know he would want me out there doing what I love." Even though Lily Rose had mentioned getting her back to work, they'd avoided telling him what her work was. The dance they'd learned to play with words as soon as she entered paleontology had taken time.

But to Jacob's credit, he hadn't pressed.

Martha wrapped her scarf a little tighter around her neck. "It's colder than I expected." She shoved her gloved hands deep into her coat pockets. With Jacob on her left and Lily Rose a few steps behind, she enjoyed the companionship.

"But look at those stars." The awe in Jacob's voice as they walked outside the lecture hall was a lift to her spirits.

With her father still bedridden and awake for a few moments here and there, she'd found herself slipping into a bit of a dispirited frame of mind. She angled her head back and followed his gaze. The night sky was clear and full of millions of twinkling stars. The vastness mesmerized her. "They are beautiful." Her breath puffed out in a little cloud with her words.

"The lecture this evening was quite fascinating, although I'm sure you probably already knew all the facts the geologist laid out." Jacob shoved his hands into his pockets as well. "Especially since you are from this area."

She nodded. "I did remember a good bit of it, but his detail into the layers and formations at the Red Rocks Park was fascinating." Turning her head, she studied him. "I don't know anything about your family . . . or even where it is that you call home."

His whole body seemed to relax with one breath. "My family is amazing. I wish you could meet them. They are back in Illinois."

That was a bit surprising, especially since he wasn't a man of means. It was a long way from Colorado. "Where in Illinois?"

"Chicago." He grinned at her. "Have you been there?"

"Many times, yes." She took slow steps, savoring every minute of their time together. Something about being in Jacob's presence made all the discouragement disappear.

"My family still lives in the same little two-room house where I grew up." He chuckled. "I wish we could go back in time so you could watch what it was like to try and play hide and seek with four siblings in the small space."

"That is difficult to imagine." She schooled her features, so the shock she felt inside wouldn't show on her face. Two-room house? She had two rooms just for her closet and bathing chamber. Her bedroom and parlor were another two.

While she was aware that there were poor people who lived like that, she'd never seen it in person. Or met someone who had experienced it. She blinked away her lack of understanding and tuned into his story.

"My brother, Daniel—the youngest—always hid in the same spot. But we took pity on him and pretended we didn't know where he was. To this day, he probably thinks he was the best at hiding." Jacob's deep laughter drew her in. The life in his voice was contagious and she laughed along.

"Having siblings must have been such a joy. I'm an only child." She stopped and turned toward him.

"There's a bench over there, would you care to sit for a while . . . that is, if you're not too cold?" The way he looked at her—with that warm gaze—was enough for her to say yes to pretty much anything he asked at the moment.

"That sounds lovely." She followed him to the bench and the three of them sat down.

Lily Rose shivered beside her but then straightened her spine. "A few hot bricks from the fire would be nice right about now."

Martha giggled at her companion and scooted an inch or two closer to her. Then she spotted her driver and waved at him.

In less than a minute, Walter placed a blanket over the ladies' laps and bowed before heading back to the carriage.

"Thank you, Walter," she called out after him. "We won't be too long."

With a glance to Lily Rose she wiggled her eyebrows. "It's not hot bricks, but it will be warmer."

"You are hopeless, Miss Jankowski." Her chin lifted a bit. "I'll be fine."

Martha turned her attention back to Jacob. "Mr. Duncan, tell me more about your family."

"Please"—he leaned forward—"call me Jacob."

"All right then, at least while we are not in public. Jacob, I'd love to hear more about your family."

His expression turned sheepish. "Would you mind if I interrupt our conversation for a moment and ask you a question?"

"Go ahead."

"A couple weeks ago, you offered me a job. Were you serious?"

She bit her lip and studied him for several moments. While she hadn't told him what the job was, he had expressed his interest in working on a dinosaur dig. And he was studying paleontology.

She *did* need the help and over the course of the past few weeks, she'd gotten to know him better. He seemed decent and educated. "I was—I mean—I am. Are you seeking employment elsewhere?"

"I am." His brow dipped and his smile slipped. "I was not a good fit at my other job."

"Oh." What did that mean? She studied him for several moments and could find no falsity in his eyes. "I will tell you about the job, but first, I have to ask you to promise that you will not share anything about this with anyone. You'll need to sign contracts agreeing to keeping the site a secret as well."

"All right." He raised his right hand in the air. "I promise you that I will not share anything about this job with anyone."

She giggled at him. "I appreciate your oath, Mr. Dun—Jacob."

Lily Rose touched her arm and she turned to look at her companion. She stared into the older woman's eyes and lowered her voice. "Do you not agree?"

The older woman leaned closer. "I was going to ask if you were certain you trusted him, but after spending time with him, I do believe he is trustworthy. I apologize for my interruption."

Martha pulled back and sent her a nod. Then looked back at Jacob. "Well, you said you wanted to work on a dinosaur dig. That's exactly what we're doing. I've been excavating an *Apatosaurus* for the last two years and proposed to the museum to have a display there."

"That's wonderful." He looked like he had more to say, but he clapped his lips back together.

"There is a catch."

"Oh?" His brow dipped.

"We are apparently in competition with another team and have been given a deadline at the end of summer. August twenty-sixth to be exact."

He blinked several times and opened his mouth and then closed it before opening it again. "That's less than four months."

"Yes." She stuck out her hand. "So . . . Mr. Jacob Duncan, will you work with me to uncover my *Apatosaurus*?"

eight

"The riches that every boy thinks will be his for this age have not yet appeared. About all I possess are books, bones, a team, a wagon, etc. I am about where I ought to have been fifteen years ago. But I am a student because that is all that satisfies me."

~Earl Douglass

Jacob sat in his roped-off section of the dig grid and worked his chisel next to the dorsal vertebrae he'd been assigned to work on. The sheer size of the fossil amazed him.

What it must have been like to see a creature like this. A wonder! With a long neck and even longer tail, the huge herbivorous *Sauropod* could have been up to seventy-five feet in length. Without anything living to compare it to, it was hard to imagine even now.

A little thrill made his arms tingle. Getting to work here was beyond his dreams. God had doubly blessed him.

Yesterday, he'd signed the contracts with Martha and her

lawyer. A lot of the same verbiage had been used as the contract from the previous dig, but there wasn't anything in the contract that made him pause. He'd even gone home and re-read the other papers just to make sure. The only thing that niggled at the edge of his mind was the fact that the other contract did have a clause about not saying anything even if you were fired or quit the dig. He'd keep his mouth shut about the work he'd done. But what if Martha found out and she pressed him?

Could he keep the fact that he'd worked on the other dig a secret? He'd given his word to them that he would. But was that betraying *her*?

The undisclosed truth lay between them like a chasm.

He'd laid the matter at the Lord's feet in prayer and decided to move forward. After all, God had opened this door for him.

A shadow passed over his bones. "Good afternoon, Mr. Duncan." Martha. Just the sound of her voice kicked his heart into overdrive.

"Good afternoon, Miss Jankowski." He squinted up at her. A thin parasol kept the sun off her.

"You've done good work already, Mr. Duncan. I'm pleased you have joined us." Her shadow moved with her as she motioned to a man behind her. "Allow me to introduce you to Mr. Parker—my assistant. If you need anything or have any questions and I'm not here, see him. But I can tell that you are experienced and know what you're doing." The smile that stretched across her face made the dimples in her cheeks deepen.

Her praise did him good and he returned the smile.

"I will check in with you before you leave today. Again, thank you for taking the job." With that, she walked away and Mr. Parker studied him for a moment before tipping his hat and following the boss.

Chinking and clanging filled the silence as the rest of the dig site worked in precise and orderly fashion.

What a different atmosphere. Chaos reigned at the other dig. Too many men working in too furious a fashion. It wasn't organized, and half the time, the men didn't even know what they were digging.

Martha's dig was the opposite.

It was a beautiful sight to behold.

FRIDAY, MAY 3, 1889 • JANKOWSKI MANSION

The bright sunlight streaming through the windows was at odds with the gloomy atmosphere of her father's room. His sickbed—even dressed with fresh linens and pouches of dried flower petals—was still a sickbed.

Martha came home from the quarry mid-afternoon desperate to speak with him, but all the positive thinking in the world couldn't awaken him. She'd been reading to him for the last hour, but he hadn't moved or made a sound.

Why hadn't she worked harder over the years to have a better relationship with her parents? Now faced with the possibility of losing Father, she wasn't quite sure how she felt about the distance that was oh-so-proper. Or so her mother stated.

Mother.

The woman was graceful, poised, proper, and could handle any situation. There was nothing Victoria Jankowski wouldn't face head on. Except maybe a conversation about her feelings.

Over the past couple weeks, Martha had tried to get her mother to talk. And failed.

Being raised in one of the wealthiest families in the country was all her mother understood. Normal to Mother was a well-dressed table, five hundred rules of etiquette for each occasion, and plenty of distance. Between Martha and her parents. Between her and any chums at school. Between her and the servants.

No one was to get close to someone of their social standing.

"Martha, my dear."

It took her several seconds to clear her thoughts. Looking up, she acknowledged her mother, who stood in the doorway. "Good afternoon."

"Would you join me in the hall for a moment?"

"Certainly." She stood, patted Father's hand, and met her mother at the door.

"It's good to see you taking the time to visit." Mother's blue eyes matched her own. They always fascinated Martha. Full of depth and secrets. Secrets that Martha wished she understood. Maybe then, she would understand her mother better. Know her more. But there was a wall around the woman that seemed impenetrable.

"I wanted him to hear my voice. I thought if I kept him updated on what was happening out at the dig, that it might help him to perk up a bit."

"That's a lovely gesture, my dear." Mother reached over and touched her shoulder. One of the few displays of affection the matriarch of the Jankowski family allowed. "I'm sure he appreciates it."

"I hope so. I hate to see him laid up." She swallowed back the lump Mother's words evoked.

"There is much to do, I'm sure, but I wasn't certain if you would be joining me for dinner this evening. It might be nice to catch up." The olive branch offered was exactly what Martha had hoped for. Prayed for. Longed for.

She'd take it. "I'll be there."

"Wonderful." With that, her mother walked away.

Watching the woman who had given her life, Martha puzzled over what to talk about at dinner. If only there were a magic formula for winning the affections of one's mother.

Entering her father's sickroom once again, she had pushed away the longing she'd had for a confidante. She was long past the age of needing a bosom friend. She'd learned how to navigate society just fine. And if loneliness was the price to pay for getting to dig, Martha would pay it every time.

Her father's nurse stood from her chair in the corner. "Miss Jankowski, if it is all right with you, I need to stretch my limbs. Might I take a stroll in the garden for a quarter of an hour?"

The woman had cared for her father around the clock.

The first few nights when Martha couldn't sleep, she'd slipped into her father's sickroom and found the woman sleeping on a sad little cot in the corner. She couldn't refuse the nurse's simple request. "Please. Go ahead. I'll stay with him until you return."

"Thank you." She left the room, the door closing with a soft click. Father's faint snores and the ticking of the clock were the only sounds that echoed through the cavernous room.

A surge of emotion welled up in her throat and the prick of tears made her try and blink them away. Grabbing her father's hand, she stared at him. "I don't know if you can hear me, but it's me, Martha." She licked her lips and tucked her lucky coin into his limp hand, wrapping his fingers around it. "You gave this to me when I was little and I've carried it with me everywhere since. Perhaps it will remind you of better days and help you to wake up."

She watched him take a couple of shallow breaths. His skin was paler than ever, the scars an even starker white. With his cheeks sunken, and dark circles under his eyes, she had a hard time thinking positive thoughts about his recovery. As tears stung the corners of her eyes, she swallowed. Perhaps if she shared her heart, he would awaken. "There's someone I would like you to meet. His name is Jacob Duncan. I met him a month or so ago at a lecture they were having at the university. He likes paleontology as well."

The more she spoke, the more she relaxed. She held tight to his hand and smiled. "I hired him to work at my dig. He's been so helpful. And encouraging. I've never met anyone quite like him. He grew up poor and has worked his way through school and life. One of the best things about him is that he makes me smile and laugh. I feel like . . ." Could she put it into words? ". . . I feel like he understands me for me. There's no pretense." She glanced down. "Oh, don't worry. There's nothing improper. He's a perfect gentleman. Rest assured. But I feel a connection with him that I've never felt with anyone else."

For several minutes, she allowed her own words to sink into her heart and mind. Her father's serene face held no judgment, so she continued. "That's why I would like for you to meet him. I know I told you last year that I wasn't interested in courting anyone. Wasn't interested in you setting up a suitable beau. I wanted to invest every ounce of energy and time I had into my work. And I meant it."

Her father stirred, but then settled back into a deep sleep.

"I guess what I'm saying—in a roundabout way—is that I believe, for the first time, that I've come to care for someone. Since this is new territory for me, I was hoping you would approve."

A low moan escaped her father's lips. And then his mouth settled into a smile.

Even though they'd never had a conversation like this . . . ever . . . Martha's heart filled with peace. "I'll take that as a yes. At least, until you can tell me differently."

Perhaps she could have the father and daughter relationship she'd longed for after all.

He just had to get better.

If the Jankowski force of will had anything to do with it, she'd make certain it happened.

147

The last week working with Martha had been the most amazing week of his life. Not only was she incredibly knowledgeable about paleontology and so many other areas, but she was organized, inquisitive, and quite striking. The more time he spent with her, the more he had to digest the fact that he was quickly losing his heart.

Not that he would ever say anything to her. There was too much separating them—mainly the rules of society.

In light of that, he'd keep his mouth shut. He didn't care about classes and social distinctions, but the world he and Martha lived in cared a great deal. Especially the world *she* came from. She might not act like a difference in class bothered her now, but one day, she could be faced with a choice that she wouldn't be able to make. Her family, their money and class—or him. He never wanted to put her through that. So he would admire her and treasure their time together. He would protect her and do all he could to see her succeed.

"Jacob?" The object of his thoughts called to him from the foreman's tent. "Would you come here for a moment?"

He set down his tools and hiked up the side of the quarry. "Good morning. How can I help?"

"Hm. That was exactly my question." Her hands were on her hips as she studied a large map on the table.

"What's this?" Walking over to her side, he recognized the map was of the quarry now that it was right-side-up. "Ah, I see." Fascinating, she'd made it into a grid. Just like the roped-off areas. He pointed. "What do these shaded areas mean?"

"Those sections have been excavated and didn't produce any fossils." She pointed to tiny checkmarks in some of the corners of squares. "The ones with checkmarks are completed in excavation and over here"—she showed him the key—"is the listing of which fossils and bones were found."

"Wow. That's impressive." She really was the best for this job. A true foreman. Organized, knowledgeable, skilled. Would he ever meet anyone like her? Likely not.

"Thank you." She released a heavy sigh. "The problem is . . . all these other squares represent what has to be done by August twenty-sixth."

He scanned the grid. "Let's not look at it as a problem."

One dainty eyebrow quirked up. "Oh?"

She was adorable when she did that. If those dimples came out, he'd have to run and splash water over his face to keep from staring at her like a schoolboy. "Look at it this way . . . you are three-quarters of the way finished."

Her light laughter filled the tent and floated out on the breeze. There were the dimples.

Oh, he was in trouble.

"That is awfully optimistic of you, kind sir, but let me remind you that I've been working in this quarry for more than two years. And the end of August is approaching faster than I would like."

"True"—he dipped his head—"but you have more help now, right?"

"Yes. But I've been doing the math for what is left. Five of the quadrants left on the grid have the majority of the bones in the quarry—so that will be more work. I hate being a pessimist, but I have to look at this realistically."

"Okay." He studied it again. "There are more daylight hours the next few months. Maybe you could ask the men if they would work more each day? I know I wouldn't mind helping." He shrugged and connected gazes with her. "Right now, they're pulling eight hours a day. I know you want everyone fresh and rested, but we could increase that to ten—possibly even twelve—hours a day until we reach the finish line."

"You'd be willing to do that? It's grueling work. Especially in the sun." The shock on her face that anyone would sacrifice for her just about knocked his feet out from under him.

A moment of bravery overtook him and he touched her arm for a second. But it was enough. "I'm pretty sure the others will agree. More hours means more pay. Money is a huge motivator."

She blinked fast several times and sniffed. Then turned back to the map. "Thank you."

"Martha, do you mind if I ask you a question?"

"Go ahead." Her sweet smile made him feel a bit guilty for what he was about to ask.

"Do you have any security for your quarry here? I mean . . . I hesitate to say anything, but there are a lot of unscrupulous people out there." With everything that had been going on, he hadn't figured out a way to talk to her about the potential spies without saying anything that would get him in trouble with the other team or in breach of contract. If any of them found out he was working for the opposing team, he'd find himself in hot water, but he prayed that wouldn't happen.

"Believe me. I know that fact better than most." She shook her head. "I appreciate you asking—and caring—about my welfare. When we purchased this property, we paid a hefty sum to have barbed wire strung around the whole of the acreage."

Huh. He thought it was just a fence at the entrance where they came in. He didn't realize they'd fenced in the entire parcel. "Wow. That's a lot of barbed wire."

"It is." She scrunched up her nose. "Especially when we're talking about fencing six feet high, half a foot in spacing. I wasn't worried about wild animals. I was worried about men."

"I take it you haven't had any troubles?" He crossed his arms over his chest and leaned against the table.

"Well, not the first two years. I hired one man to patrol the entire fence line daily. As soon as he saw someone snooping back in April, I hired more men."

The thought of having the funds to employ all these people took him back for a moment. What kind of wealth did she come from? To employ this many people. The more calculations he did in his head, the drier his mouth got. His family had never known anyone comparable. "How many?"

"There are eight total. They rotate. Four are always on a patrol." She went back to the map and laid her palms flat on the table. "You think we can do it?"

The last thing he wanted to do was give her false hope, so he studied the grid again. "If we extend hours, work every day but Sunday, and don't run into any major hitches, I think we can."

For several moments, all she did was look over the map. Then she straightened and snagged his gaze. "I guess that means we won't have time for any more lectures for a while."

Even though she was teasing, the remark struck him in the heart. Had she looked forward to them like he had? "You're probably correct."

"Well, it is a bit of a disappointment, but I'll take the fact that I get to see you every day now as consolation."

His jaw dropped a bit, but she'd turned on her heel so quick she probably didn't have a chance to see the impact of her words.

Good thing, too, because he wasn't sure what he would have done if she'd stayed.

SATURDAY, MAY 11, 1889 • ALONG THE COLORADO/ WYOMING TERRITORY BORDER

All her life, she'd lived in the background. The shadows. Because it had been safer. Gave her the cover she needed. She enjoyed living a double life. Wanted nothing more than to fill her purse and get rid of the people in her way.

But something inside her begged to change things up.

The world was shifting.

If those two bone swindlers could get acclaim for all their dishonest deeds, then she could swoop in and take the limelight for what she'd accomplished. Show the world what a *real* fossil hunter was.

Or she could keep selling everything in secret and make even more of a fortune.

Either way, she was the winner.

As she gazed around the sparse terrain on the horizon, she focused on the ranch to the west. Another man awaited her. Wealthy. Handsome. Willing to give her whatever she wanted.

By tomorrow, she'd own another thousand acres and three hundred head of cattle. Not to mention easy access to the train for her men.

Not bad for a day's work.

nine

"I want my better days to be full of work and to do something to encourage and help my suffering fellow men. May my inspiration continue."

~Earl Douglass

The look on Lily Rose's face as she headed Martha's direction did *not* bode well.

Taking a deep breath, she met her companion. "You don't appear to have good news."

"Your mother received a telegram this morning." Martha stiffened. "The powers that be are doing all they can to keep it out of the papers, but that probably won't happen. Thankfully, she knows people, and they informed her. She doesn't want this hurting you. . . ." It had been a long time since she'd used her stalling tactic.

It wasn't working. "Spit it out. Whatever it is, it can't be that bad." Although, if the feelings in the pit of her stomach were any indication, she was in trouble.

"A number of bones have disappeared. From digs in Wyoming, Utah, Colorado, and some even from Montana. As in—they are being stolen as they are shipped to their respective museums or universities. The officials have no idea who is stealing them or how."

"How many is *a number?*" Martha swallowed. Everything in her stomach threatened to creep up her throat. If Mother had been alerted, it had to be a large amount since she and Father still invested heavily in paleontological digs.

"Train cars full. Over twenty train cars full."

"What?" This was no doubt a result of the feud between Cope and Marsh. Why was this atrocity allowed to continue? "How can this be happening? It doesn't make sense—"

Her companion's huff stopped her. "It's happened over the past five years. With correspondence being so slow back and forth from here to the East, it has taken time for all of it to come to light. Especially since everyone has wanted to keep a low profile and not let anyone else know what they have found until they put it on display."

Another reason to blame those two for all the grief they'd caused the paleontological community. Anytime those two men came to mind, her anger built. "Have they found the bones that were stolen?"

"No. That's the thing. They've never found any of them. They've probably been sold to private collectors." Lily Rose's face hardened. "No surprise, the wealthy always do whatever they want."

The comment stunned Martha. Was that bitterness in the older woman's voice? She'd never heard her speak in such a manner.

"Don't forget it is a wealthy family who pays your *generous* salary," Martha snapped. Goodness. She sounded exactly like Mother.

Lily Rose's jaw tightened, but she gave a short nod. "My apologies, Martha. I am out of sorts today."

Martha gave her a sharp nod, her thoughts going back to the stolen bones. If they were with private collectors, they might never be found. A year or so down the road, someone could claim to have dug up a specimen and use the bones they purchased to claim the find and get their name out there. Or the rich collectors could simply keep the bones in their homes as a prize. A medal of honor. Is that what her scientific field was coming to? The richest of the rich hoarding—poaching essentially—whatever they wanted so they could put it on display. It disgusted her.

She shouldn't be surprised. It had been happening with jewels and art and archaeological artifacts for centuries . . . why not with dinosaur bones? It was a commodity that wasn't available anymore. Whatever was in the fossil record was *it*. No more. The simple matter that they were rare and scarce made them desirable.

She almost lost her lunch with the thought. Maybe she should switch to studying something else. It's not like they had the resources in their community of scientists to double-check where each specimen came from to stop the thievery. And she was sick and tired of all this mess. If she ever had the chance to speak to Mr. Othniel Marsh or Mr. Edward Cope, she would give them an earful.

"Um . . . Martha, you're about to shred that paper."

Lily Rose's gentle tone, so opposite her earlier derision, stopped her. "Hm?" She looked down. While she'd been thinking, her hands had made a mess of her notes from this morning. "Oh, heavens." Working to smooth the papers back out, she did her best not to smudge them any more than she already had. "There are days I simply want to give up."

"You don't mean that."

Lily Rose's scolding look was almost comical. It seemed

whatever was bothering her companion before had passed. Martha shrugged. "You're right, I don't mean it. But sometimes I have to say it anyway." She chewed on the inside of her cheek. "To get away with those thefts, people would not only have to know who is digging what where, but they'd have to know the exact time bones were loaded and transported and then know the train schedules inside and out."

Lily Rose grimaced. "It would take someone clever to figure all of that out."

"And someone with lots of money. Let's not forget that. The financial cost of mounting such a ring of organized theft is beyond my imagination." That kind of wealth wasn't unheard of out here in Colorado, though rare. Perhaps someone on the East Coast was behind it all, hoarding the earth's treasures for their own pleasure, rather than sharing it with the world. Or offering it for view at an exorbitant price.

She shook her head. What was she doing? She was giving the crooks exactly what they wanted. Her own lack of focus on her project—the worry and conjecture—could give them the openings they needed. Whoever *they* were. "No matter. It's not worth my time and energy to even think about. My bones will not be delivered by train. I'll hand deliver them if that's what it takes to keep them secure."

"Good." Lily Rose nodded. "What would you like me to help you with today?"

"Would you check on each of the men and their quadrants? I'd like to be updated on the progress morning and afternoon. Even when I'm out digging myself."

"I'll be *with* you when you're digging, Martha. Let's not forget that. You know it's imperative to protect your reputation. Your parents insist."

"Yes, yes. I know." Lily Rose was a wonderful companion, but sometimes it would be nice if Martha could delegate more to her instead of always needing the hovering of a mother hen. The more hands they had, the better.

The older woman sent her a knowing smile. "Still. What your parents don't know can't hurt them. I shall start a check on your quadrants and catch up to you at your dig site. Does that sound fair?"

Martha kept her surprise in check. "I appreciate a bit of freedom today, Lily Rose. Thank you." She waved goodbye as her companion walked southeast.

Her gaze dropped back to her grid, and she looked it over one more time. No matter how redundant, every day she redid her calculations. They had little margin for error if they were to finish on time. If anyone got behind, it put the entire dig in jeopardy.

"Good morning, Miss Jankowski."

Jacob's voice from her left brought her attention up. Oh, what that lopsided grin did to her insides. "Good morning, Mr. Duncan. Are we back to formalities?"

He glanced around. Her perch where she'd positioned her tent to observe the dig was in everyone's view. "Well, you *are* my boss. And the whole dig site can see us." He put a hand to the side of his mouth. "And probably hear us too." The last words were hushed.

"First and foremost, I hope you think of me as your friend." Feeling bold, she wiggled her eyebrows at him. "You are definitely *my* friend, Jacob."

"Certainly. You are my friend. Martha." The way he said her name made her feel . . . special. "Have you thought about hiring a couple more workers to dig?"

Her happy little bubble popped. Back to business. "I have. But I don't think I can risk it. Finding people I can trust is getting more difficult by the day."

"That's understandable." He stepped beside her and examined the map and grid. "For now, I'm confident we can get it

157

done. I know how important it is to prepare for contingencies. If even one of your workers gets sick or injured, we'll be in a heap of trouble scrambling to make up for the loss."

"I know. I can't say that I haven't worried about that. But can I risk someone stealing from me? Spying on me? Or sabotaging the dig?"

He winced.

"Oh, I trust *you*, Jacob, I do. But I'm sure you can understand my concerns."

His eyes now held a bit of hesitancy. "I'm here to help you in any way that I can. I promise."

"Thank you." She looked back down at the map. He was obviously troubled over the whole matter as well. Otherwise, he wouldn't have asked about her having protection. Wait until she told him about the news Lily Rose had shared with her. "I'm glad you're here, Jacob."

"Me too. I appreciate you giving me the opportunity." He looked down, a hint of red creeping up his neck as he fidgeted with a pencil on the table.

She watched him for a second and bit her lip. If she shared with him the rules from the competition, perhaps it would make him feel more comfortable. He might even have some good ideas to help her. "Jacob . . ."

His head jerked up. "I'm sorry. I was lost in thought."

She pulled the paper out of her case. "Each worker knows the rules I have set out for our team, and they know that we are bound by rules from the owner of the museum. You read my rules when you signed the contract. But the rules from the owner of the museum are very specific for what will disqualify us from the competition. My rules for the team are based on them."

"I'm glad the museum owner did that. It should keep everyone honest."

With a nod, she lifted the paper. "Here . . . why don't you read them."

He took the paper from her and she watched his lips move as he read over it.

She crossed her arms over her middle and paced back and forth.

His mouth pinched as he folded the paper and handed it back to her. When their eyes met . . .

Goodness! His face had gone pale and his eyes wide.

Then his gaze snapped to the ground. Like he couldn't look her in the eye.

"What's wrong?"

"There's something I need to tell you." His Adam's apple bobbed as he swallowed.

"All right." What on earth was wrong?

"I'm afraid—"

"Martha!" Lily Rose rushed up beside them, her breath coming in gasps and her hair in disarray from running. "I just ran into Isaac again. Your mother sent him. We need to head back home. Your father has taken a turn for the worse."

"Father?" Martha bent over his bed. "I came as soon as I heard." She glanced up at Nurse Krueger.

The older woman simply shook her head, lips pressed into a thin line.

Her father's breathing was slower than it had been. More labored. With an awful rattle in his chest. What did that mean? She squeezed his hand and clenched her jaw as tight as she could. She had to be strong. But the tears threatened to overwhelm her.

Nurse Krueger stepped out of the shadows in the corner. "Miss . . . we've called for the doctor, but . . ."

"But *what?* You don't think he's going to get better? Is that

159

it?" Why was she taking her emotions out on the one person who had cared for Father?

The nurse stepped closer. "The doctor will be here soon. Let's not jump to conclusions." How the woman kept calm in situations like this was beyond Martha's comprehension. The older woman wrapped Martha in a brief hug.

The touch, the human contact, filled all the cracks and crevices in Martha's crumbling outer shell. It filled her with a fresh peace.

"Thank you." She pulled away. "I'm sorry for my outburst."

"It's completely understandable."

Martha scanned the room and saw her mother sitting in a chair in the corner. She stared out the window, a twisted handkerchief in her hands.

Nurse Krueger leaned close to Martha's ear. "I'm worried about her."

"Me too." But what should she do? Should she try to comfort her? Or would Mother shoo her away?

"Hush. Both of you." Mother snapped out the words. "I don't need your pity."

Shuffling sounded at the door and Martha shifted her gaze. Dr. Murton entered with his black bag.

"Miss Jankowski . . . Mrs. Jankowski." He removed his hat and strode over to Father's bed.

Not a word or acknowledgment from her mother.

Martha stepped back.

So this was how it was going to be. Feeling more alone than she'd ever felt before, Martha watched the doctor change the bandage on her father's head.

The wound there was much worse than she'd realized. Bile threatened to make its way up her throat. With a hand to her mouth, she forced herself to swallow it down.

Oh, for someone to comfort her. To hold her while she cried.

Tearing her gaze away from Father's sickbed, she searched

out the chair in the corner, but rather than moving closer to her mother, her feet took her to another large window on the other side of the room.

She'd have to face this by herself.

~~~~~

THURSDAY, MAY 16, 1889 • DENVER

"You, my dear, will be the queen of all this when you are older. You'll be able to buy yourself whatever your heart desires." Papa's voice sounded so pleased. So happy.

She watched him closely. Glanced around the room at all the chests of jewels and gold coins. The idea of always having whatever she wanted was wonderful.

Then he grabbed her arm and squeezed it tight.

"Ow, Papa, that hurts." She kicked at his leg and missed.

He dragged her along into the next room. "Your tantrums will do no good against me, my dear."

With a grunt, she leaned her head over and bit his hand.

"Why, you little—" He sucked in his lips over the last word. His grip tightened.

"Ow!" She stomped her foot. Pitching a fit had always been to her benefit in the past. She'd gotten whatever she wanted.

But Papa wasn't cooperating. He grabbed her other arm, squeezed even tighter, and then shook her. Leaning down, he was almost nose to nose with her now. "Don't even think of trying to bite me again." He stared her down. "Now . . . are you quite finished?"

Lifting her chin, she turned to face the other way.

"Fine." He dragged her toward another door and swung it open. "This"—he shoved her toward a smelly man lying on the floor—"is what will happen to you if you decide to disobey me again."

She stumbled and fell onto the man. His open, unseeing

eyes made her scramble backward as fast as she could. She'd seen dead men before but had never gotten used to it.

"As long as we are clear, my dear."

"Yes, Papa." She swallowed hard. "I won't disobey you again."

"Good. No more tantrums?"

"No, Papa."

"I'm glad to hear it."

With a shiver she worked herself back to her feet, but as she turned, Papa closed the door and locked it. "This is simply to give you a chance to think about your actions, my dear. And to remind you of the consequences."

Kneeling down, she looked through the keyhole. "Papa?"

But he turned and strode away—

"No!" She woke with a start and sat up. Sweat on her forehead and neck. The memory from her childhood always came back in her dreams.

This time she'd woken up before she saw the blood. And before she screamed along with her seven-year-old self.

Rubbing her arms, she pushed the pictures in her mind away. Her father had been a harsh man, but he had indeed given her the world. And all his knowledge. Every scheme. Each bargaining tactic that had won him his fortune.

Now she was enjoying the life she lived. The parts she played. Continuing the legacy and building the fortune.

Papa had been harsh, yes, but he'd taught her that she could have whatever she wanted.

No matter who stood in her way.

ten

"With songs and hymns these rocks ne'er rang;
These hills the prophets never trod,
Nor sages e'er these wonders sang
Nor seers have heard the 'voice of God'
Yet here the Spirit dwells, divine,
That spake with men in Palestine."

~Earl Douglass—
From his *Hymn of the Wilderness*

As she read aloud the last portion of Gregor Mendel's paper, *Experiments in Plant Hybridization*, Martha's thoughts tumbled over each other. Ever since hearing the lecturer who'd gotten himself practically booed off the stage, she'd wanted to read this paper that he mentioned.

It was in German and not easy to get her hands on, but she'd finally acquired it, thanks to a hefty sum. Good thing she was fluent in German—and French, Italian, and Latin, for that matter. All thanks to her tutelage growing up.

Over the past week, she'd read snippets of it to her father.

163

Hoping that he could hear her, but knowing it was doubtful he would understand. Father had never been fond of other languages.

But the paper, which had been read at meetings of the Brünn Natural History Society more than twenty years ago, was a wealth of knowledge. Why it hadn't gotten more attention was beyond her. This was a treasure trove of biology and the curiosities of organisms.

"Father . . ." She swallowed the lump in her throat. If only he'd wake up and answer her. "What do you think of this part? 'It is willingly granted that by cultivation the origination of new varieties is favored, and that by man's labor many varieties are acquired which, under natural conditions, would be lost; but nothing justifies the assumption that the tendency to formation of varieties is so extraordinarily increased that the species speedily lose all stability, and their offspring diverge into an endless series of extremely variable forms.'"

She took a moment to chew on her lip. "It seems that with all his work on tens of thousands of pea plants, he concluded that while there can be variety, it simply can't up and change to say . . . a squash plant. Or a tomato." Should that surprise her? There was so much they were learning every day as science and experimentation advanced. But the intricacies of life—even in plants—was extraordinary.

She tapped the papers against her hands, ignoring the quivering in her stomach. Ever since Monday, her father had barely moved. Lifting her chin, she refused to be like her mother and think the worst. So she'd continue her conversation with Father, even if it was one-sided. "I haven't studied it at the extent that he did." Obviously. Twisting her mouth back and forth, she shook her head and walked over to the window.

"I don't wish to be ignorant. I want to be educated and open-minded." She paced her way back to her father's side.

"You taught me that. That's why I wish to keep studying and learning. Will that make you proud?"

Father groaned and she leaned closer to him.

"Are you responding to my query?" She squeezed his hands.

Another groan.

Martha stared at her hands intertwined with his. She couldn't remember the last time that she'd held his hand before he fell ill. Perhaps when she was small, before his accident. What made her long for the touch now?

Stepping back over to the window, she longed to see his eyes again. She picked up the family photograph she'd left there late last night. The only one Father had allowed after his accident.

All the daguerreotypes of him before he was scarred had been removed. But she could still faintly remember what he looked like.

The difference was the humor in Father's eyes. It had been there before but disappeared a long time ago.

What she wouldn't give to see that again.

Looking over her shoulder, she studied him. Watched his slow breaths.

She returned the photograph to the dresser and went back to his side.

Grabbing his hand, she whispered, "I miss you." Her impulse to say those words struck her in the heart like a needle. It pinched. Burned. Made her uncomfortable.

Whether she missed the man she remembered from her childhood, or the thought of getting to know her father as an adult bothered her, she wasn't sure. But the weight of her words grew heavier with each passing second.

Regret was awful.

Father's hands tightened around hers.

A glimmer of hope shot through her. "Father?"

He convulsed on the bed.

Nurse Krueger rushed to the bedside and shoved his shoulders down. "Quick." She jerked her head to the side table. "Get that strap between his teeth so he doesn't bite his tongue off and swallow it."

Martha grabbed the strap and fought to get it in between his teeth as Father flailed on the bed.

Tears pricked her eyes.

Nurse Krueger held Father down as best she could but jerked with him several times.

Martha's knees buckled as she watched. Grabbing the arm of the chair she'd occupied as she read, she sat back down, her heart racing.

Father's movements lessened. Then stilled.

Cold seeped through her veins like ice chilling her from the inside out.

He went completely limp.

She shivered. Why couldn't she feel a thing? Her fingers, her arms, her legs . . . all numb. She couldn't move. Couldn't speak. Couldn't breathe.

Nurse Krueger stood there for several moments, her hands still on Father's shoulders. Then she laid her head on Father's chest. When she righted herself, she put a hand in front of his nose and then shook her head. "I'm afraid . . . I'm afraid he's gone, miss." She stood tall and stiff and straightened her skirts with her hands. "I'll go inform Mrs. Jankowski."

Martha's jaw went slack. Just like that? It was over? Her father was . . . dead? All the questions that had plagued her since he'd fallen rushed through her mind.

There would be no chance at a closer relationship. He wouldn't be around when her dinosaur was put on display. He wouldn't be there for her wedding, or the birth of her first child.

Antoni Jankowski was gone.

Footsteps sounded in the hall. Much faster than normal.

Mother's voice echoed from the doorway. "No . . ." and tapered off in a whimper.

Martha walked over to the window and stared out at the blue sky. The weather should be dark and gray. The heavens pouring out their own sorrow in droplets of rain.

But no. It was sunny. A cloudless day.

Happy weather.

She wasn't sure how long she stood there, but her fingers had gone numb as she'd squeezed her arms tight around her ribs.

Nurse Krueger and Mother exchanged words, but Martha didn't understand them. Her head was full of cotton. Nothing made sense. Was the room spinning or was it her? The doctor was surely on his way here now.

Would they take Father's body away and she'd never see him again? Was that how all this worked?

"My dear . . ." Mother's voice floated over to her as she wrapped Martha in a hug.

That was the last straw. Martha burst into tears and turned into her mother's embrace. They cried together and Mother whispered soothing words . . . more than Martha had ever heard from her mother in her lifetime. Martha drank the terms of endearment into her heart like they were water to a parched throat.

Which made the ache grow within her.

Mourning the loss of the man who was her father.

Mourning the loss of any relationship with him in the future.

And mourning the lack of a relationship with her own mother, even as she stood in her arms.

SUNDAY, JUNE 2, 1889 • JANKOWSKI DIG SITE

Jacob sat on top of the ridge and looked down at the quarry site. It was quiet today. No chinking of metal against rock.

No rhythmic swishes of brushes clearing rock and dirt. No voices.

After church, he'd come here. Alone with the wind and the picturesque views behind the sandstone, limestone, and mudstone.

The mountains were glorious. A bit of snow remained on the highest peaks, and the foothills were still a little chilly in the morning. He breathed deep of the clean air and picked up a blade of dried grass. There was no doubt, in the heat of the day, that summer had taken hold in the Rocky Mountains.

Splitting the grass into several thin, tan strands, he stared off into the distance. Two weeks had passed since Martha lost her father. Ever since, he'd promised her to do his best to keep everyone inspired and working diligently at the dig.

She'd promoted him to foreman in her absence. With Mr. Parker to assist. Why she'd done it, he didn't understand, especially since he was the newest member of the crew. But the men didn't balk. He hadn't heard any rumblings. Hopefully it would stay that way.

His fellow workers were good men. They'd worked harder and longer each day, helping Martha in her time of sorrow.

Lily Rose had even come out to the dig a few times with Martha's driver, scribbling the updates on a pad of paper to take back. They had hovered and intimidated the workers with some harsh words, but Jacob couldn't really blame them. They were protecting Martha—trying to help in the best way they knew how in her time of grief.

More than anything, he wished Martha would come back to the dig. Not only so she could be a part of what she'd started. But he missed seeing her every day, talking with her, discussing intellectual ideas, sharing excitement over each fossil brought out of the ground. And her smile. Oh, he missed her smile.

Stop it! Martha was in mourning.

Even so, from everything they'd talked about, it didn't seem like Martha had been close to her family. In all honesty, it didn't sound like she'd ever been close to anyone.

Other than Phoebe. Martha had mentioned her governess a few times, but he wasn't sure how to bring her up again. Not that he had a right to push his way into anything.

They were friends.

That was all.

He shredded another blade of grass and then another.

God, I don't know what You have planned for me, but I'm thankful for this opportunity. I'm thankful for the job. And thankful for everything that I get to learn through this. The longer I'm around Martha, the more I'm drawn to her, but please protect my heart. I don't want to do anything out of Your will, and I definitely don't want to overstep.

Footsteps on the rocky path behind him cut the prayer short and made him jump to his feet.

What if it was someone from the other team coming to spy? They'd recognize him! Martha's work would be jeopardized, and it wouldn't do him much good either.

He dove behind a large boulder. Maybe whoever it was hadn't heard him.

"Thanks for coming with me, I know this was supposed to be your day off."

Martha! As much as he longed to see her, Jacob stayed behind the rock. He couldn't jump out now—that would scare her.

"I don't mind. I'm glad we're out here again." Lily Rose was with her.

If they discovered he was hiding, well . . .

He shook his head. It didn't matter what they thought of him.

Oh, but it did. The thought of being seen as weak or deceptive wasn't exactly the image he wanted Martha Jankowski to carry around of him.

Vanity. Yep. It was all vanity.

Once the women were past the boulder, he rounded the backside as quietly as he could and came up behind them on the trail. "Afternoon, ladies."

Martha whirled around and put a hand to her throat. "Jacob! You scared me!" Her shoulders dropped as she shook her head.

"My apologies. That was not my intention."

"What are you doing out here?" Her brows were scrunched up, her lips pinched.

Shoving his hands into his pockets, he stepped a bit closer. "I thought I'd come out after church and enjoy the quiet."

"Oh. It is serene out here when no one else is around." She moved toward him, her parasol shading him a bit. "I'm glad you're here. Thank you for all your hard work. Lily Rose has kept me apprised and I must say that I am impressed with how much you have accomplished."

"It's not me." He shook his head. "The men have been going above and beyond to help you in your time of grief. You've hired yourself a good crew, Martha. They are loyal and hard-working."

Her head turned toward the quarry. "They *are* good men. I am indeed fortunate." Her voice cracked a bit on the last word. As her chin lifted, Jacob noticed the sheen in her eyes. "I'll be back to work tomorrow."

"Oh, that's wonderful news." He wanted to jump up and down to see her again. But a twinge of guilt hit him. Was he being selfish? "Are you sure it isn't too soon?"

Her head bobbed up and down. "I need to be here. Need to be working. The house is a giant echo chamber. As soon as we buried Father, Mother was never around anymore. And I find myself lost in grief with nothing to do. I need for my hands to be busy."

"Whatever you need to do, I'll be here to help."

"Thank you." Turning to face him fully again, she pressed her lips into a thin line. "I have a request though."

"Anything."

"Will you continue on as foreman—along with me? I mean, just in case. If my mother needs me, or if I find something is too difficult . . ." Her lips pinched into a tight circle.

He held out a hand toward her. "I'll be here for you, no matter what. I promise." Dipping his head, he stared at his boots for a moment. "To be honest, I've enjoyed the job."

"I'm glad to hear it . . . and thank you." She took a long inhale. "I know my loss will always be there, but I need to see this through."

The sound of horse's hooves clopping up the trail made all of them whip around.

Jacob stepped in front of Martha, just in case this new visitor had ill intentions.

"Miss Jankowski." The tall man's face was shadowed by his hat.

Martha stepped beside Jacob. "Mr. Grissom." She put a hand to her throat. "You startled us." She shifted toward Jacob. "I'm sorry. This is one of the men I've hired to patrol the perimeter."

He released a breath, but it didn't make him feel all that better. The news written across the man's face wasn't good.

"Not my intention, miss." Grissom's low voice was scratchy. "But I saw your carriage out front and came to find you. We've got a problem."

"What is it?" She stepped closer to the man.

"We found blood on the southeast fence line. Someone cut through two rows of the barbed wire."

Martha gasped beside him. "Did they get through?"

"We've searched the entirety of the area and haven't found anyone, but that doesn't mean much. There's plenty of places for someone to hide. But they're injured, and I wouldn't want to be out here with the wildlife and an open wound."

"Have you fi—"

"Sorry to interrupt, but yes, we've fixed the fencing. Our intruder is either trapped inside or never made it in." He sidled his horse closer. "We're going to need more men, Miss Jankowski. I don't like the fact that someone was brazen enough to cut the wire."

Martha's shoulders stiffened. "Hire as many as you need, Mr. Grissom. And post men at the front gate around the clock, please. If the intruder shows himself, take him straight to the police chief."

Grissom rode away and Jacob took Martha's elbow. "Are you all right?"

Fury filled her face. "I'm fine. I just find it despicable that someone would try to do this right after I've lost my father."

Lily Rose stepped forward, placing a calming hand on Martha's arm. "They probably don't know who owns this, Martha. They just wanted to find out what we're doing."

"But it's against the rules. Don't you see? I have to report this to the museum director immediately."

He'd never seen her so fired up.

Lily Rose *tsked*. "I don't think that's a wise idea. That could anger whoever is behind this and they might retaliate."

Jacob frowned and studied Martha's companion. "Not a wise idea to report criminal activity that's clearly in violation of the rules of the competition?" Why would she even suggest such a thing?

The older woman looked over at Jacob, her lips pulled tight with irritation. Was she offended he'd challenged her? Jacob glanced away, alarm tightening his shoulders. Something was not adding up here.

Martha shook her head. "I know you are trying to protect me, Lily Rose. But this isn't college, where someone is trying to steal my paper. I agree with Jacob, this is against the law and I'm going to report it. The other team might not play by the rules, but I will." She spun around and headed back down the trail.

"And I *will* win," she tossed over her shoulder.

eleven

"I want to plow, to sow, to reap, to garden, to have fine
animals about me, to see things grow and blossom. I
want to get at the real significance of things and help my
fellow man to arise and come into the light of freedom
and truth. I want suitable surroundings for this. We have
had hardships all our lives. I want those around me, who
have borne the heat of the day, to have calm and rest at
evening."

~Earl Douglass

MONDAY, JUNE 3, 1889 • DENVER

The museum truly was a beautiful building. And the contents
were quite valuable, as they were in any museum. But it was
all a sham. A cover for what she really did.

She reveled in another plan playing into her hands with
precision.

The two digs were unearthing some of the world's largest
fossils. One would go on display and bring her the recognition
she deserved. The other would get stolen in transportation
and bring her a tidy sum.

174

With the little competition she'd thrown together gathering all the attention, no one was the wiser of what she had going on behind the scenes.

And she was right in the middle of it all.

They were all blind.

And stupid.

But if she'd learned anything from her own papa, it was that pulling a con meant staying in control and knowing everything that was happening. The best way for her to accomplish that was to be one of the players on the chess board.

An innocent, harmless, beautiful player.

Walking up the steps to the museum's entry, she had to laugh at her own thoughts. Innocent and harmless.

How many people had she duped over the years?

It never got old.

Saturday, June 8, 1889

For more than six weeks, Cole had followed the trail. All over Colorado, Wyoming, and even into Utah. Some of the leads had turned out to be nothing. But a few gems had stood out. Three other murders with a lady's white kid glove over the man's chest. Spread years apart. With nothing connecting them.

Mr. Gilbert was willing to do whatever it took to catch his son's killer. But convincing Hart—Cole's boss—to give him more money and time had been torturous. It wasn't until he mentioned the multiple murders that Hart agreed to at least keep him on the case.

The last two weeks had been discouraging. One dead end after another. Even so, he'd come back to Denver to see what else he could find out, specifically about Edwin.

He was missing something. Something important. But what?

Perhaps he just needed to get out on foot and interview anyone and everyone he could. It would give the town gossips plenty of fodder and get the word out that he was investigating. Besides, at this point, what other choice did he have? He was a Pinkerton. And a good one too.

A half an hour later, Cole walked into the McGovern Tavern. It was the middle of the afternoon, so the clients were scarce. The barkeep chatted with a portly man at the end of the bar. Two men sat at a corner table on the opposite side of the room, a card game spread between them. Someone played the upright piano opposite the two men, but the person was obscured from view.

Cole sat on a stool a few down from the portly man at the bar.

"What'll ya have?" The bartender slapped a towel over his shoulder and leaned forward.

Cole waved a hand. "Too early in the day for me. But I did have a few questions about a man who used to come here. If you have a moment."

The man pushed off the bar. He glared at Cole. "You the police?"

"No. Just a friend of someone who is concerned about his son."

"Who?"

"Edwin Gilbert."

"Ah."

That response was about as helpful as a buggy on a sand dune. "Did you know him?"

"I did. He came around few times a week for different poker games."

Cole pulled the photo from his pocket. He wanted to be sure. "This him?"

The man leaned forward and nodded. "Gilbert was good people."

"Was he a drunk?"

"Nah. He loved his cards, gambled away most of whatever money he had for the week. But he wouldn't touch any drink."

"What about women?"

The man at the end of the bar stood and came to sit by Cole. "I'm Bobby Polk." He stuck a hand out and Cole shook it. "I played cards with Ed many times. And let me tell you, he loved the ladies. Didn't he, Vince?"

"He did. New dove on his arm every night almost." Vince rubbed a glass out with his towel and placed it on the shelf. "Well, he used to. He'd been seeing some new woman for about a month afore he died. Real pretty thing. All blonde hair and blue eyes."

Bobby tossed back what was left of his whiskey. "Nah, she had light brown hair, didn't she? But definitely blue eyes. She could stare through you like you wasn't even there. Who knew what she saw in old Eddie, but she stuck to him close."

Cole drummed his fingers against the thick oak bar top. The variance in descriptions wasn't helpful, but if they could get a general sketch of the woman, he could have someone at the office draw it up and share it across the wire between here and Colorado Springs. He needed to question this woman.

"You gentlemen have been very helpful. Just one more question. Have you seen the woman recently?"

Bobby shook his head. "She ain't been round here since Eddie died."

"Yeah, she was. Two days after the funeral. She came in and talked with Slim." Vince raised an eyebrow. "They looked mighty cozy. But she ain't been back after that."

"Slim?" Cole made a mental note of that.

"Come to think of it, haven't seen him in a bit neither." The barkeep frowned and then shrugged.

Hm. Cole had quite a bit to do when he got back to the hotel. "Appreciate your cooperation." He tossed a couple coins on the bar. "Have a drink on me." He tipped his hat and left the tavern.

He stood on the wooden sidewalk for a minute, putting the information he'd just learned in order in his mind. It was clear that Edwin Gilbert was well liked by most who knew him and had kept his promise not to drink. So there was no longer any doubt in Cole's mind that someone made Edwin's death look accidental.

But it was murder. By someone who'd committed several other murders. Which meant the killer was far more danger-ous than he'd originally suspected.

Of utmost importance now was to track down this Slim and the mystery woman. Maybe the two of them knew some-thing that would be helpful. Or maybe they were his culprits.

One thing was certain.

The faster he found them, the better.

SATURDAY, JUNE 15, 1889 · JANKOWSKI DIG SITE

A yellow-bellied marmot raced across Jacob's worksite as he was setting out his tools. Each morning, he liked to be the first one on-site. And each morning, the critter would eyeball him and race off.

He'd even given the animal a name. Reginald.

Whether the little guy was looking for food or simply upset that the dinosaur dig was in his path, Jacob couldn't say. But he'd started having conversations with it.

"Good morning to you too, Reginald!" he hollered after it. "I look forward to our discussion today."

Yesterday, Martha had interrupted one such conversation and had laughed for a solid two minutes at Jacob's tone of voice with the animal.

He worked out the kinks in his neck and smiled. Working side-by-side with Martha the past couple weeks had been superb. The best days of his life to be honest. Not only was she a great teacher when it came to paleontology, but they found a rhythm like they had been working together for years.

Jacob noticed it. Lily Rose noticed it. Martha even commented on it.

But today . . . well, he had other plans. Last night, he'd lain awake for hours developing a strategy. It might be foolish of him to even ask, but Martha needed a change of scenery.

They both did.

Martha and Lily Rose arrived followed by a herd of the workers.

Jacob finished his preparations and wiped his palms on his work denims.

Taking a big breath, he removed his hat from his head and walked into the tent where Martha was coordinating the work for the day. "Do you have a moment?"

She darted her gaze to him and then back to her papers. "You don't have to ask, silly."

He didn't have her attention yet. But hopefully soon. "Since we are relatively ahead of schedule the past couple days, I was thinking it would be nice to do something to refresh our minds and spirits."

"Oh?" She didn't look up, penciling something else in on the grid.

He was invested now. "The guest lecturer—the one on the Bible and science going together?—has been invited back with a promised mediator. Apparently a lot of folks complained that they wanted to hear what he had to say. He'll be back this coming Monday evening."

She didn't respond, just kept studying the papers in front of her.

Jacob licked his lips and plowed on ahead. "We could leave a bit early Monday, get cleaned up, perhaps have some dinner, and then head to the lecture. What do you think?"

Her head slowly turned in his direction, expression thoughtful. "That would be lovely, Jacob. Thank you for asking." She surveyed the quarry and turned back to him. "You're correct, we need a break. A moment to refresh. I'll make sure that Lily Rose is available. If I remember correctly, she told me she needed to run an errand on Monday."

Oh. Disappointment rippled through his chest. He understood the need for propriety and a chaperone. But Martha's companion unsettled him for reasons he couldn't quite pinpoint. Still, any time he could get with Martha would be a treat, no matter who was with them. "Great. I'll look forward to it." He plopped his hat back on his head and grinned the grin that was sure to look that of a smitten schoolboy. "I better get back to it."

"I'd like for us to finish up quadrant J15 today, if you think it's possible?"

"Certainly." He tapped his leg. "I'm almost done with it, so with your help, it shouldn't be a problem."

"Perfect." Her tone was enthusiastic. "Let me ensure everyone knows what their tasks are for today and I'll be over with my tools."

Jacob headed back to his little square of the quarry and began the tedious process of chiseling, brushing, blowing, and then starting all over again. Within half an hour, Martha had joined him in the upper right corner of the square. From what they could tell, there were two more bones that needed excavating. One appeared to be a vertebra from the tail—a caudal vertebra, to be exact. The other one they weren't sure about since it appeared to be perpendicular in the rock layer rather than horizontal. Those were the ones that took the greatest amount of time.

Martha worked on the vertebra while Jacob continued the time-consuming work on the larger bone.

The next hour passed in the sounds of chinking and a little bit of conversation.

The wind whipped up several times and produced little dust devils that swirled around them and covered everything in a fine mist of red dirt. But they'd brush it aside and focus on the tasks at hand.

"Aha!" Martha's exuberance was palpable. "I've got it." She held up the vertebra and several of the workers in the quarry applauded.

Jacob grinned at her. "Excellent work, boss."

Getting to her feet, she handed the bone to Lily Rose. "Would you take this to the tent so that I can catalog it in a little bit? First, I need to double-check and make sure there isn't anything in the layer underneath."

Lily Rose attempted to take the bone with her gloved right hand and keep a hold on her parasol with the other. It didn't work.

Fear shot up Martha's spine. She jerked the precious bone back from her friend's grasp, clutching it close. "Drop the parasol, Lily Rose!" Irritation laced her command.

The older woman's gaze landed on Martha with a split second of anger. The emotion had flickered across her pretty features so quickly, Martha thought she might have imagined it.

Lily Rose snapped her parasol shut and leaned it against a smaller boulder. "I apologize for my carelessness." She held out both her hands and Martha placed the bone in them, making sure Lily Rose's grip was tight. "I'll return momentarily."

Martha turned back to the digging area with a deep breath.

Her nerves were on edge more than usual. Still, Lily Rose's lack of caution in handling an important piece of the dig grated on her. If the bone was dropped and it shattered, it wasn't like they could just conjure up another one. Hopefully, she'd learned her lesson just now.

Releasing a long sigh, she plucked out her small hammer and pounded away at the thin layer of rock on top of where they'd found the vertebrae. From experience, they'd learned that there could be fossils three, four, even up to six layers deep. There weren't any other bones or fragments in that foot-wide section, so she worked to remove it.

Jacob waited to continue his own chiseling until she was done. No sense having the vibrations mess up the delicate work he was doing. The thin bone he was working on seemed to go quite deep. Which made him think it might be part of the pelvis or even the scapula. Either one would be exciting since they didn't have them yet.

"Well, that is disappointing." Martha raised up from her kneeling position.

"What?" Jacob studied her.

"I was hoping there might be more fossils underneath here. Not that we need to add to the workload, but there's still several bones unaccounted for. The skull being the most important. I'll go another layer down when you're finished." She walked over to where he worked. "How's it coming?"

"Pretty well. This one goes deep, though, so it will take a while."

She clapped her hands together and then wiped them on the apron that covered her skirt. "I will catalog that bone and check the grid. Then I'll be right back to help."

"Sounds great. Thanks." He pointed his gaze back at the rock. To work in close proximity with her on the same bone made his palms slick with sweat. He wiped them on his denims. Somehow, he'd have to keep his focus and his grip. Especially when her perfume wafted over him. Sweet Verbena, she'd told him. The scent would forever be matched with Martha.

Steadying his chisel, he took a long breath. It was best to focus on the work at hand.

But as soon as the hammer hit the chisel, he felt it. The rock beneath him cracked. He worked the chisel carefully around the bone and pulled it out.

Sure enough, the fossil had broken in two.

"What's happened?" Martha's quick footsteps sounded behind him. "I heard the crack." Her voice held tension.

Jacob had to tell the truth. "When I chiseled"—he pointed to the exact fissure—"right here, the whole rock cracked. Including the bone."

Her eyes closed as her lips pinched together.

Oh boy.

She'd be mad. That was completely understandable. Even though this kind of thing happened, they all took precautions to *not* allow it to happen. His heart sank. "I'm so sorry, Martha."

The time it took her to open her eyes and look at him seemed like an eternity. "Is the rest of the bone still in the rock?"

"I believe so."

With a nod, she kept her gaze away. "I'll take it from here."

~~~~~

Monday, June 17, 1889 • Castle Rock, Colorado

She watched until the group of ladies left with their bolts of fabric. A quilting bee must be coming up.

Once everyone was out of the mercantile, she entered and went about completing her odd list. Sometimes it was an annoyance to travel such a distance to do business, but it kept her on her toes. Glancing down at the watch on her shirtwaist, she cringed. She was running out of time and needed to get back to Denver before tonight. And that was thirty miles.

She checked her list and pulled the rest of the items from the shelves.

Up at the front, the clerk smiled at her, his large mustache twitching. "Good morning."

"Good morning."

"Is this all you need?" He began to tally the items. Perfume. Lye soap. Ammunition. Needles. Thread. Rope. Knives. Chisels.

She kept an eye on the door as he continued with her odd assortment of tools.

"Yes, sir. I appreciate your fine business here." She could pour on the charm when she wanted.

He scribbled for several minutes. Then let out a low whistle. "That'll be seven dollars and fifty-two cents, miss." He glanced over her worn dress and threadbare shawl, then up to her brown bonnet with orange flowers that had small holes in them. "I don't think we've met before. Are you new in town?"

"Yes, thank you."

"I can't offer you a line of credit if I don't know your family. That's a hefty sum." His eyes seemed sympathetic.

She didn't need his sympathy.

"It's not a problem." She reached into her drawstring purse and pulled out several coins. Handing one gold eagle over to the clerk, she flashed him a smile. "Here you are."

His puzzled look as he took it didn't bode well. He'd seen that she had more. The ten-dollar piece wasn't normally carried around by common folk. "That's a lot of gold coin to be walking around with—especially for a woman of your . . . station."

Nosy man. She repressed a frown. "God has been good to me."

But his brow lowered. "Where did you say you were from?" He went to the cash register.

"I didn't." He was getting too intrusive.

He held the coin up to the light.

Exasperating man. "It's real, I promise."

All he did was stare at her.

This was taking entirely too much time. Rude man. Stupid, stupid man. Pulling out her knife, she marched around the counter, grabbed his collar, and stabbed him.

His eyes widened as he crumpled behind the counter. Good enough. Now to get out before anyone else saw her.

She yanked the knife out, wiped it on the ugly brown shawl, and slid it back into its hiding place in her skirt. Then she reached into her drawstring bag and pulled out a glove. She hadn't planned on using this today, but it was best to be prepared. With a wry grin, she laid it on the man's chest.

Grabbing her purchases and the coin, she lifted her chin then strode out the door. It only took a few minutes to pack her horse. Once in the saddle, she glanced over her shoulder. The streets were quiet.

Huh. Perhaps she'd visit again.

~

MONDAY, JUNE 17, 1889 • UNIVERSITY OF DENVER

Martha paced the sidewalk outside the lecture hall. Neither Lily Rose nor Jacob had arrived yet.

Walter called down from his seat on the carriage. "Would you like me to wait, miss?"

She shook off her irritation and smiled at him. "No need for you to delay your dinner because of me. Please return in two hours."

"Yes, miss." He set the horses in motion and the carriage rolled away.

As she watched, she noticed Jacob heading toward her. Finally. She released her breath.

As promised, he carried a basket and a blanket. His pace was quick and he was at her side in no time. "My apologies for the delay, it took a bit more time to arrange everything than I imagined it would."

"It's not a problem." She took his offered elbow and walked with him over to a grassy patch under a tree.

He laid out the blanket and she took a seat while he removed all the goodies from the basket. "It's nothing fancy, but it should do."

Over their picnic dinner, they discussed the work of the day. Jacob shared how he'd been so nervous she would fire him over the broken fossil. Once they'd gotten the rest of the bone out, they saw how easy it would be to repair and piece back together. But until that moment, he'd been nervous.

"I don't wish to scare you, Mr. Duncan."

He laughed at her teasing. "Oh believe me, you scare us all plenty. You're the boss, remember?"

Their laughter joined and seemed to roll over the grassy area in a wave of happiness. It was an altogether new feeling for her. She loved every minute of it.

If this was what courting was like, she could understand its popularity.

Of course, that probably had to do with one's companion. Over a sip of lemonade, she watched Jacob. Yes, the company was definitely the deciding factor.

Jacob checked his pocket watch. "Oh my, we need to get this cleaned up. I didn't realize it was almost time for the lecture to begin."

Martha peered around the small grassy area. Where was Lily Rose? It was odd for her companion to be late like this.

By the time they had their picnic packed away and cleaned up, there was still no sign of Lily Rose. "I guess we better head inside. At this rate, I won't be able to see over any of the gentlemen's heads anyway."

"I already took care of that." The glimmer in Jacob's eyes was curious.

"Oh? What did you do?"

"Before I grabbed the picnic, I asked a groundsman to allow me in. I laid my coat and a couple of blankets over three seats at the front."

What a wonderful gesture. "That's impressive, Jacob, but what if someone moved them? It is cutting it close."

He shrugged. "I figured we could deal with that once we are inside." He held out his elbow again. "Shall we?"

When they were almost to the door, a voice rang out behind them. Martha turned to see Lily Rose running toward them.

She held her hat on with one hand and another to her chest. "My deepest apologies for my late arrival."

"It's fine." Martha shared a glance with Jacob. "Jacob took good care of me."

Her companion eyed him and lifted her chin a bit as he held the door for them to enter. What on earth was that about? Martha shook her head and followed Lily Rose inside, tipping her head in thanks to Jacob for his courtesy.

An hour later, the lecture was in full swing. So far, while there had been a few heated questions from the gallery, it had gone well. And Martha found each exchange fascinating.

Neither the atheists in the crowd nor Mr. Langford had exact proof of either of their points of view. But Mr. Langford was in much better spirits this time. Probably because he hadn't been ambushed and the university had provided a mediator.

From everything Martha had studied, the model of a Creator was still her favorite. It made the most sense. Even though the papers and ideas behind other theories also had a great deal of science backing them up, there was still so much they didn't know. Not yet. In the great big picture of life, they had about as much information as the same space the Earth occupied within the known universe. Which wasn't a lot.

That's why she loved science, loved learning. She wanted to continue with her education as long as she could. To explore all the unknowns. Search for truth. Find beauty in every detail of life around them.

The lecture came to a close without a major argument erupting or anyone coming to blows. That was nice. Martha surveyed the lecture hall and noticed that each of the reverends and their wives had stayed. That was good. Good to show the community that they could come together with differing ideas and discuss in a calm, logical manner.

Today, anyway.

Tomorrow was another story.

Their trio walked out after the crowd dispersed. Once they were past the outside doors, Jacob raised an eyebrow at her. "What did you think?"

She paused for a moment. Where should she start? "It was educational. And I agreed with the speaker on many counts."

"May I inquire which ones?"

She pursed her lips and pulled her shoulders back. "Yes, of course. First, I would have to say that his understanding of the young earth model and the Creator—God—made sense to me. It's logical. From what I can ascertain as a scientist and paleontologist, a global flood catastrophe—Noah's flood—accounts for what we see in the fossil record."

He nodded and the three of them continued walking.

"Second, to back up the Creation theory, it makes sense that God created the earth *old* and fully developed. It wasn't like He plopped a baby planet in our solar system that wasn't ready for anything yet. I can wrap my brain around that."

"All right." Apparently, he was waiting for her to finish expressing her ideas before commenting.

"Third, what I haven't figured out yet is when the dinosaurs lived. Many believe that it was millions of years ago and then they went extinct long before humans were on the planet. And I must admit that I can understand their point of view. On the other hand, I've read Scripture. And I've read lots of historical documents and writings from other cultures around the world that all testify to the world being thousands of years old, they all have an account of worldwide flood, and they each speak of creatures that are massive beyond anything we have now. I've seen a fossilized tree upright through multiple layers of geological stratum. What should be a timeline for millions of years and yet the same tree is there. To me, there is science behind both the evolutionists' and the creationists' points of view. I can't explain it. I've never heard anyone be able to. Thus, all sides have to have *faith* in what they believe is true."

Jacob nodded. "You're right. My family was worried about my studies in paleontology, afraid I would be tainted by the world. But I don't believe science—or the study of it—to be bad. If we believe in a Creator, then He created science for us to discover, learn, and explore. It wouldn't be all that fun if we were born with all the answers to everything. What would there be to explore? To learn? To discover? I don't know about you, but that sounds pretty boring to me. In all my years studying Scripture, I never once—"

"Stop!"

Martha started at Lily Rose's sharp tone. She'd never heard such a tone from her friend before.

Lily Rose's beauty was marred by two bright red spots in her cheeks. Her eyes were narrowed, and her hands fisted on her hips. Anger made her shoulders rigid. "Stop it. I'm not listening to either one of you spout any more."

Martha placed a hand on her friend's arm. "What's wrong?"

Lily Rose shook her head with such force that Martha was afraid she might injure herself. She pushed Martha's hand away. "All my life, I've endured listening to people who live false lives talk about their artificial faith. Yet they live how they want to, not caring how they treat others. Or talking about God on Sunday and living however they want every other day. Don't try to convince me that their sham is worth believing. I'm done. I don't believe there is a God." She turned to Martha, her face rigid. "I'll send Walter over with the carriage. I'll find my own way home."

With that, she stomped away.

twelve

Thursday, June 20, 1889 • Jankowski Mansion

Mother had left her a note Monday evening that they needed to talk. By the time Martha returned from the lecture, her mother had already gone to bed. Martha hadn't seen her since.

So she arranged to come home early this evening, but no sign of her mother.

What was going on? Their conversations had been shorter and stiffer than usual. Was that how grief worked? If so, Martha didn't like it. Not one bit.

It had been much better when her mother had wrapped her arms around Martha and they'd cried together. That was something she could cling to. Understand. But after that one time, the walls between them were even higher. Thicker. Impenetrable.

To make matters worse, Lily Rose kept her distance and had spoken all of twenty words to Martha since her outburst at the lecture. Fifteen of those words had been to ask for an extra day off. Figuring they both needed the space, Martha gave it to her. For all their lack of deep friendship, the rift bothered her, and she didn't know how to make it right.

The chimes for the doorbell rang and Martha glanced at her watch. Who could that be?

She waited in the library. Her favorite room. Built-in mahogany bookcases lined each wall and were filled to the brim with books.

Knowledge. Information. Answers.

If only she had the answers to all her questions.

Their butler knew where she was if needed, but people didn't come to see Martha. They came for Antoni or Victoria Jankowski.

She stared out the window as the sun set behind the mountains. Where could her mother be? Not that she usually kept tabs on her, but she'd never gone this long without seeing her. Had she?

Sad. She couldn't remember.

Martha rubbed the bridge of her nose as the door to the library opened. She turned, expecting her mother, but it was Gerard.

"Miss. There's a Leonard Foster here to see you."

"Me?" That was unexpected.

"He came to see the missus, but she's not here."

"Why would he want to see me, then?" She swallowed against the dryness that overtook her mouth.

Gerard cleared his throat. "He's a reporter, miss. Says it's urgent. About your father."

A reporter? She blinked. "Um . . ."

"Shall I send him in? He refuses to leave until he speaks with one of you." One bushy eyebrow spiked on Gerard's forehead.

Reaching for the glass of water beside her, she puzzled over the situation. She took a sip and the cool water bolstered her for a moment. "Please. Send him in."

Their butler ushered the man in and made introductions.

But as soon as Leonard Foster entered the room, Martha smelled a rat. His top hat was scuffed, and when he removed it, he gave an all-too-pretentious bow. His smile was as oily as his hair.

She forced a cool greeting. "What can I do for you, Mr. Foster?"

"Ah, the young socialite wishes to give me the cold shoulder. Just like your parents." He sauntered awfully close and pointed his top hat in her direction.

Gerard paused at the door and stayed.

Martha appreciated that and sent the man a pleading look. "You have one minute to state your business, Mr. Foster, before I am forced to have you removed from my property."

"Spirited, too. Like your mother." He sauntered his way around the room. "I won't take up your time. I simply came here to get a comment from you for an article I'm writing."

"I doubt I will have anything to comment, Mr. Foster. Now if you will please—"

"Was your father ever prosecuted for blowing up priceless fossils at a dinosaur dig in Wyoming?"

She surged to her feet, her blood pounding in her ears. "My father did no such thing!"

But the dreaded societal mistake of showing her emotions had been made. She'd played right into his hands. Foster slapped his hat on his head and slinked out of the room as fast as he'd entered.

Martha jerked awake. Pain shot through her neck. With a groan, she sat up in her chair and pressed her fingertips into the tight muscle. The clock on the mantel chimed midnight. Where was her mother?

But then, footsteps sounded out in the foyer.

Martha rushed out there and spotted the older woman heading up the grand staircase. "Mother!"

"Heavens, child." She put a hand to her chest. "What are you doing up at this hour?"

Martha lifted her chin. "I could ask you the same thing." She'd never spoken to either of her parents like that.

Mother narrowed her eyes. "Young lady, you better have a good explanation for speaking to me in such a way."

"A reporter, Mother." She spat the words. "He came here and said he's writing an article about how Father blew up fossils in Wyoming!"

Mother paused, placed her hand on the intricately carved handrail, then descended the stairs with slow, steady steps. Her lips were pinched in a thin line.

How could Mother be so calm? The thought of Martha's own flesh and blood stooping to the levels of sabotage and connivery made her sick to her stomach. "Father would have never done that."

"We will not speak of it now. I don't have time for this." For the first time ever, Martha's mother looked . . . weary. Aged. Mother had always been a beautiful woman, but the lines around her mouth and eyes had deepened since Father's death.

"But Mother! He was a reporter. Won't he tar—"

"Enough!" Mother's raised voice was like a slap. "I will deal with this reporter. What was his name?"

"Leonard Foster." The name even tasted rancid on her tongue.

"Very well."

Had she pushed too hard? She rushed to her mother, hoping to embrace her and cry together like they had before, but Mother stepped back and held up a hand. "I'm tired, my dear. Things have been difficult since . . ."

Feeling the ache of her own grief compiled with the stabbing pain of being refused, Martha straightened. "I understand." But she didn't. And she never would.

On wooden legs, she carried herself to her room, threw herself on her bed, and sobbed.

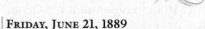

FRIDAY, JUNE 21, 1889

Martha knew Jacob's address by heart, not that she would have ever dreamed of coming here on her own before today. But at this moment, she didn't care that she was without a companion or chaperone. She didn't care what people thought. She didn't care if anyone recognized her.

All she wanted was to talk to Jacob.

As she looked up at the two-story apartment house, she couldn't stop the tears. She'd been like this the entire night and the only person she could think of talking to was him.

The sun wasn't even up yet, but she waited outside the building watching the mountains in the west as the sun's rays hit them.

"Martha?" Jacob's shocked voice from behind her was followed by footsteps on the porch. "Is everything all right?"

She turned her tear-stained face toward him and shook her head. "No. It's not all right."

He pulled a handkerchief out of his back pocket and handed it to her. With a hand to the small of her back, he led her across the street.

As she wiped her eyes, his gaze darted around. "Perhaps we could go to the hotel and have breakfast there?"

"I'm not hungry." She shook her head and sniffed.

"I'm not either. . . ." He continued to look around. "But if we keep standing out here alone, with you crying, I'm afraid your reputation will be sullied."

Blast the horrid rules of society! She hated every one of them at the moment. "Walter is waiting over there." She pointed to the end of the street. "Let's take the carriage to the quarry."

"All right." The protective way he shielded her and watched the streets as they walked together was sweet.

Here, this man had nothing to gain from their acquaintance and he cared more about her than her own mother. It saddened her and infuriated her all at the same time.

At the carriage, he helped her up into the seat.

"Walter, please head to the quarry. But take it slow."

"Yes, miss."

Jacob looked at her. Worry filled his eyes. "Where's Lily Rose?"

"I'm not sure. She hasn't spoken much to me since Monday." Tears made trails down her cheeks, but she didn't care.

"Tell me what has you so upset." He turned himself in the carriage seat so that they were almost facing one another.

As she poured out the entire story of the changes in Mother since Father died and then of the reporter coming to the house last night and his creepy insinuations, her heart felt like it was breaking in two. This couldn't be happening.

Jacob leaned a bit closer and took her hand. "I know this is difficult for you, but you told me that you're not all that close with your parents. Why is this upsetting you so much?"

She reared back, her shoulder slamming into the carriage seat. "How dare you even ask that? Can't you see . . ." But then she clamped her mouth shut. See *what*, exactly? His question wasn't hurtful. It was an honest one.

"I'm sorry." He squeezed her hand and then pulled away, leaning as far back into the other side of the carriage as the seat would allow.

She blinked away the tears gathering in her eyes and reached for his hand. "No. *I* am sorry." Inching a little closer to him, she kept hold of his hand. "You're correct. And I apologize for snapping at you like that." She straightened a bit and swallowed. "You've been good for me, Jacob Duncan. Always asking solid questions. Helping me to grow and learn."

He released a sigh. "But we're from two different worlds, Martha. It wasn't my place to say anything like that."

"Oh, but it is. You are my friend and I treasure that." His handkerchief in her left hand was soggy from her tears. "I confronted my mother when she came home last night. But she refused to speak of it. So what am I supposed to think? All these years, I've railed against the atrocities that Marsh and Cope paid their men to do, all so they could outdo one another. Compete over who wrote the most papers or named the most dinosaurs. I've sat up on my high horse looking down on anyone who wanted to associate them-selves with their practices or praised them for all they did for the field of paleontology. Frankly, it made me sick." A sad laugh escaped her lips. "And wouldn't it be ironic if my own father was one of those people? What will they say about me then? Will my name be dragged through the mud along with his?"

He squeezed her hand again, the callouses on his fingers pressing into the back of her hand. They were rough on her skin, but Martha found it didn't repulse her. In an odd way, those callouses were comforting, a reminder that Jacob didn't shy away from hard work. "From what I know of you, Miss Martha Jankowski, you have done everything you can to con-duct your dig with the utmost of respect for the field. You have expected the best from your workers. It doesn't matter what that reporter says about your father."

All feelings of comfort dissolved. "It will, though. You don't understand. I think the reason my mother wouldn't speak of it is because she's afraid of what this will do to her. What people will say. I've never seen her like she was last evening, and it concerns me."

He sat in silence with her for several moments.

She watched his face go through several expressions as he seemed to ponder what to say next.

"I guess I can understand that, but, Martha, the best thing you can do is keep going. Keep doing things respectably. Focus on what the Lord would have you do in this situation."

"I don't even know how to do that." Her words were pitiful, even to her own ears. "If it doesn't entail digging in the dirt, I don't even know where to start."

His laughter filled the carriage. "Then dig in the dirt. That's okay too."

She wanted to laugh along with him, but the tears started up again. "And if my father did what that man said he did? If he literally blew up fossils so no one else could find them? What do I do then?"

Jacob scooted closer. "We will deal with that when it comes, okay?" The tender way he looked at her made her feel cherished. Something she'd never felt before.

"Okay . . ." She breathed the word. "Thank you."

"I'll be here for you. I promise." His thumb rubbed the top of her hand.

"Thank you."

"I'm glad you came to me this morning." The warmth in his gaze drew her in.

"Me too." For the first time she understood what it meant to feel butterflies in her stomach.

thirteen

"I have loved more or less many times an ardent but transient affection that perhaps aroused something holier and nobler in my nature. But each has been somewhat different. . . . The earth seems brighter and my life for some time has been happier. It is the sweet pleasure of a calm love which seems to be growing deeper."

~Earl Douglass

FRIDAY, JUNE 28, 1889

It had been the best week of his life. Funny how that happened so often this summer.

All because of one person.

Martha.

Working by her side made every day richer. The work at the dig was grueling but extremely satisfying. They were on track to finish ahead of schedule.

A little laugh together here, a glance there, a secret smile shared every hour or so. Every day she'd found a way to grab his hand and hold it in a private moment together.

Was this what love felt like? And even though his common sense told him that he was treading on thin ice, he couldn't believe that God would bring them together like this then tear them apart.

Oh, they were a long way from stating their affection aloud. The dig had to be first and foremost. But Jacob was hopeful. He'd spent a good many hours praying about it.

Tomorrow was Saturday and they would have another long day at the dig site, but then Sunday, they'd planned to go to church together and have another picnic.

Having something like that to look forward to was enough to put a skip in his step, even at this late hour.

Shoving his hands into his pockets, he whistled a lively hymn as he made his way the last few blocks to his apartment house.

Even though Martha had endured a lot, she'd gotten stronger this week. Lily Rose was still distant, but Martha was slowly breaking down the other woman's walls. There was no word about how things were with her mother, but the story about her father's alleged criminal activity had been printed and run. The same day, there had been a horrible accident on the train tracks in Denver and it had taken over people's conversations and almost all of the newspapers the next few days.

The story would surely come back to light at some point, but perhaps people were getting tired of all the nonsense with the so-called Bone Wars.

When he reached his building, he couldn't wait to get out of his dirt-encrusted clothes and clean up in the wash basin. His bed was calling to his aching body.

He climbed the stairs two at a time and walked down the hall to his room. A noise behind the door stopped him in his tracks. The door was ajar.

What was going on?

He pushed the door ever so slightly. "What are you doing?"

The figure jumped and turned toward him. Abe. One of the men he'd worked with at the other dig.

Jacob scanned the room. His belongings were strewn across the bed. "Abe, I'll ask you again. What are you doing?"

The scrawny man blinked several times. "I need a place to stay." He glanced down at the bed. "And some clothes to wear."

"Why? What happened?" Not that Jacob didn't want to be compassionate, but something had the hairs on the back of his neck prickled.

"I need to get home to my ma. She's sick."

"So you thought it would be okay to come into my room without permission and rifle through my clothes?" They weren't even close to the same size. Jacob was a good five inches taller than the other man. And a good bit broader too.

The man ducked his chin. "I'm sorry. But you always said that if I needed anything, you would be there for me."

A bit of the anger left him. He *had* said that. To many of the other men too. He'd tried to befriend them, be the light of Jesus to them. He'd told them he would be there for them. It was important to follow through. "I assume it's just for one night?"

"What? Oh yeah, one night." Abe swallowed. "I'm leaving tomorrow for home."

"All right then. Let's clean up this mess and I'll see if we can get you some food over at the hotel."

"Thanks, Jacob." The man's shoulders slumped. "You're a good man."

After getting a sandwich from the hotel, they walked back to Jacob's apartment house.

Jacob nodded to Abe. "You can have the bed tonight. You'll need some good rest to travel tomorrow and be able to help your mother. I'll make a pallet on the floor."

Abe didn't respond.

But when they reached Jacob's room, the door was wide open and his landlady stood there with hands on her hips. "I don't know what happened. I heard a ruckus but by the time I got up here, the men were gone."

"Men?" Jacob narrowed his gaze. His bed was overturned. The dresser drawers dumped all over the floor.

It wasn't like he had a lot of possessions, but what little he had was destroyed. "I'll clean it up, Mrs. Williams. I'm sorry for the noise."

She patted his arm. "You're a good man, Jacob. I'm sorry this happened. I'm not sure how they got into the house to begin with." She walked away.

Jacob stared.

Abe drew up beside him. "Look . . . I'll find another place to stay tonight. Don't worry about me."

He nodded. Most likely, Abe had something to do with this. He'd been the distraction. But Jacob didn't have the energy to deal with it. Anger wouldn't get him anywhere. He walked into the room and started to pick up the mess.

"Let me help you. It's the least I can do." Abe was beside him and they worked in silence for the next few minutes.

Once they salvaged what they could, Abe went to the door with his hat in his hands. "Thanks for the sandwich, Jacob. You didn't have to do that. But you did."

Jacob swallowed. Weariness kept him from saying anything.

"I'm sorry about all this." And then he left.

Jacob slumped down onto his bed. If his gut was correct, the guys from the other dig were behind this. To find what? Had they found out that he was working on the other dig? If so, they were probably looking for the location of Martha's dig site. Or information of any kind on the competition.

The fact that he couldn't tell Martha about working at the

other dig ate at him. Especially now. What if he'd put her in danger?

Dressed in her best dress for church, Martha made her way down the hall toward her mother's chambers. The events of the week had given her a bit of gumption and she was determined to put the accusations against her father aside. Today was not a day to allow her thoughts to get her down.

Jacob was meeting her at church, and it would be a great chance for him to meet Mother. That was, *if* Martha could convince Mother to attend church. She hadn't been since Father's death.

With a deep breath, Martha rapped on her mother's door.

Harriet, her mother's maid, answered. "Good morning, miss."

"Good morning, Harriet. I'd like to speak with Mother, please."

She moved out of the door and allowed Martha entrance.

"Mother?" She took bold steps toward the sitting area.

"Yes, my dear."

"I think it's high time you joined me for church again." Perhaps using the confident tone would help.

Mother turned toward her. The slow movements seemed perfectly choreographed. One eyebrow arched up. "Look who's enjoying her job as foreman." The slight amusement on Mother's face was better than the somber looks of late. She stood. "But no, my dear. I will not be heeding your orders." Head high, shoulders back, her mother glided across the room.

Martha huffed. "I'm not ordering you, but it's time. It's been long enough since Fath—"

"Don't say it." The words were hissed.

"But—"

"I said don't! Don't say anything at all! Understood?"

Her mother whirled on her, and the rage in her eyes burned into Martha. She gulped and did her best to keep the tears at bay. Mother hated tears.

"I don't have time for this, Martha. Don't you understand?"

Enough was enough! "Don't have time for *what*, Mother? Church? Talking about Father? Me? What exactly don't you have time for?"

Her mother's eyes widened and then narrowed. The ensuing silence settled over Martha like a heavy blanket.

"I'll forgive you for your tone of voice, daughter—this once—because we are in mourning. But don't ever speak to me like that again. Go on to church without me." She turned and walked away.

Several seconds later, the door to Mother's private study clicked shut.

"Allow me, miss." Harriet led her back out to the main hall. Another door shut.

And Martha was left with her thoughts in the cavernous space. Alone.

Again.

~⌇~

GARDEN OF THE ANGELS, RED ROCKS PARK

"Are you going to tell me about whatever it is that has put that crease in your forehead, or should I just pretend everything is fine, eat my lunch, and sip my tea like a good gentleman?" Jacob waved a hand in front of Martha's face.

The carriage had stopped rolling and he wasn't sure whether she was in the mood for the picnic or not. Had he pushed too hard?

Pink filled her cheeks and she glanced down at her hands. "I'm sorry, Jacob."

"Well? Should we head back, or do you want me to get out the food?" He perched on the edge of the seat.

When she didn't respond, he hopped down from the carriage and held a hand out for hers. "Come on. This will be good for both of us."

"You're right." She took his hand and he helped her down. Then he walked her over to a grassy area that wasn't too prickly looking. "You wait here. I'll go get our things." He jogged back over to the carriage and nodded at Walter. "Would you like some food? I brought plenty."

"That is much appreciated, Mr. Duncan, but I'm not sure Mrs. Jankowski would approve," the man stated from the driver's seat.

Jacob rubbed his jaw. There had to be a way around the stiff rules of society. Aha! "I've got it. Since you are technically playing the role of driver *and* chaperone, then you should be allowed to eat. The chaperone always does."

The slightest of smiles worked its way up Walter's face. "Well then, I agree." The older man climbed down from his perch and assisted Jacob in unloading the carriage.

Once he had a colorful checkered cloth on the ground, Jacob placed the basket in the center. "Shall we eat?" He offered a hand to Martha as she gracefully lowered herself—and her massive skirts—to the cloth, and then took a seat on the ground and crossed his legs. "Help yourself, Walter." Jacob handed the man a plate.

The driver's eyes twinkled. "I will wait until you two have served yourselves."

"Nonsense, Walter." Martha waved a hand. "Please. We can all fill our plates. Let's not stand on ceremony today, all right? It's wearisome."

"Yes, miss."

All three of them helped themselves to fruit, cheese, tiny little sandwiches, and pickles. Then Jacob filled three glasses with the lemonade he'd brought. "Mind if I pray?"

"Not at all." Martha's sweet smile caught his attention.

He gave thanks for the food and then their little trio echoed in amens. Walter nodded at them and took his plate and glass back to the carriage. "I'll be over there if you need me, miss."

"Thank you, Walter." Martha popped a grape into her mouth.

With the sky as blue as it could be, the red rocks around them towered and soaked up the sunshine. The afternoon would be quite warm.

Jacob had already begun to sweat in his summer suit.

Martha finished off a sandwich and took a sip. "I'm sorry for my attitude earlier." She wrinkled her nose. "My relationship with my mother continues to perplex me."

This was unknown territory for him. One, he wasn't used to courting a woman, and two, he had a close relationship with every member of his family. What should he say? "I'm sorry it's been such a struggle."

"If you haven't already guessed, that was the reason for the crease in my brow as you so graciously put it." A light laugh accompanied her words.

He smiled at her and picked up another sandwich. "You know . . . I had a feeling."

She released a huff and relaxed her shoulders. "I don't know what's wrong with me. Before this summer, I never really felt the need to pursue a closer relationship with my parents. Then I met you. My father fell. Then my mother . . . well, she changed. Then when Father passed, Mother and I had this moment of connection. At least, I thought we did. But since then, she has kept me at arm's length. Everything is secretive. She's gone a lot more than usual. Or at least more than I noticed before. Instead of bringing us together . . . my father's passing has pushed us further apart. I didn't realize how much I'd hoped for the opposite until this morning. She refused to come to church and basically shut the door in my face." Once all the words were out, she pointed her blue eyes in his direction and shrugged. But the tears shimmering in the corners couldn't be missed.

Jacob held her gaze, wanting to reach out and comfort her but unsure of his instincts. What was allowed in polite society? "I didn't realize that happened this morning . . . I'm sorry." He stared at his plate for a moment and then back at Martha. "Is there anything I can do?"

A sad smile lifted her lips. "That's sweet of you to ask, but no. You simply being here is balm to my heart. I appreciate it more than I can say."

Throwing caution to the wind, he scooted closer to her and reached for her hand. "I *am* here for you, Martha. I wish I could take away the pain I see in your eyes, or give you the kind of relationship with your mother that I have with mine, but I know that God is the one who can meet your needs better than I."

Her brow did that crease again.

"Do you not agree?"

She shook her head. "It's not that I don't agree with you. It's simply that I don't understand. I do believe in God. But He's the Almighty." Sucking in her bottom lip between her teeth, she squinted at him. "Please don't think less of me, I truly am seeking understanding. But my relationship with God has always been as distant as that with my parents. Are you saying it can be different? I've never heard that taught in church."

His heart ached for her. To never have known familial love and closeness . . . it made sense that she never expected it from her Heavenly Father. "It can be the closest relationship you've ever had. Jesus, and God the Father, they long to have a deep, abiding connection with each one of us."

The crease in her brow grew as she pinched her lips together. "I don't understand. No reverend I've ever known has said such a thing." Her frown deepened. "But then, I haven't had an association with anyone that even ventured toward *close*. Not as an adult. Except maybe . . . you?"

His heart did a little flip. How he longed to bridge the gap for her. He opened his mouth, but snapped it closed as a new understanding hit.

He'd come to care for her far more than just a friend. Had hoped to say something to her today about his feelings. Class differences, societal rules . . . they all flew out the window. But if she didn't understand love . . . she couldn't understand God's love.

Then how could they ever be together?

NORTH OF DENVER

With her two hulking bodyguards beside her, she waited for the wiry man to approach her desk.

"What do ya need?"

"It's simple." She slid a piece of paper across the desk. "Don't hurt any of the fossils, but damage anything else you please. Take their tools. Make a mess." She waved her hand in the air. "I don't care. But don't get caught and don't tell anyone who hired you."

"I've never let ya down afore."

Pulling an envelope out of her desk, she looked at him sideways. "Be that as it may, this should ensure you get the job done and keep your mouth shut."

He waited for her to slide it across. Once he peered inside, he chuckled. "That'll do it."

She stood. "I've got plenty of work for you over the next few weeks." Then she leaned over the desk, steepling her fingers on the shiny surface. "But rest assured, I'll kill you myself if I even *think* you've let anything slip."

The terror in his eyes was all she needed.

He knew who he was dealing with.

fourteen

"My experience as a student has been something un-
usual but I have had a never failing desire that has borne
me through at last. There have been months and years
of suspense and waiting and hoping and disappointment. There have been times when the heavens looked
dark. But I can credit myself for only part of the victory. Had it not been for my friends I never could have
done it."

~Earl Douglass

MONDAY, JULY 1, 1889 • COLORADO SPRINGS

Cole bid his wife good-bye once again.

He hated leaving her for long periods of time, but this case
had gotten under his skin, and he couldn't let it go.

It wasn't just Edwin Gilbert's death—it was the death of
several men. His count was now up to six.

The local law enforcement in each area had been eager to
help—well, all except for Denver—when it came to Edwin's
death.

The thought that a murderer had gotten away with killing over and over for so long . . .

He gritted his teeth so hard they ached.

This wasn't a case of bank robberies and notorious gun-toting criminals who didn't care if their name was known. This wasn't about men who enjoyed killing, thieving, and doing whatever they pleased. Who taunted law enforcement to catch them.

No. This case was much worse.

It was about someone smart.

Someone conniving.

Someone who kept a low profile but taunted nonetheless.

And why leave a lady's glove? Had the killer been jilted by a lover, and this was his way of getting back?

The more he thought about it, the more his anger grew, and the less he slept at night. Why couldn't he figure this out? Even though there had been a bit of a trail after he found out about Slim and the woman, it was cold now.

At this point, the only hope of catching this killer was . . .

No. He hated to even think it.

But it was true. His only chance would be to wait until . . .

He swallowed back the bile that rose in his throat.

Until the killer stuck again.

❧

| TUESDAY, JULY 2, 1889 • JANKOWSKI DIG SITE

Staring down into the quarry, Martha watched the men pack up for the day. Another long day at the site should have invigorated her, especially with how much they had accomplished, but she couldn't let go of her anger and confusion.

Mother had left her a note Sunday evening. A *note*. They lived in the same house, and the woman couldn't have the common decency to come talk to her?

Martha pulled the paper out of her pocket and read it again.

Martha, my dear,

I think it's best if you keep your distance from that Duncan fellow. He's nothing but trouble. Those of the lower class always are. You are doing amazing work out at the dig; we wouldn't want that to be hampered by a shady character in your life.

Mother

If Martha hadn't had the refreshing time with Jacob, the note would have sent her over the edge.

The gall of the woman.

Of course her mother knew every last detail of her life. She always had.

Martha put a hand to her stomach. All these years . . . had Lily Rose gone to Mother and told her everything? Of course she had. Mother loved control. After all, her companion's salary *was* paid by Mother.

But still. For her own mother to try and tell Martha what to do when she had pushed her away that very same day . . .

It didn't make sense.

That's what bothered her about the whole situation. *Nothing* in her world seemed to make sense anymore.

In the past, her mother's actions always had a reason behind them. Even if Martha didn't agree, she could count on her mother to be constant. Predictable. They were predictable. Martha could deal with the distance and the coldness because that was normal. But this?

Her mother was clearly not dealing with her grief over losing Father.

To be honest, neither was Martha.

Losing her father had brought up so many feelings she'd never faced.

Opening up to Jacob had been one of the hardest things

she'd ever done, but she didn't regret it. Especially not after he told her there was hope for more in this life.

She folded the note and shoved it back in her pocket. One of these days, she'd have to figure out how to deal with the situation. Right now, she would keep her head down and plow ahead with her bad mood. It kept her driven and focused.

Everyone said their good-byes for the evening and Jacob and Lily Rose waited for her at the head of the trail. Martha paused and studied her two friends. There was a strange tension between the two of them. They weren't talking. They weren't even looking at one another. What had changed?

Even though Martha and her companion hadn't patched things up per se, things were on a better footing. But this distance between Lily Rose and Jacob bothered her. At one time, she seemed to get along with Jacob, at least. But now the air was heavy with discomfort. Was it because Jacob was so open with his faith? Martha's head hurt even thinking about it. When had her life gotten so complicated?

Jacob walked beside Martha on the trail back to the carriage. "So I was thinking that perhaps we needed something to boost morale around here."

"I know I haven't been in the best of moods, but I don't think your attempts to cheer me up are doing the trick. I need to stay focused." Oh, why did she keep snapping at him? He was trying to help, but she didn't *want* his help. There was so much to do, and her mother's words wouldn't leave her alone. How was she supposed to put distance between herself and Jacob? Not that she wanted to, but she needed her mother's financial help.

Martha pressed her fingers to her throbbing forehead. Everything was a mess.

"Focused?" He stepped a bit farther away. "You mean focused on your anger?"

Lily Rose gasped behind them.

213

Martha took a quick glance over her shoulder.

"How dare you speak to her like that," Lily Rose exclaimed. "You should learn to mind your manners, young man!"

"Lily Rose, you—" Martha was cut off by Jacob lifting his hands, pausing in the path.

"I apologize for being so blunt, but Martha, this isn't you. I don't know what has put you into this mood, but let us help you. We're your friends. Remember?" He reached for her hand.

The simple touch melted the edges of her fury toward her mother, and she stopped and turned to him. Stared deep into his eyes and saw the concern and truth there. She nodded. "I'm sorry. Yes, we're friends."

"Good. I don't believe friends should allow their friends to stay in a foul mood for longer than, oh, say, an hour." He pulled out his pocket watch. "You've definitely exceeded that time so why don't we figure out what we need to do to move into a better frame of mind." He gave her that lopsided grin and then winked.

A blush crept up her cheeks. Did he know what that did to her insides? She'd have to teach him about proper etiquette. A man didn't wink at a lady. It was entirely too . . . intimate. "Jacob." With a sigh, she glanced at Lily Rose.

The older woman's gaze was locked on their clasped hands, her nostrils flared with anger.

Martha pulled back, feeling the heat creep up her neck, but she forced a smile in Jacob's direction. "I'll try to do better and not be so grumpy tomorrow." Maybe that would be good enough for now.

They reached the last curve in the trail and she saw her carriage with Walter in the driver's seat.

Wait. There was another figure by the gate.

Oh, ick. That despicable Leonard Foster.

So much for getting rid of her bad mood.

"Mr. Foster"—she didn't even try to hide her distaste—"how did you find me?" That he had tracked down her property brought her rage to the surface.

"Miss Jankowski. How lovely to see you." He bowed and reached for her hand. "I followed your driver."

She put her hands at her sides and stepped back, thankful Lily Rose and Jacob were by her side. "What do you want?"

"I'm here working on another story about the Great Dinosaur Rush—the Bone Wars—and how it is still ongoing today. My editor would like to expose the corrupt and criminal activity once and for all."

"Oh?" She didn't have time for—

Good heavens. Now she sounded like her mother. Even in her head, she couldn't escape the woman's influence.

He pulled out a notepad. "Did you know"—he slithered forward, and put his pencil to his tongue and then the paper—"that Mr. Duncan here was originally hired for your competitor's team? And he was fired?"

"What?" She spun and looked at Jacob. "Tell me this isn't true."

But the red in his face, and the sorrow in his eyes, told her all she needed to know. "I—"

"You despicable man! I don't want to hear it." Her insides heated and she stomped toward her carriage even as the world around her seemed to stop. Within seconds, she reached it, but the door was closed, the step folded away. Walter sat atop the driver's seat with his mouth agape.

With as much fire as she had within her right now, she was pretty certain she could make the leap without assistance, if not for her blasted skirts. "Walter!"

At her screech, motion began around her again.

Her driver blinked and hurried down. "I'm sorry, miss."

Jacob ran toward her.

No, no, no. She stomped her foot like she had when she was

a little girl and wanted her way. Because if she didn't keep her fury burning, she would curl up in a ball and cry. Right here.

This couldn't be happening. Not like this.

Not Jacob.

Walter fumbled with the door and the step—his nervousness at her ire all too apparent. Lily Rose scrambled up into the carriage and pushed her skirts aside so Martha could sit. "Let's go, Martha. You don't need to give that man another second of your time."

Lily Rose was right. But she felt paralyzed. Almost like she couldn't breathe.

Her heart ached in her chest. It felt trampled. Beaten. Bruised. She cared for Jacob. More than anyone else. How dare he do this to her?

Walter held out a hand and helped her up in the carriage, but a hand on her arm kept her from taking her seat.

She spun around to face Jacob. "Leave me alone, Mr. Duncan." Movement beyond him caught her eye.

That horrible Mr. Foster. He seemed to take pleasure in her situation. She wanted to scream at him too and threaten to swipe that smirk off his face, but a gentle tug on her arm brought her attention back down.

Jacob's face was grim. "I can't leave you alone, Martha. Not like this."

"Do you deny that you worked for the other team?"

"I do not."

She yanked her arm away and plopped onto the seat. "Walter—"

But Jacob moved the large man aside and stepped up into the carriage. Martha felt Lily Rose stiffen beside her, and she put a hand on her companion's arm. She would handle Jacob. It was not Lily Rose's place.

Jacob gripped the side of the door, his face pale. "It's unfair for you to not allow me to defend myself."

"What is there to defend?" Her words were choked. She wanted—no needed—for there to be a great explanation for all this. For Jacob to not have betrayed her.

He didn't cower under her rage. His face was set. Determined. Honest. "I signed a contract to work for the other team before I ever met you. Before I knew anything about you or your dig. In that contract, I was obligated to not speak of the dig to anyone. Even if my employment was terminated, I couldn't talk about it. I'm a man of my word, Martha. I would hope you would know that by now."

"You were terminated?" How much more of this could she take? "For what?"

He slumped in the seat and ran a hand down his jaw. "I'm not sure. In my mind, it was because I spoke up about things happening at the other dig that went against the competition rules. They sure didn't like that . . . but they didn't give me a reason when they fired me."

Oh, how she wanted to believe him. His words were sound. He'd never been untruthful with her before, had he? She shook her head. "I need time to think. It's best if you go." Everything in her deflated, and her limbs felt like they carried the weight of the world. At that moment, all she wanted was to close her eyes and pray for sleep to erase all the pain.

"I'll be back to work in the morning."

"I don't know if that's a good idea—"

"I signed a contract for you, Martha. You need my help, and I'm not going to let you down. Not even for a sleazy reporter who wants nothing more than to stir up trouble and ruin my reputation. But I'm not worried about what others think. I worry about what *you* think. I am on your side and will be until . . ."

Several seconds passed as she waited for him to finish. "Until what?"

"Until you tell me that you no longer want me there."

FRIDAY, JULY 5, 1889

The sun glinted off the rocks, heat rippling across the quarry. Jacob peered at the site with a pit in his stomach. Should he even be here? The last three days had been some of the worst in recent memory. The look in Martha's eyes when that reporter told her about his employment with the other team haunted him. He couldn't bear to think of them leaving things unresolved, but he'd seen her face. The disbelief. Distrust.

He had done that. By not telling her the truth from the beginning. But wouldn't that have made him in breach of his contract?

What was the right thing to do?

Sleep hadn't come.

He'd poured out his heart to the Lord, studied Scripture, and wrestled. Martha felt betrayed. He couldn't blame her. He'd left things the best he could and he'd come to work and kept his head down. The best thing he could do was show her who he was with his actions. Anything else he could have said in the moment would have been lost. He'd walked away to give her space. And to clear his own head and heart.

Jacob looked down at the piece of paper in his hand. The contract. It was the one thing he had to show Martha to prove that he hadn't been lying to her. Hadn't tried to deceive her. That, before the Lord, he was honest. He hoped that she would give him time and hear him out. Everything. Nothing withheld. With a final deep breath and a prayer, he made his way toward the tent.

Martha was there, huddled over the quadrant map. Her shoulders slumped. There were lines around her eyes, she looked tired. More than tired . . . exhausted. Jacob swallowed and cleared his throat.

She glanced up and did a double take. Her whole body

went rigid. Anger flashed in her blue eyes before she schooled her features into a polite mask. "Mr. Duncan. What do you need?"

He winced. Gone were the pleasant notes of trust and friendship. Hopefully he could fix that today. Taking off his hat, he fiddled with the brim, the contract crinkling under his fingers. "I came to talk to you about . . ." He cleared his throat again. *Lord, help me.* "About my previous work."

Martha's lips tightened but she said nothing.

He studied her face, now so familiar to him. The fact that his actions, or lack thereof, had wounded her and destroyed the trust building between them broke his heart.

"Marth—Miss Jankowski, I want to apologize for not telling you about my work for the other team. I know it sounds hollow, but I did want to tell you about my previous job. But"—he sighed and held out the papers—"I signed a contract and was legally bound to not say anything. To anyone. Plus, there were all the rules from the museum owner about the dig. I didn't know what to do, if I could say anything. So I stayed silent. Well, I was going to tell you once, but we were interrupted. Then I realized I couldn't go against my word."

Martha licked her lips and stepped forward, taking the paper from him.

Please let her believe me, Lord. How do I tell her it wasn't my intent to hurt her? He waited as she read the document, the seconds ticking between them.

She sighed, setting the contract on the rough tabletop, and glared at him. "I can see how this would legally bind you to not say anything, but you do understand why this information was not only shocking, but hurtful." She turned away.

Jacob took a chance and stepped toward her, closing the distance. "Martha"—his shoes scuffed the dirt and rocks as he stepped toward her, desperation in his voice—"the last thing I wanted to do was hurt you. Please believe me. I am asking for your forgiveness. I never shared anything with the other team. I was fired. They couldn't—well, wouldn't—tell me why."

Her lips pinched and then relaxed. The look on her face indiscernible. "I'm sure my offer came at the right time."

"It did, but not for the reason you think. Your offer gave me the chance to spend more time with you. To get to know you. To learn from you." Jacob shifted and took one more step toward her. He ached to hold her hand, but he didn't dare. He wanted her to hear his heart, that she was precious to him. Even though there could be nothing more than friendship between them now, he still cared for her. "I know you're hurt and you have a lot going on with your father's passing. I'm sorry this is one more burden for you. But I hope you know I truly never meant to hurt you or keep secrets from you. And if you'll allow me, I want to finish the dig with you."

His eyes searched her face. Those blue eyes bored into his with the intensity she brought to all areas of her life. Emotion sparked between them.

Her shoulders relaxed. "I know it wasn't easy for you to come and apologize. Especially after my treatment of you the other night. You're right. I am hurt. And I'm angry. At you, at the whole situation." She turned back to the table and picked up the contract. "Losing my father has brought out extreme emotions in me, and I know that I overreacted and allowed my temper to take over. Not without good reason, mind you." The slight grin she sent him helped ease the tension. "Thank you for showing this to me. I do see now that you were in an impossible position. I don't envy you that. But now I don't know . . . if I can trust you."

Jacob waited, silent. He would respect whatever she said next. But hope flared in his chest that she might be willing to let him back in.

"Jacob, I—"

"Walter is ready with the carriage, Martha!" Lily Rose's voice floated into the tent as she walked through the open flap. The older women stopped short at the sight of the two of them together, her face flushing red. "What are *you* doing here?" She all but spat the words as she stepped between Martha and Jacob.

Startled by the woman's rage, Jacob took a step backward. "I needed to explain to Mar—Miss Jankowski what happened. I thought I owed her that."

"Don't you think she's been hurt enough by you?" She wagged a finger at him. "She doesn't need the pain of seeing you again. You've broken her trust, and at a time when she was especially vulnerable." Lily Rose let out a short laugh, full of derision. "That was probably your plan all along. No surprise. People like you—"

"Lily Rose, that's *enough*!"

Jacob looked at Martha, noting her hat and gloves were on, her drawstring bag over her wrist. His heart dropped.

"I will meet you in the carriage, Lily Rose."

"This is hardly acceptable. And your mother—"

"I said I will meet you in the carriage." Martha's volume increased, startling Jacob.

Her companion stopped short, her eyes darting to Jacob. "Fine!" She stomped out of the tent.

Martha turned back to him, her shoulders rigid. There was no warmth in her gaze. Her fingers threaded through the fringe on her bag, nearly ripping it from the seams, much like the first night they met. Only it was anger agitating her movements, not nerves. This precious woman was slipping through his fingers.

"I appreciate your boldness and honor in your commitment to the dig here, Mr. Duncan. I know this couldn't have been easy." Her voice was distant, that polite society mask back in place. "But I need time to think about this. To consider everything you've shared with me. Please give me time. I will contact you when I have an answer. You don't need to come back to the dig until then."

His heart sank. "I understand, Miss Jankowski. I will wait for you to contact me. And will abide by whatever you decide. But"—he paused and gave her a smile—"please know, no matter what happens, our time together will be held in my fondest memories. And I will always be praying for you."

A sheen of tears filled her eyes. She nodded shortly and fled the tent.

"Well, Lord . . ." Jacob sighed as the clack of wheels filled the now empty space. "It is in Your hands."

fifteen

"Above the firm foundation of the hills, above the
wooded glens, above what we call the realities of life,
and in spite of the hard things we call facts, one feels
that far off, somewhere, somehow, good and truth and
love will conquer and there is peace."

~Earl Douglass

MONDAY, JULY 8, 1889

After all the mess with that slimy reporter, Martha was about
done with the whole Bone Wars narrative. As much as she
wanted to bring a reputable name to the field . . .

She shook her head. Was it worth it?

She paced around her table at the quarry. The articles about
her father's alleged sabotage hadn't been all that enlightening
or condemning, but people were still talking about them. She'd
noticed a few sideways glances in her direction.

Then there was an article that didn't name Jacob directly
but mentioned one worker who'd secretly worked for both
teams competing for the prestigious spot at the museum. The

223

suppositions printed were all negative. Had the man been hired to spy? To sabotage? What would the owners of each dig do?

The museum director had sent word that he would be checking into the situation with Jacob. The horrid reporter was no doubt behind informing the director of the worker's identity.

And now inspections would be held at each dig weekly. That was fine with her. All the troubles needed to stop.

But to be honest, she couldn't deny that the best thing that had ever happened to her was meeting Jacob. He'd already been working for the other dig then. He hadn't tried to hide anything but had held up his end of his contract. That was trustworthy, right? Surely the museum director would find no wrongdoing on Jacob's part.

She pressed her fingers to her temple and rubbed. Trying to rub away the headache and all the worries and concerns that caused it.

She had to face the facts of the probable consequences of this latest article. With word out about the competition, all the eager observers would be in search of the sites wanting to watch, steal a souvenir, or find a job.

Not what she needed right now.

That should be her primary focus: protecting her work. But it wasn't. Jacob was at the forefront of everything. She missed him. A lot.

His work ethic was incredible.

He was a huge help.

He was her friend.

She winced. Friend . . . Everything inside her wanted to be more than simply friends—

Stop it! That couldn't happen. Not with everything that had transpired. No. It was best to focus on the matter at hand. Jacob was right. He hadn't lied to her. She'd never asked if he worked for the other dig, and he'd been honor bound not to talk about it.

He was also right that in everything, he'd been on her side. From the very beginning.

So. It was time.

She'd send for him. He was the best worker she had and she needed him.

After she penned a note to him, she headed over to Michael. The young man was wiry and fast on his feet. Ever since she'd hired him, she'd used his love of running to her advantage. He always got the job done. "Could you deliver this to Mr. Duncan, please?"

"Yes, miss. Right away." He dipped his hat at her and took off at a run.

Watching him run off down the trail, she felt like a gigantic weight had been lifted off her shoulders. It would be much easier to get back to work now.

Lily Rose approached with her parasol, a pleasant smile on her face. "Which area would you like to work on today?"

"Follow me. It's one of the tougher grids. A lot of fossils appear to be jammed together. That's why I saved it for me."

"Smart approach." Lily Rose followed her and then provided shade while Martha lowered herself into a sitting position on the ground.

It took her more than an hour to make a tiny fissure in between two of the fossils. This would take much more time than she'd anticipated. She leaned back and studied it. There had to be a better way. But how? None of the proven methods could speed up this process, and if she made the slightest error, she could damage more than one bone.

"Miss Jankowski!" Michael's shout from the ridge above brought her attention up.

She smiled as she spotted Jacob, but neither he nor Michael were smiling. That couldn't be good.

Lily Rose helped her to her feet and Martha brushed the dust from her apron as the men jogged down the ridge toward them.

"What's wrong?"

Their expressions were grim.

Jacob winced. He removed his hat and curled the brim in his hands. "I'm sorry to come back with bad news, but the museum director asked me to visit him this morning. He wanted to ask questions because of Mr. Foster's article."

"I see." She knew this was coming. Her stomach tied in knots. "And?"

"He told me that the other team has experienced some vandalism on site. He asked me if I did it." The sadness in his face broke her heart. "But I was at church when it occurred. There was a policeman who questioned me. They spoke with the pastor."

"So they know you didn't do it?"

"Yes." He glanced at Michael. "I don't want to add to the pressure you must be feeling right now, but I have to tell you. . . ." He cleared his throat. "They thought you might have been behind it . . . because . . . because of what your father did."

"What?" Of course it would come back to this. Her father's reputation was now hers. She stepped backward. Her foul mood turned blacker.

"I'm sorry, Martha. I told them you wouldn't do anything like that. I was emphatic about how honorable you wanted to be in all areas." The angst in his gaze matched the feeling in her gut.

She bit her lip and her breath stuttered. "Did they believe you?"

"I'm hopeful." He shook his head. "But we need to be on guard. If someone went after them, and we know it wasn't anyone from our team, does that mean that same someone could come after us?"

"I look forward to seeing what you have to offer me." The man tossed several golden eagles down on the desk.

She raised an eyebrow at him. Cretin. "I don't take bribes, monsieur."

He waved it off. "It is not a bribe. Let's call it a gift. I know the power and control that you wield. It is worthy of a little . . . *lagniappe*." His mustache wiggled with the word.

A little something extra . . . She let her lips turn upward. "*Merci*."

"I will eagerly await word from you." He set his lavish, gold-capped cane down on the floor and dipped in a bow. "Good day."

She watched him walk out of the room.

He'd traveled all this way from Louisiana to check in with her. Gentlemen like him were few and far between.

She liked to think of him as one of the old-timers. Like her father.

Life in the world of underground smuggling had been prestigious. Dignified. Generations of her family had built an empire on the trade of prized goods. Diamonds, rubies, emeralds, gold. Fine works of art. They'd become smugglers during the Napoleonic Wars and had made a fortune.

Once they came over from England, her father had expanded the business in America. She had grown it even more. And loved the thrill of something new and exciting around every corner.

From the time she was a blossoming ten-year-old, he'd taken her under his wing and taught her the business. Perhaps it was a little ugly for a young lady. But he'd often told her that understanding the harsh realities of life—and death—made them smarter and stronger.

And if they had to take a life to get what they wanted, what of it? Most of the time, the life given up wasn't worth anything. In the grand scheme of things, her family had simply put souls out of the misery that was to come to them.

What a remarkable heritage she had. Oh, to be able to pass it down to a new generation, but would that day ever come?

With a shrug, she shook off the dismal thought and went back to her desk. Many so-called irons were in the fire right now. It gave her a little thrill to be juggling all of them. It kept her on her toes. Kept her sharp.

Venturing into the fossil business had been easy enough. A priceless commodity that couldn't ever be produced again. For two decades, she'd enjoyed adding that little side business.

But apparently, there were others on the prowl.

She hated it when the peons tried to encroach on her territory. Time to show them who was queen in all this.

WEDNESDAY, JULY 10, 1889 • JANKOWSKI DIG SITE

Sweat dripped off Jacob's nose and into the red clay. It was past one, and the heat of the day was taking its toll on everyone at the dig. Though lunch had been a brief respite from the pounding sun, wind still whipped through the tent, salting their food with dirt. He wasn't complaining though. With gentle swipes, he brushed more dust and rubble from the three vertebrae he'd found the day before.

It was a wonder Martha let him return. He *would* prove that she could trust him and that he was here to help her accomplish her dream. But no matter how much he longed for things to be as they were before—or to show her how much he cared—any trace of warmth between them was gone.

Martha had become a firm, ambitious woman who had a deadline riding her and no patience for anyone. He didn't even have an ally in Lily Rose anymore. All he received from that quarter was icy silence and angry glares.

Not that he could blame either one of them.

Even so, Martha's companion had made him wince more than once since he returned. Her feelings toward him seemed to swing on a giant pendulum. He couldn't predict it any more than he could predict a tornado dropping out of the sky.

Jacob chiseled another hard rock from the edge of the bone, his eyes burning from the glare of the sun.

He'd messed up. When it came right down to it, he never should have taken the job with Martha. That would have prevented any appearance of wrongdoing on his, or her, part.

But no, he'd taken the job, and he'd hurt her. No wonder Lily Rose was downright rude to him. She wasn't about to forgive him for that. But he suspected he'd been in her bad books ever since his conversation with Martha the night of the second lecture—when they had discussed the Lord and creation.

He grabbed his canteen and took a swig of water, then grimaced. Even the water was hot today. Letting out a sigh, he wiped his brow once more. He had to get these vertebrae out. They were behind as it was. His fault because he hadn't been here to keep the men motivated. Men around camp were starting to chafe against the pressure, and the growing tension and uneasiness among the workers worried him.

It was an environment that could make men sloppy. Pressure to work fast often created broken or chipped bones, which wouldn't help Martha at all—

He grunted. Wouldn't help Miss Jankowski.

I need Your help, Lord. I'm grateful for the work, but You know my heart. How do I help Martha? How can I be a good . . . I don't even know what, Lord. Please . . . help.

A shout went up from the quadrant over. Jacob stood up and saw a group of men shouting, dust swirling up between them. He carefully put his tools together and covered them before heading over.

He nudged a shorter man on the fringe of the scuffle. "What's going on?"

The weather-beaten man scratched his face, leaving streaks where dirt had been. "Can't rightly say."

Jacob resisted the temptation to roll his eyes. A bad or antagonistic attitude wouldn't get him anywhere with these men. He hesitated. He wasn't an assistant to the foreman anymore. It wasn't his job to monitor the men. But a fight like this would only put them even further behind.

He threaded into the group and looked at the men now being held separate by three others. "What's happened?"

The men turned and looked at him. One of the fighters sneered at him, his nose dripping in blood. "Why do you want to know? Gonna run off and tell your friends at the other dig?"

Jacob ignored the barb. "We're on a deadline. Fighting and scrapping won't do Miss Jankowski or us any good. We need to be focused on our work."

"Get back to your own side, Duncan, and leave us be," another man spat. "We've got this handled."

"I—" He stopped and looked around, then paled. Martha was approaching the edge of the group, her face a blaze of fury.

"What is the meaning of this?" She strode into the middle of the men. Lily Rose was right behind her, parasol up, eyes hard as flint.

Bloody Nose spoke up first. "Well, miss, you see Jasper over here was working and Miller stole his tools and—"

She held up her hand. "And so you decided that fists were the way to settle this?" She glared at each man in the group, including Jacob. "Our deadline is six weeks away. Six. Weeks. If we cannot complete this dig, then all bonuses for you are off the table. The prize money is gone! And our chance to show this beautiful specimen to the scientific world is up in smoke." Martha pulled herself up to her full height.

Jacob fought the smile attempting to break through. She was beautiful all fired up. But behind the façade, he could see the exhaustion in her eyes.

"Beyond that, I hired you all because you were honest men with good reputations who refused to make this dig underhanded. You've all been respectable to this point. Consider this a warning. If there is one more fight, you will be fired immediately. But I know all of you want this dinosaur out of the ground as much as I do, so I suspect this will be the last of it."

"Yes, miss."

The group grumbled and slowly broke apart.

Jacob started back up the hill toward his dig but Martha's voice stopped him. "Mr. Duncan, a word."

Ice shivered down his spine despite the heat. He turned back to her. "Yes, Miss Jankowski?"

Cold blue eyes bored into his own brown ones. "What do you think you're doing?"

Jacob rocked back on his heels. "Doing?"

Martha fisted her hands on her hips. "You are not the foreman, Mr. Duncan. It is not your place to step in and direct the men."

"I understand. I was trying to defuse the fight and help you—"

"The only help you can possibly give me right now is getting those dinosaur vertebrae out of the ground. Now!" She marched past him up the hill.

Jacob watched her disappear around the bend. Hurt and frustration coursed through him. Was being on this dig worth it if things were so strained between the two of them? Jacob rubbed his mouth with a hand then grimaced as dirt covered his lips. He took out his handkerchief and wiped at it haphazardly.

"I tried to tell you, Mr. Duncan."

Lily Rose's voice startled him out of his thoughts. He glanced to his left and saw her standing there, staring at him.

"She doesn't want you here. She doesn't need you here. You're nothing but trouble and always have been."

The parasol fluttered in the summer breeze. The older woman took a step toward him, her eyes never leaving his. "I'm watching you." Her words hissed out on a low whisper. "You are here to help with the dig because you are under contract. It's plain to see you are good at what you do. But one misstep toward Martha and I will make sure you never see her again." Turning on her heeled boot, she left.

Jacob felt rooted to the ground. Had Lily Rose just . . . *threatened* him? He shoved his handkerchief back in his pocket and followed the path back to his spot.

After all Martha had been through, all the hurt, the betrayal, the loss . . . she had every right to be harsh and upset.

Which left one question burning in his mind . . .

Would the woman he cared about be able to overcome the darkness that pressed in?

sixteen

"Think a moment, stop, and listen. Think how swiftly the moments fly. Youth is short and age is dreary; cheer these early days with a song or thou wilt grow sad and weary if the journey should be too long. Up and arm the fort, the battle for the strife with you."

~Earl Douglass

MONDAY, JULY 15, 1889

A knock at his door brought Cole to his feet.

He opened the door.

"Telegram for you, sir." The young boy waited with his hand out.

Cole dropped a coin into the boy's palm and the lad took off running. Ripping into the envelope, he closed the door with his boot.

It was from the sheriff in Castle Rock. A man had been murdered . . . and a white glove had been left.

Two hours later, Cole tied his horse to the post outside the sheriff's office. He'd been fuming since receiving the missive. Why hadn't he been contacted sooner? As soon as he knew about the killer's signature, he'd sent alerts through all of his contacts.

He stomped into the building. "Sheriff?" he shouted into the room.

A man came from the back, a deep frown on his face. "That's me. What's got you all fired up?"

Cole brought the telegram forward. "Why didn't you wire me sooner with this information?" He hated the accusatory tone in his voice, but this case was trying his patience.

"Simmer down, son. I just got the alert yesterday. As soon as I saw it, I sent you a telegram."

The answer defused his anger a bit, but the blasted delay might make him lose the killer. "I apologize for my abrasiveness. This case has my anger riled. And now it's been almost a month since this murder."

"Understandable. That's why I contacted you as soon as I found out you were on the case." He stepped over to his desk. "Maybe this will help you. In addition to the white glove left on the body—I have a witness who came forward."

Energy rippled through him. A new lead. Exactly what he needed. "What did the witness say?"

"Sadly, he was in the shadows himself. So he didn't have a lot more information than the description." The sheriff leaned back in his chair.

"In the *shadows*?" What was that supposed to mean? The witness actually admitted to hanging out in "the shadows"? Didn't anyone know how to do decent police work anymore?

The sheriff cleared his throat and leaned forward, his expression hardening. "No need to take that tone. He'd just come from the brothel."

Cole shook his head. So the witness was of disreputable

character. Great. "Never mind that. I apologize once again for my frustration, but there's a killer on the loose. What did he see?"

"He saw a blonde woman come out of the mercantile and get on her horse. She was the only one to leave the mercantile around the time of the murder."

His jaw dropped. Women were often involved in crimes, but a murderer? "A woman? Was he certain?"

"Yep. And she headed north when she left." The sheriff appeared pleased as punch. "I've got this drawing, if it helps."

Cole took the paper and studied it. "It does. Thank you." He folded it and walked out of the sheriff's office, his gut churning.

If a woman was behind the murders, his case just got a lot more complicated.

And dangerous.

The wagon back into town was unusually silent. Ever since Martha's dressing-down of the men a few days before, the mood had shifted to a surly silence. The work was getting done, but attitudes were worsening. At some point the tension was going to break, and Jacob feared what the outcome of that would be.

Not only was Martha on edge every moment she was at the dig, but her companion was even more severe. Which oozed out to all of the men.

Their friendly, happy atmosphere was gone.

Thankfully, no one else had brought up his working on the other team again. He didn't need that reminder while doing his best to make this dig a success for Martha.

But they were behind. Plain and simple. Martha was surely feeling the pressure. What could he do to help fix this mess?

He sighed. He'd caught glimpses of Martha since she'd

snapped at him, but he hadn't dared try to talk to her. Lily Rose was constantly with her and, true to her threat, she watched his every move at the dig. Jacob shifted on the uncomfortable seat. Something was not right with that woman, but what?

Am I imagining things, Lord? Or is she just protective of her friend? I need Your wisdom, Jesus.

Finally, town loomed into view. A few minutes later, Jacob gingerly stepped off the wagon. His muscles screamed at him. The bumpy journey and all the ways he had to twist and turn to excavate bones were taking their toll. He was twenty-five, but tonight he felt sixty-five.

He hadn't reserved the tub for this evening, but maybe his landlady would be lenient and let him have it after everyone was done. He could dig again tomorrow if he had a good soak tonight.

He made his way down the street, then slowed his pace. A group of men huddled outside the door of the local hotel, angry voices raised.

"My tools were stolen, I'm telling ya!"

That was Jones, one of the men from the other dig. He was yelling into the face of a small man with a bowler hat on.

"Snatched in the light of day while I ate lunch."

"And a smaller fossil I found was smashed to bits."

Jacob couldn't see who was speaking that time.

The small man shuffled. "Now, gentlemen, I will take your grievances to the owner, but—"

"But *what?*" This from a tall man Jacob didn't know. "The rules were clear! No sabotage! The owner needs to do something about this!"

Shouts of agreement echoed around the businessman. Jacob felt bad for him, but it was best to steer clear of the group. The last thing he needed was to get pulled into an argument that had nothing to do with him. Besides, being associated with that team had given him enough trouble.

Still, had the other dig been sabotaged? Who would attempt to steal tools and smash bones in broad daylight? Who was that bold?

Jacob rubbed the side of his face.

He prayed for the men he'd worked with before. They needed Jesus as much as he did. He didn't have a right to bitterness and anger, but the memories of the conversations he'd overheard rang through his mind. To his knowledge, that team hadn't followed through on any of their threats to Martha's team. But those who'd made the threats couldn't be trusted, that much was sure.

He rounded the corner, and at the sight of the boarding-house looming into view, he sighed. Hopefully the dinner his landlady had tonight would be filling.

A foot crunching on gravel behind him startled him from his thoughts. He glanced behind to see who it was, but something hard connected with his jaw. His head snapped back with the force of the punch, but before he could get his bearings, another fist slammed into his right eye. Pain coursed up his chin and through his head as he tumbled onto the ground. Blackness danced around the edges of his vision.

Jacob tried to prop his body up on his elbow to see who was punching him, but he had no time.

A boot slammed into his stomach, stealing his breath. Another fist slammed the top of his skull. Agony rippled down his spine as another foot slammed into his back. He curled into a ball and tucked his hands over his head.

Punches and kicks rained down on him. How many men were there? Two? Three?

"Think you're better than you should, Duncan." Another punch to the head.

"Putting on airs, think you're fancy as the foreman of another team?" A hard kick to the shoulder.

"Shoulda known your betrayal would come back on you. We know it was you. Smashing bones, stealing tools."

Oh Lord God . . . please help me. Please, Jesus. I can't take much more . . .

The prayers slipped in and out of his consciousness until suddenly, the pounding stopped. Each breath was painful as he slowly, carefully unfolded himself from his protective ball. The street was silent.

Jacob's eyes twitched. Something trickled through his lashes down onto his cheek. He couldn't focus, couldn't see where he was. He rolled onto his back with a moan and coughed. Searing heat flushed his side and he eased his fingers over his chest and stomach. He managed a glance at his fingers. Blood . . .

Then, mercifully, the darkness overtook him.

<hr/>

Wednesday, July 17, 1889

This was ridiculous. Martha hadn't seen Jacob since Monday night and no one knew where he was. Lily Rose said they shouldn't care, but that was her protectiveness of Martha coming through. And Lily Rose's own prejudice. Her companion had recently confided to Martha, after the situation with Jacob, about a beau she'd had. He'd been duplicitous and had broken her heart. No wonder Lily Rose had no qualms about giving a dishonest man the cold shoulder. Still, Lily Rose's growing boldness in voicing her opinions was concerning Martha. She bit her lip at the thought. Was that wrong? Did she not want to hear her companion's opinion because she was . . . just that? A paid chaperone? Did class matter that much to her?

Martha sighed. It hadn't with Jacob. But that relationship was a bit less complicated than with Lily Rose.

At least, it had been.

Of course, Martha had been peeved at Jacob for not telling

them the truth from the beginning. Not that he could have. His hands had been tied. That was plain enough to see.

But her companion had been all fired up—which had gotten Martha all fired up. However, it hadn't done her any favors. Her emotions had been a wreck. She felt she was teetering ever so close to the edge of sanity.

Last night, she'd remembered Jacob's words about sharing a deep connection with God. He'd said to put God first, but what did that mean? The longing that she'd had for closer relationships with her parents . . . had that all been because she wasn't allowing God to reign in her heart and mind? Was it possible?

Could God fill that need—that hole—within her?

The one person who could help her understand—she'd pushed away. And now? All this time without any word from him . . .

It didn't make sense. Jacob would never go away without telling her first. Something was wrong.

Pushing all doubts about him away, she focused on what she knew.

Jacob was a good and decent man.

She cared about him more than anyone else she'd ever met.

She . . . trusted him.

She shook her head. Time to stop wallowing in her fear and anger. She needed to find Jacob and fix what was broken. What *she'd* broken.

She searched the quarry and spotted Josiah, another lanky fellow who was quick on his feet. She called him and waved to get his attention.

He ran up to meet her. "Yes, Miss Jankowski?"

"I need you to run into town and check on Mr. Duncan. Can you do that for me?" She handed him a slip of paper with Jacob's address. "Take one of the horses from the shed if you need to. But you mustn't tell anyone where you're going.

If anyone asks, you're doing an errand for the dig." Martha paused. "I will give you a fifty-cent piece if you keep it a secret."

Josiah's eyes rounded. "Sure thing, Miss Martha." He took off running.

After what seemed an eternity with no word from Josiah, she checked her watch. Only an hour had passed? She turned back to her work, only to check her watch again after ten minutes.

This was useless. She couldn't focus on anything other than the question nagging at her mind and heart. . . .

Had something happened to Jacob?

No use trying to work anymore. She went to stand at the top of the ridge. When she finally spotted Josiah returning, she went to meet him.

His grim face sent tremors through her.

"What's happened?"

"He's in bad shape, miss. Someone clobbered him good."

She took off at a full run toward the trail to town.

"Wait! Miss Jankowski!"

But she kept running. If Walter wasn't there at the gate waiting with the carriage, she would run the whole way to Jacob's if she had to.

The door to his room creaked. Jacob forced his lids open but couldn't push them up very far. Through the haze of his lashes, he spotted two figures. But in the dark, they were just shadowy blobs.

Had they come to finish the job?

Closing his eyes, he tried to shift in his bed, but that didn't work. A moan pushed its way out of his lips. His heart picked up its pace.

"Jacob?"

If he wasn't dreaming, that was Martha's voice!

"Hm? Martha? Is that you?" *Please, God, let it be her.*

A match was struck and he heard the sizzle of the flame coming to life. Then a gasp. "Oh, *Jacob!*"

He forced his eyes to open again, but he could only see through little slits.

She'd lit a lantern, and an unknown man stood beside her. "Jacob, I'm so sorry this happened to you, but I brought help. This is Doctor Murton. He's going to help you."

Jacob told his tongue to move, but his lips were swollen and cracked. It was hard to get words out. "A doc in town . . . came to see me . . ."

"You still look like this after a doctor tended to you? That's shameful!" The doctor came closer, set his bag down near Jacob's feet, and opened it up. "Well, Miss Jankowski has hired me to make sure you receive the best of care. And I shall do precisely that, son." He turned and washed his hands in the washbasin. "Miss Jankowski, I need to ask you to step out of the room for a few minutes so I may inspect all of his injuries."

"Is it all right if I speak with him for just a moment, Doctor?" The sweet concern in her voice melted his anxiety. He relaxed into the bed and swallowed.

"Certainly. I'll wait out in the hall." The man walked away leaving the door open.

"Martha—"

"Jacob—"

They spoke at the same time.

She shook her head. "Just listen for a moment, please?"

He nodded and winced. Every movement hurt.

"I'm sorry. So sorry. I know how I treated you was abominable. I trust you and know you didn't do anything to harm me. If anything, you were trying to protect me, and I appreciate that. Will you please forgive me?" She grabbed his hand.

Even though it hurt like the dickens, he welcomed her touch. "I will. As long as you forgive me."

Another shake of her head and her hair tumbled around her shoulders. He'd never seen it down before. It was lovely, even if it was in disarray.

She released his hand and reached up to tuck her hair back up into her hat. "I must be a mess. I ran as soon as I heard you were injured and didn't care what a mess I made of myself. And there's nothing to forgive. You didn't do anything wrong. I know that."

When her hair was safely in place, she took his hand again. The warmth of her touch seeped through him.

"Jacob, life has been a struggle for me lately. And I'm ashamed to say that I've taken out my tumultuous emotions on everyone around me. I'm sorry for that too."

"Martha . . ."

"I care about you, Jacob Duncan, and I couldn't bear the thought of anything happening to you." Her words were almost a whisper but they smoothed over him like a healing balm. Their hands trembled together.

"I care about you too." His voice sounded like his mouth was full of grit, but he had to let her know.

"Before I go . . ." She glanced down and then back up at him, her eyes sparkling with a sheen of tears. "How do I have that kind of deep relationship with God you spoke of?"

Every hope and prayer he'd had for her rushed to his mind. Even through all the pain, his heart thrilled for her. "Read His Word. That's how He speaks to us and teaches us. Shows us His love for us. And pray. Lots. That's our communication with Him."

"Any time I want? I don't have to be in church?"

A half chuckle came out before he groaned. "Ow, I probably shouldn't laugh for a while. But no, you don't have to be in church to pray."

"All right. I'm going to ask the doctor to come in, but I had to know."

"I'll pray for you."

"Thank you." Her voice was soft. Much softer than it had been when last they spoke. "I'll be right outside, Jacob. I won't leave."

"Thank you." He croaked the words and the door clicked shut.

"Now then"—the doctor brought a cup of water to his lips— "let's get you something for your parched throat. You're going to need to answer a good many questions for my examination."

seventeen

"One of the greatest things said about Christ was that He went about doing good. Oh, that we may follow in His example."

~Earl Douglass

Dipping her prized gold pen into the inkwell, she smiled at the blank piece of paper.

Then she began her missive.

Dear Police Chief Masterson,

Since we have been good friends for so long, I hope you will take this news to heart. It is not in my disposition to throw accusations at innocent men, so you may trust my words are true and sound.

As you know, there has been a lot of turmoil with the competition out at two dig sites. The museum has given them a deadline and staunch rules to follow, but there are always criminals in our midst, sadly.

244

It has come to my attention that a Mr. Jacob Duncan is the mastermind behind the trouble we are seeing now. I would ask that you look into him.

He has worked for both of the teams.

Thank you for taking the time to listen to my concerns.

Your longtime friend,

She reread the note and then signed her initials. After blotting it and waving it in the air for several moments, she folded it, placed it in an envelope, and sealed it with her special wax seal.

On to the next thing on her to-do list.

Eliminate another thorn in her side.

***

THURSDAY, JULY 18, 1889

"I demand to see Mr. Spalding. Right now!" Martha had prepared a speech, but at this point, it had flown out the window along with her manners. The reason for her visit conjured up images of a bruised and battered Jacob and that had her infuriated again.

The museum was quiet, but her yelling echoed through the halls and made it sound as if a crowd of elephants had invaded the space.

"Yes, Miss Jankowski." The man behind the desk was clearly afraid of her temper because he took off at a brisk pace.

Mr. Spalding appeared with an equally quick gait. "Miss Jankowski, I'm a bit shocked to see you—"

"We shall dispense with the pleasantries. One of my men was beaten to a pulp this past week, and I insist that you bring the foreman of the other dig in immediately."

"That will take some doing, I don't thin—"

She stomped her foot and he fell silent, looking much like

he'd swallowed a bug. "I don't *care* what you think right now. And it won't take any doing. The men who beat my employee accused him of smashing bones and stealing tools. They also berated him for being promoted on the *other* team." Martha pointed to the man she'd scared the wits out of. "If that doesn't tell you my competitor is behind this, then you are more ignorant than I thought. Send for him. Now. And I do mean *now*, Mr. Spalding. I am not leaving here until this is rectified."

"This is highly—" The director's gaze shifted to the door then back to Martha.

"Miss Jankowski." Lily Rose's voice was out of breath. "Good heavens, was the museum on fire?"

Trailing her companion were two of her parents' hulking guards. That Mother and Father insisted on keeping such a force around their grounds had seemed . . . excessive. But today? She hadn't given the men a choice. Just ordered them to come with her.

They didn't hesitate. No wonder. After a sleepless night formulating her plan, her mood upon rising had been dark and determined.

Armed now with her two guards, a highly peeved companion, and her own temper, Martha turned back to the director. "Well?"

His face went ashen. "Very well." He licked his lips. "I will also speak to the owner of the museum about this."

"I insist that you do."

An hour later, a man named Joe was introduced to her.

He appeared harmless enough, but Martha wasn't fooled. She stepped so close she could almost knock him down with the brim of her hat. "Back off."

"Excuse me, miss?"

"Don't make me get the police after you, or worse yet, my mother. She'll own your whole dig and fire the lot of you in a moment's notice if I tell her to." Probably not true, but at this point, Martha just didn't care. And if Mother argued, well, she'd better look out too.

Joe held up his hands. "I have no idea what you're talking about!"

"One of my men—Mr. Jacob Duncan—was beaten nearly to death by some of your thugs—"

"Now wait a minute." The thin man held up his hands. "None of my men have gone near Jacob. And how do I know it wasn't *you* ordering your people to damage our dig?" He stepped closer.

So . . . he wasn't afraid of her and her entourage. She stepped even closer and placed her hands on her hips. This time, she *could* knock him down with her hat if she had the mind to do it! "How dare you! I would never!" She spewed the words at him. If she wasn't a woman, she'd slug the man right now. *If* she knew how to punch. Instead, she let him have it with all the information she had. The words that had been spoken to Jacob as he'd been beaten. "He could have been killed. Do you want murder on your head"—she searched for his name—"Joe?"

The foreman blanched.

The director did his best to put an arm between them and then tried to wiggle his way in. "Perhaps we could all sit down and discuss this in a calm and friendly manner."

"No," she spat. Never in her life had she ever spoken to anyone in such tones. But this was for Jacob. She'd do anything for hi—

Goodness.

Her eyes widened.

She would. She would do anything for him!

Gathering her wits, she straightened her shoulders and eyed Joe. "I'm headed back to my dig. I have done nothing out of line, and neither have any of my men. I run an aboveboard organization, sirs. But if anything else happens to my men or my dig, I promise you, you will face my wrath."

And while that might have been an empty threat in the past, today it was more than a threat. It was a stone-cold promise.

She turned and marched out of the museum.

***

| SUNDAY, JULY 21, 1889

He could take a deep breath again. Merciful heavens, that alone was reason to rejoice. Jacob drew in another breath and breathed out a prayer of thanks to the Lord. Despite five broken ribs, a stab wound to his side, and a face that looked like . . . well, he wasn't sure what. But based on the looks from the doctor and Martha when they'd first seen his injuries, it wasn't good.

He shifted again and grunted. Pain was still his constant friend. But he could feel the healing happening, especially in the small stab wound. The doctor had told him he was fortunate the knife hadn't been large. It had missed important organs.

He'd had no idea he'd been stabbed.

The kicks and punches had held his focus.

The bruises on his stomach and chest would linger for a while, and his black eyes would take some time to heal, but all things considered, he'd fared better than other men who'd been attacked and outnumbered in the wild city of Denver.

Only the Lord could have spared him. Each trial seemed to be worse than the one before. And though he didn't always understand the ways of the Lord, he needed to trust Jesus. Trust His Word. He looked down at the worn Bible on his lap. His fingers brushed over the pages, and he read out loud, "But we have this treasure in earthen vessels, that the excellency of the power may be of God, and not of us. We are troubled on every side, yet not distressed; we are perplexed, but not in despair; persecuted, but not forsaken; cast down, but not destroyed. . . ."

He sighed as the truth of God's Word washed over him. Some of the mess he was in was of his own making. But Jacob had been taught as a young man, and now understood, that, through faith in Jesus and walking with Him, trials came to strengthen his faith. He smiled faintly. *I can see I needed to learn to trust You, Lord. This is hard, but I know You're with me.*

A tap on the door interrupted his prayer and he glanced up.

Martha's face appeared in the small opening. A bright smile curved her lips and her blue eyes shone in the afternoon light. "Well, hello there." Her tone was bright. "Are you up for a visit?"

Jacob closed the Bible and shifted. "Martha! Come in." Placing the black book on his small side table, he then shimmied into a sitting position. Thankfully, the doctor had helped him clean up and look presentable during his visit earlier in the morning.

Martha left the door to his room open enough for propriety then settled on the hardbacked chair by his bed, placing a wicker basket on the floor. She was a vision in a pretty light pink day dress. The ease in her smile and the light in her eyes did Jacob's heart a world of good. Certainly better than those foul powders had done for the pain.

"How are you feeling?" Her light laugh accompanied a nose scrunch. "That's probably a silly question."

He grinned with the side of his face that didn't hurt as much. "I'm better. In fact, I was thanking the Lord I could get a deep breath again."

"Oh, that's wonderful!" Her fingers brushed his shirtsleeve, then his wrist. With a shy look, she took his hand in hers. "Your face is still quite the sight. But I'm glad to hear you can breathe. I've brought you some treats, fresh from our chef. His desserts are delicious. But I thought his chicken soup would help you feel a bit better." Pulling the basket up by the handles, she set it on the end of the bed and then started pulling out items. A snowy white napkin was spread across the blanket on his lap, and a soft hunk of bread, cheese, and apple slices followed. But it was the pretty blush in Martha's cheeks that had his rapt attention.

Warmth bloomed in his chest. He was touched by her thoughtfulness and told her as much.

She waved his thanks off. "You need to get strong." She smiled. "We still have so much to do together."

Together. That word meant more to him than she could ever know. The time he'd had in bed, after coming to consciousness, had been full of thoughts of her. Prayers for her. Seeking the Lord as to what He was saying regarding their relationship. Jacob loved Martha. He was in love with her. Could he tell her? He knew the Lord didn't care about class or station.

But Martha did. Though she tried to hide it, it mattered more than Jacob thought she realized. Still, they could be happy together.

". . . I still can't believe how forward I was in speaking to the museum director." She shook her head after relaying the story. "But I received word that he will be visiting and inspecting each dig site every week—*personally*. Without warning and unannounced, so that should keep everyone on their toes and honest."

One thing was for certain, Martha was used to getting her way. A force to be reckoned with, as his mother would say.

"That's quite the look." Martha's words broke through his thoughts. "Are you in pain?"

He glanced at her and shook his head gingerly. "No. I mean, well, yes. But I'm thinking. And praying."

"About?"

Jacob took a steadying breath. "Us."

Martha's hands stilled in the basket on her lap. She looked down, as if she was refusing to meet his steady gaze. "Us?" She echoed the word with a squeak.

Fighting a laugh—and the pain it would bring—he nodded. "You see, I've been praying a lot about us this last week. Asking the Lord what He wants for us. If there can even be an us." He cleared his throat and picked a small slice of apple from the plate on his lap. He popped it in his mouth and chewed slowly before speaking again. Even that small act hurt.

"I know there is a world between us. You've grown up in a wealthy household with servants and had a wonderful education granted to you." At her sharp glance he held up a hand. "I am not jealous of it, my dear"—the endearment slipped from his lips naturally, but he continued, unsure if she caught it—"I'm grateful for all I've learned from you. I know I come from a poor background. A big family and a small house. I've pinched and scraped and saved to get where I am, by the grace of God."

She placed the basket on the floor and gripped his hand with both of hers. "Those things don't matter to me. I've told you that."

Jacob glanced down. Her fingers looked so delicate compared to his, yet their hands fit comfortably together. "I know that. And getting to know you has been a joy. Learning with you and from you, talking about faith and science, digging up dinosaur bones . . . Martha, these last few months, even with their ups and downs, have been precious to me. I've come to care for you . . . dare I say . . . *love* you."

Her smile filled the room. "Oh, Jacob. They've meant so much to me too. Even though you didn't tell me about working for the other team, I've forgotten about that. I know you'll keep showing me that I can trust you again. I've . . . come to care for you—love you—too."

Those words should have lit up his heart. Instead, they gave him pause. *Lord, give me wisdom.* "What do you mean, show you that you can trust me again?"

She looked at him with a smile. "Well, you must earn back

my trust, Jacob. It was an awful thing for you to keep from me, but we're already on that journey, dearest."

Discomfort settled in his gut. Jacob pulled away from her in the pretense of shifting again to find comfort. "But Martha, I told you, I was under contract. I *couldn't* say anything." He paused, searching for the right words. "I didn't deliberately hide something from you."

She sat back, shoulders rigid. "Jacob." The way she said his name was back to her foreman tone. "You worked for another team, then came to work for me. With the pressure of the dig and the deadline, and the rules laid out by the museum owner, that was information I needed to know, no matter what the contract said. I'm willing to look past it though and begin again. Why can't you let it go?"

He stared at her. The chasm between them was still there. She, the wealthy owner and foreman. He, the poor employ—

No. He couldn't think like that. "I was bound to that contract by my word and my signature. I care for you. Deeply. And you say you care for me. But is this issue something you will hold over my head? When I've asked for forgiveness for hurting you?"

"I've given you my forgiveness." But her shoulders were stiff, her eyes narrowed.

"Have you ever hurt anyone, Martha?" *Please, Father, let her hear me and not become defensive.*

She pushed the chair back farther and laced her fingers together. "We all hurt each other in some way."

Jacob nodded. "That's true. And when you hurt someone, like maybe your mother or Lily Rose, how do you resolve it?"

"Resolve it? There's nothing to resolve. Maybe sometimes Mother will remind me about a past mistake, but she does that to help me remember not to make the same one again." She sighed and gave him a small smile. "You're not a bad person, Jacob. Is that what's concerning you? That I now think you're a bad person?"

His eyes dropped to the quilt over his lap. Was that the issue here? His own pride? He paused for a moment then shook his head. "No, that's not the concern. I know I'm a bad person, Martha. I know I'm a sinner. That's what Scripture says."

"Oh Jacob—that's not true. You're—"

"The Word of God tells all of us that we are sinners who have fallen short of the glory of God." As much as he cared for her, the truth stared him in the face. Had he been ignoring it because of his feelings? It rocked his entire being. . . .

She didn't truly understand faith and salvation.

"Without Jesus, we have no hope of being reunited to God. Jesus is the one who loves us and has given Himself for us that we can be cleansed from our sins."

Martha nodded. "I remember Phoebe telling me that. Jesus died and now I'm saved." She shifted in her seat and started playing with her drawstring bag, her fingers plucking at invisible strings. "Why are you even bringing this up?"

He sighed. He took a long look at her, his heart open to her with all its love ready to spill out. But he ached for the battered and bruised heart of the beautiful woman before him. "There is so much more to it than knowing Jesus died. He wants us to come to Him and know Him. Do you know what Scripture says about love and forgiveness?"

"Well, I'm sure many things. I've heard many a sermon over the years." Her voice held a sarcastic edge.

"It does say a good bit on the subject, but one of the things it says is that love bears all things. And when we love one another, we strive after Jesus's example, forgiving one another because He has forgiven us." Jacob swiped a tired hand over his face. Where was his grandfather at a time like this? He would have the right words. Know the right theological things to say.

Tell her about My love. Tell her about My forgiveness.

The thought whispered around his heart.

Yes, Lord. "Martha, Jesus loves you. And He wants you to

know Him. To know that love doesn't mean keeping a record of wrongdoing or holding things against one another. But to love someone means forgiving when it hurts, believing the best about the other, and holding each other to what the Bible says."

Martha stood. Her body rigid. "I can see that my visit has taxed you and you're tired. You need to get some rest. I need you back on that dig, Jacob. You're my partner out there. When this dig is all over then we can talk about other things. But right now, the dig is the most important thing." She plucked the napkin off his lap, the bread and apples flying.

The confusion on her face nearly broke him. He didn't want to push her away, but they could not be together if they weren't on the same page spiritually. *Lord, help me.*

Jacob captured her wrist in his hand. He folded her fingers in his. "I love you, Martha, but Jesus loves you more than I ever could. I'm praying you will come to know Him and to experience His real, beautiful love."

Martha looked at him for a long moment, tears spilling over onto her cheeks. Silently, she slipped from his grasp and plucked the picnic basket from the chair. The click of the door closing echoed into the silence.

His own tears flowed.

"Lord, help . . ."

eighteen

"If prophet, genius, sage, and seer
Would flash deep truths in human speech,
Would read the revelations here,
The Spirit's inspiration teach,
Their words would live through tempest shocks,
Their thoughts survive these crumbling rocks."

~Earl Douglass—
From his *Hymn of the Wilderness*

| MONDAY, JULY 29, 1889 • JANKOWSKI MANSION

Martha stared out the window as dusk settled over the mountains to the west. The deep purple faded to the black starry sky as the moon rose.

She turned her attention back to her desk and the open Bible that lay there.

Things had been quiet between the two digs since her confrontation with Mr. Spalding and Joe. There'd been no more reported smashed fossils or stolen tools, her men hadn't found any more cut barbed wire, and no one else had been attacked

255

in the street and beaten. But the more she thought back on the altercation with the two men at the museum, the more she regretted her temper and her words.

Especially after spending time each day reading the Word. When she'd asked Jacob about how to get closer to God, she had never expected that the answer would be so simple.

Even so, each morning and evening she committed time to reading the Scripture. If she truly believed that Almighty God had created all of this, and if Jacob believed that one could have a real relationship with Him, then she had to put her best efforts forth.

She'd always been an avid reader and researcher. Loved learning. Loved taking notes while she read.

Well, she'd taken dozens of pages of notes in the last week alone, but it was hard to understand and even harder to put aside all her habits, which she was coming to realize were bad.

Being raised in a wealthy home was one thing. Being raised by Victoria and Antoni Jankowski was another. Neither of her parents took no for an answer. Especially Mother. She was always in charge and in control. No one dared speak back to her.

Had Martha picked up that habit too? She cringed thinking about how she'd spoken to people. Jacob, Joe, Mr. Spalding . . . Gracious. She didn't want to be a tyrant. And she most definitely didn't want to be known for her fiery temper.

To be honest, she was used to getting what she wanted. Plain and simple.

Yesterday was another fine example of that. She'd gone to a different church than the one she'd grown up attending and cornered the reverend afterward. Her bold approach with the man showed her that she was all too willing to plow over everyone to get her way.

The man—who'd wanted to be called a pastor, not a

reverend—had waited quietly while she burst in with her demands to have her questions answered.

When he hadn't said anything, she stared at him, and he'd responded. "Let's start over, shall we?"

He led her down a hallway where his wife waited in a little kitchen with a table.

For the next two hours, she'd prodded and questioned.

He answered. Each time calm and patient. Like he was speaking with a child.

Which, she admitted now, she'd acted like one.

They'd pored over many verses together and he helped explain them in a way she understood. A verse he went back to was in Proverbs chapter seventeen.

When he'd first read it aloud, it didn't make sense to her.

"He that covereth a transgression seeketh love; but he that repeateth a matter separateth very friends."

"I don't understand?" She'd rubbed her brow. "Covereth?"

"There's a great depth to the meaning in this one verse, but let me tackle one piece at a time. When you forgive someone, you should hide it away, never to bring it up again. Because when you repeat it—bring it to the person's attention time and again—it will separate you from that person. Put a great distance between you. Perhaps for good."

She sat at her desk and thought about those words. And her conversation with Jacob. Not only had she lorded over him the fact that she was his employer, but she'd basically told him that he'd have to earn—and maintain—her trust. As if it were all his work to do if they were to move forward because she was in the right and would always be.

How selfish and unloving was that?

After spending the afternoon with the pastor and his wife, and then reading in the Scriptures for herself, Martha was convinced of several things.

One, she was a rich snob and needed to rid herself of the

bad habits she'd allowed herself to develop. She wasn't better than anyone else. She shouldn't demand her way. She should extend love and forgiveness, just like Christ.

Two, she had no clue how to change. The way she'd been raised had shaped her. She'd never known anything different.

Oh, but that wasn't completely true. When Phoebe had been her governess . . . things were different. Even wonderful. Someday, she should track the woman down and thank her for the beautiful example she'd been to a little girl.

Flipping through the pages of her Bible, Martha went on the hunt for Ephesians.

The pastor and his wife had encouraged her to study that book before coming to church next week, since that was the passage he would be preaching on.

She read through the entire book and then went back and read it again. The last verses in chapter four jumped out at her: "Let no corrupt communication proceed out of your mouth, but that which is good to the use of edifying, that it may minister grace unto the hearers. And grieve not the holy Spirit of God, whereby ye are sealed unto the day of redemption. Let all bitterness, and wrath, and anger, and clamour, and evil speaking, be put away from you, with all malice: And be ye kind one to another, tenderhearted, forgiving one another, even as God for Christ's sake hath forgiven you."

She'd been so introspective of late, especially where her faith was concerned. But as she reread those verses, a night from her childhood played in her mind. Only weeks before Phoebe left, Martha had cried over the crucifixion and resurrection accounts in the Bible. Phoebe had talked her through what it meant to receive salvation from God.

As though it was happening now rather than a long time ago, she saw herself kneeling by the side of her bed and praying.

Martha closed her eyes and felt it—that unmistakable sense of utter joy.

The only time she'd felt it in her life.

In fact, ever since, she'd essentially been searching for a way to get it back.

No question. What Phoebe had was real. And she'd felt it that night for herself.

Martha folded her hands and rested her forehead against them.

Father God, I want what Phoebe had. What I had. After she left, I didn't have anyone who could guide me. I believe. God, I believe. I have since I was a child, but now I'm ready to grow and no longer be a child in my faith. Please show me the way.

A single tear slipped down her cheek and she smiled out the window. This was right. This was good.

She looked back down at the passage in Ephesians. Jacob told her if she wanted to know God, she needed to read His Word. She'd been forgiven. It was her turn to pass that on. Truly learn about forgiveness.

And love.

Prayerfully soon she would have a chance to speak with Jacob. Her mother had forbidden her to go back to the boardinghouse, but he was healing. She would pray for him to heal enough to come back to the dig.

Knocking sounded at her door and she turned in her chair.

Lily Rose entered. "Good evening, Martha." Hands clasped in front of her, she quirked an eyebrow. "What are you working on?"

"I'm reading the Bible."

"That again?" Her companion's chin lifted as her shoulders stiffened. "I will leave you to it."

"Please, won't you stay? It would be nice to discuss it with someone."

But Lily Rose was already turning toward the door. "I cannot stop you from what you wish to do, miss, but I also don't have to subject myself to it." The words were sharp, cutting.

Martha stood and went after her friend. "What is it that you have against God? You've never behaved this way before. Which reminds me, the way you've treated Jacob has been horrid. I won't allow it any longer."

"The way I have treated Jacob?" Lily Rose held her gaze. "I apologize if my behavior is offensive to you. And since you have seen fit to remind me of my position, I will remind you that ultimately, I am in your *mother's* employ. We have discussed Mr. Duncan at great length. She thinks he's after your family's money and doesn't like him. Neither do I."

"I thought you said he was trustworthy?" Martha held her hands out. Pleading. "What changed your mind about all this?"

Lily Rose shrugged. "Money. He has none. And those who have not will always take advantage of those who do." She glanced at the Bible in Martha's lap. "As for God . . . I prefer to make my own way. God doesn't exist. End of story. But please, get back to your reading, I won't keep you."

Stubborn woman. "Fine. I wish to get to the dig site earlier tomorrow, so please be ready by six."

"Fine."

The door clicked shut.

Lily Rose's revelation reverberated through her.

Mother had talked to Lily Rose about Jacob? Her heart sank.

She'd dismissed the note her mother had left for her about Jacob because she was certain that Mother was just being prejudiced about the lower class. But now? It hurt to think that her own mother was talking about the man she'd come to love in such an unfavorable manner. What did Victoria know of Martha's feelings though? She didn't. Because the woman couldn't even find time to talk with her only daughter.

Hot tears burned her eyes as the anger in her gut swelled again.

TUESDAY, JULY 30, 1889

Apparently the Duncan fellow wasn't going to die from his injuries.

Such a shame. It would have been easier that way.

But . . . on the other hand, she could use him still. He'd make a perfect scapegoat.

Little Martha would get over it. Eventually.

Oh, but she had plans for Martha. And for all the bones.

Her enterprises were expanding daily, along with her bank accounts.

Wouldn't Papa be proud?

WEDNESDAY, JULY 31, 1889

Martha stared at her reflection and scowled. Even with her wide-brimmed hats and parasols, her face was getting tanner by the day. Their shadows often caused her problems with what she wanted to dig, and she pushed them back. She stretched her head to the left then the right, trying to relax. She rubbed the skin on her jaw and grimaced. It was dry. If she wasn't careful, she'd end up looking like some of the ranchers that came to town: leathery and wrinkled.

Martha opened a small pot of facial lotion that her mother special ordered from France and smoothed it over her face with quick strokes. Wiping the residue from her fingers with a soft cloth, she leaned close to look at her face in the mirror.

Satisfied she hadn't missed a spot on her face, Martha turned her attention to her hands.

They were worse than her face. Her fingernails were jagged from digging out vertebrae earlier that afternoon. Her work gloves were cumbersome and hindered some of the more delicate bone excavations. It was a good thing Mother wasn't around right now. The unkempt look of her only daughter would send her into a fit.

She filed down the rough edges around her nails and buffed them with a leather strap until they gleamed. Plucking a slim, purple glass bottle from the various beauty products on her vanity, Martha unscrewed the top and inhaled the sweet scent of verbena. She tipped a small amount of the lotion into her palm and smoothed it into her skin.

Her beauty routine complete, Martha relaxed into the back of her chair. Had Mother been there, she would have scolded her about being more conscientious about her complexion. About looking like a young woman of means.

She shook her head. Mother had invaded every bit of her mind the past couple days, and it had made her angry each time.

Time spent reading the Scripture had fallen by the wayside.

Why did she care so much what Mother thought? They hadn't spoken in days.

Soft skin and delicate hands paled in comparison to feeling the sun on her face. The wind in her hair made her feel alive in a way that society functions and fancy dresses didn't. It was like the dirt and the mountains and the bones were part of her. Couldn't this be who she was? The quarry was becoming the only place she felt like herself.

That and any time she spent with Jacob.

She inhaled sharply. Jacob. She'd been doing her best to keep thoughts of him at bay while he recovered. But she couldn't. His voice, his comments haunted her. He sounded like Phoebe. Talking to her about God like she didn't know Him. Yet, talking about God like he did.

Her eyes drifted to the black book on her bed. She'd ignored it for long enough.

When she was younger, Phoebe read it to her, or they read it together. Those stories and people felt so alive and real when she was ten.

Now? If she thought about it for a moment longer than was comfortable, Martha had to admit she didn't know what she believed anymore. When she was digging, there was no doubt that evolution couldn't have just happened. God had to have made the heavens and the earth. It was so clear to her.

But in the silence of her room, in the stillness of the morning, Martha felt alone and afraid. Was God like the reverend at her church said He was? Around, but not interested in her everyday life? Or was he more like what the pastor of the little church she'd visited portrayed? A loving shepherd for His sheep. A Father.

She chewed the inside of her cheek and got up from her dressing table. Fingers trembling, she picked up the Bible.

She sat down on her bed and clutched the book to her chest. Tears pricked her eyes. But the pressure and the loneliness were too much to take. With a tremulous breath, Martha looked up. "God . . . are You there?" The words came out in a hoarse cry. "I . . . I . . ." She bit her lip and felt the tears release down her cheeks. "I want to know You. Truly *know* You. Like Phoebe and Jacob. But I don't know how. I remember praying . . . and I remember that joy. I long to understand. Long to have a relationship with You."

Still the silence sat, heavy and full. She looked at the Bible and, with a firm nod, opened it. Somewhere in here there had to be a place telling her how she could know Jesus. She flipped through the fragile pages—then stopped. What did that say?

Her finger slid across the words: "And this is eternal life, that they might know thee the only true God, and Jesus Christ, whom thou hast sent." Her eyes scanned the page. The book of John. A memory came flooding back to her like it happened yesterday. . . .

"Read it again, Phoebe! Read it again!" Martha squealed, her hands clapping together.

Phoebe smiled at her. "I will, my girl. Listen closely though. This is the beginning of the greatest story ever told. 'In the beginning was the Word, and the Word was with God, and the Word was God.' John 1:1."

Martha stared at her governess. "In the beginning? There were words?"

Her governess's delicate laugh rang through the nursery. "No, dear one. In the beginning was one Word. Jesus. He is the Son of God and He came to earth to teach us His gospel and redeem us from our sins." Phoebe gathered her close. "Let's start again. Let's read the book of John together, and then you will see the Lord's great love for His Father and His children on display."

As the memory faded, tears fell, dripping onto the pages. Martha slipped her fingers through the pages until she came to the beginning of the book of John. "Jesus, Phoebe said You were real and right here with us. Jacob talks about You like You're real and his dearest friend. I want to know that for myself." She wiped at her tears and let out an unladylike sniff. "My anger has exhausted me. And I'm beyond myself in knowing how to handle the situations thrown at me of late. I haven't handled them well."

A glance at the clock said it was eight in the evening. Mother was gone. She was never home these days. And Martha had no clue where Lily Rose was. She was always off on one errand or another of late. Besides, Martha couldn't take these questions or thoughts to her companion. Not after what she'd said.

She flicked her thick blanket back and climbed into bed, the lantern burning bright enough for her to read. Settling against the pillows, Martha looked at the Bible again. Then, with determination in her heart, she did what she did best.

She started to dig.

SATURDAY, AUGUST 3, 1889

Pacing the grand library, she enjoyed the rhythmic taps of her footsteps.

Things had been too tame. Too boring.

That's why she liked wearing costumes. Pretending to be other people. Traveling to different towns and planning elaborate ruses.

It was time to up the ante. The little dig that had a head start—well, their foreman was sweet little Martha. The poor thing didn't need all this tension.

So why not throw a nice, big wrench in the works for the other team? They had more workers to begin with. They had no business excavating anyway. It was hers.

It didn't matter to her because she'd have the dinosaur in the end anyway, but why not let the underdog have a little victory. Martha deserved it.

Perhaps it was time to make matters worse. That should make things a bit more interesting.

The clock chimed.

Footsteps sounded behind her.

Right on time. As usual.

She turned.

When he got close enough, she leaned forward and whispered in his ear.

He grinned. "I'll take care of it."

"Good. They already suspect that Duncan fellow and he needs to go away. Permanently."

It felt good when everything came together. Martha could have her day. Jacob would be gone.

All in the name of true love.

nineteen

"The winter seems broken at last."

~Earl Douglass

Jacob stared at the quarry. The sight had never been more beautiful. Red rock, sparse greenery, the blue of the sky. He inhaled—and winced. His ribs were healing, but still tender. The doctor's caution stuck with him. He wouldn't overdo it today. Even so, he was determined to be out of bed and out-doors, where he belonged.

Humming his mother's favorite hymn under his breath, Jacob followed the familiar rocky path to the tent. He'd be lying if he said his nerves weren't tight. He hadn't seen Martha since that day in his room when he'd declared his feelings. He could feel the flush rising in his neck. He wasn't ashamed of it. Or of what he had said to her. He'd prayed for her every day since. No matter what happened between them, he wanted Martha to know the Lord. Even if it meant they couldn't be together.

267

But now he fully expected an awkwardness to exist between them. "Best get it over with," he muttered and stepped into the tent. Martha was at the table again, talking with her new foreman.

She glanced his way and gave him a tight nod. "Mr. Duncan, you are familiar with Mr. Parker. He's the foreman now and will have your assignment for today."

Martha's tone was even, matter-of-fact.

It stung.

But he could deal with it. He nodded at her and followed the foreman out, listening as the older man pointed to the northwest side of the quarry. The men had found what they believed to be the skull of the *Apatosaur* and needed someone with his detailed skills to help get it out.

A thrill shot through Jacob. Often the head was the hardest fossil to find. Many skeletons had been sent to museums without the skull or with a mismatched skull. To find a skull intact, that matched the whole skeleton . . . He couldn't stop his grin—or the twinge of sadness. Oh, to celebrate this find with Martha. But she still needed space. He would respect that.

"Mr. Duncan!"

His name on the wind gave him pause and he turned, spotting Martha picking her way down the path. Hope flared within him. She came to a stop in front of him, breathless. "Have you grown hard of hearing since your accident?" She smiled. "I called your name four times!"

Her smile was easy and full, a complete contrast to the reception he'd gotten moments before. Heat crawled up Jacob's face. "I was lost in thought. Did you need me?"

Martha nodded and took a deep breath. "I'm sorry about just now. I wasn't sure . . . I mean I had hoped . . ." She stopped and clasped her hands together. "I was determined to be professional and calm. But I wanted you to know, I am happy to see you, Jacob. I'm glad you're feeling better, and I'm thrilled you're back on the dig."

He blinked. He studied her face, the openness of her expression, and swallowed. There was no pretense in her words. Her blue eyes shone with a peace he had not seen there before, and his heart thumped. That's what it was. The shadows he so often saw in her face were receding. He smiled at her. "Thank you for your well wishes and kindness. And congratulations. Mr. Lewis told me about the skull find."

Martha went up on her toes. If possible, her smile grew. "Can you believe it? I nearly fainted when we found it a few days ago. I wished so much to tell you right away, but my mother wouldn't allow me back at your boardinghouse." She glanced down to the ground and let out a breath. "There's so much I've wished to talk to you about lately."

Those words warmed him, and he tucked his head down to catch her gaze. "I've missed you." He kept his words tender.

Martha blushed. "I've missed you as well."

"Would you . . . that is, are you available to talk?" The words rushed out of Jacob in a whoosh. A crunch of boots on rock signaled someone else was joining them and he wanted to make it quick. "There's a little café two blocks from my hotel. Would you like to meet for dinner tonight? After work? Around six thirty?"

Happiness shone from her blue eyes as she nodded, lips pressed together, making her dimples appear. "I would enjoy that."

"Hello again, Mr. Duncan."

Lily Rose's voice cut through their moment.

"I'm surprised to see you so well recovered from your injuries."

Jacob schooled his features into a pleasant smile. He wouldn't feed the ill will of this woman. "Thank you, Miss Ducasse." He turned back to Martha. "I'll see you later tonight."

He walked away, but Lily Rose's outrage followed him on the wind.

"Where are you going with that man tonight?"

"We are having dinner. There is nothing untoward, and there are some things we need to discuss. You are welcome to join us."

Martha's voice stayed calm. Good for her.

"Well, don't expect me to accompany you. He's not a man of means, Martha. I would think you would listen. Especially after your mother . . ."

Their conversation drifted out of his earshot. What about Martha's mother? It was the second time Lily Rose had referenced her in regard to him. He made a note to ask Martha about it at dinner tonight.

Several hours later, home and freshly bathed, Jacob slid an arm into his suit coat and snagged his hand on a thread in the lining. Disentangling his fingers, he groaned. Several threads now hung from his fingertips. He pushed them inside his cuff. He would have to fix it some other time. He didn't want to be late for dinner. Smoothing his hair back, he settled his hat on his head and made his way downstairs.

"Oh, there you are, Mr. Duncan!" His landlady came up with a folded piece of paper. "I was on my way to find you. A telegram came for you. Rather urgent."

Jacob took the paper from her.

In Colorado Springs. Need help. Injured. Meet me at the Antlers Hotel. John

Cousin John was in Colorado Springs? His mother hadn't mentioned that in her last letter. Only that he was mining up in the mountains. Jacob read it again. Injured. Things must be bad for him to be taken to Colorado Springs and send a telegram. Sighing, Jacob smiled at his landlady. "Thank you for giving this to me. I'll be gone a few days. My cousin John is in Colorado Springs and has asked for my help because of an injury."

The older woman patted his arm. "What awful luck for you and yours! And you recovering from your own injuries. Be safe, Mr. Duncan. I'll hold your room for you, pay it no mind."

"I appreciate it. Also, do you have a sheet of paper? I need to pen a note."

Jacob wrote of the situation to Martha. Surely she would understand his absence for the next few days? If not, well, what could he do? His family needed him.

He handed the note to his landlady and checked the clock. "Could you see that this note makes it to Miss Jankowski at the café on Main Street right away? If I have any hopes of catching the train, I'll have to run to the depot."

"I will. Safe travels, Mr. Duncan."

Jacob nodded his thanks and bounded back up the stairs. Thankfully, between his first job and Martha's generosity on this dig, he had a bit to spare for a train ticket.

He threw a few things in his small pack, closed and locked his door, then ran back down the stairs. He was expending more energy than he had in a while, but at least his wounds weren't on fire.

His landlady waited at the bottom of the steps. "Here, take one of my horses. I'll have Ronald fetch it at the station after he delivers your note."

"Thank you." Mounting the horse, he took another deep breath and then prodded the horse down the street.

Poor John! To be injured and so far away from any family. He understood that feeling now more than ever. *Lord, please protect John and help him to heal.*

He would just have to see what he was up against when he arrived.

As he rode, his thoughts returned to Martha. He couldn't wait to return and hear what had been happening with her.

The change in her was encouraging and he hoped their next conversation would be a step toward their future.

By now, surely she had received his note. He closed his eyes as he reached the station. Hopefully she would understand and forgive him for missing their dinner.

~~~~~

WEDNESDAY, AUG 7, 1889 • JANKOWSKI DIG SITE

Pacing the tent at the dig site, Martha fidgeted with her handkerchief.

Her world had spiraled out of control.

Again.

Lily Rose had left the dig site after their little spat and hadn't returned.

Jacob never showed up for dinner. She sat at the café until Walter came in to fetch her and take her home.

She couldn't order anyone to do anything about it. Mother had refused to be seen since she was having a fit of her headaches. Summer and the heat seemed to bring them on and keep her in her bed.

Walter had checked at the boardinghouse yesterday, but no one had seen Jacob.

Lily Rose's room was pristine and her things were still present, while their owner was missing.

What was happening?

Martha had tried to read the Scriptures to find comfort the past couple days but then little thoughts would niggle at the back of her mind that everything had been fine until she started searching for more about God.

Without anyone to talk to, she'd done her best to pray. Even when she didn't have the words, she'd lift her face toward the ceiling hoping that God understood her heart.

After those moments, she'd felt peace.

Until her mind started spinning again.

Between worry and uncertainty about the two people that she cared about the most, she had worn thin.

She wanted to have faith. Longed to have God work in a miraculous way so that everything would be all right. But she was tired.

A cheer rose up from the southwest quadrant.

She left the tent, lifted her skirts, and rounded the dirt path.

"Look!" One of the three men lifting the fossil was all smiles. He spotted her. "Miss Jankowski! We have the skull!"

Whoops and hollers echoed around her at the site. She put her hands to her mouth—they'd done it. They had the skull.

She placed one hand on her stomach and forced her jittering nerves to calm. She walked closer, ready to hold the skull for herself.

She did. Well, with the help of the others. The skull of an *Apatosaurus* was small in comparison to its body, but massive in comparison to a human.

As she inspected the fossil, more men gathered close. There was a little bit of the mandible missing, but that was to be expected. Other than that, the cranium was there.

She lifted her gaze to the men, blinking away the tears of joy that threatened to multiply. "Thank you. All of you. You have done a magnificent job."

"Won't Jacob be excited to see this?" Josiah came closer. The poor guy probably didn't even realize Jacob was missing.

Her elation plummeted, but she couldn't allow them to see that. They had less than three weeks to complete the dig and they still had several cervical ribs, a humerus, an ulna, and the sternal plates to unearth. There were other pieces in progress that would be completed soon, but those others hadn't even been started.

The crowd began to disperse as the men figured out the best way to haul the skull up and get it wrapped for storage.

Martha made her way back to the tent, tired of all the ups and downs in her emotions.

"Uh . . . Miss Jankowski?" Mr. Lewis removed his hat. "There's a policeman out at the gate asking to see you."

Her heart drummed in her chest, faster and faster. "Thank you. I'll go see what he wants."

Whatever it was, it couldn't be good. The police didn't usually arrive with good news.

She took steady, quick steps down the path toward the gate, and sure enough, there was a man standing there. Looking somber.

"I'm Miss Jankowski. You asked for me?" She eyed the man, willing herself to stand still and remain calm.

"You need to come into town with me, miss. One of your employees has been spying on another dig."

"Pardon me?" Placing her hands on her hips, she narrowed her gaze.

"A Mr. Jacob Duncan. An official report has been filed." He tugged on her elbow. "Come with me. Now."

twenty

"I have got to leave these scenes and this country which have grown so dear to me."

~Earl Douglass

Friday, August 9, 1889

The train rolled into the depot with a loud hiss and burst of steam. Muttering excuses and apologies, Jacob pushed his way through the crowd. He had to get to Martha. Nothing else mattered.

The entire trip had been a bust. Frustration boiled in his gut. A train ticket was expensive enough for a trip that was planned, but an unexpected trip? It was a luxury. Then to make it to Colorado Springs and find that his cousin wasn't even present? Infuriating. The lost money was secondary in his list of frustrations, however.

Something wasn't right.

With plenty of time on the train to think, Jacob had outlined the various situations he'd been in the last months. And

275

now no cousin. A long trip taking valuable time away from the dig.

Jacob stopped in the middle of the planked pathway in front of Martha's house.

He rubbed his face—someone wanted him away from the dig. Was that it? But who? Why? He wasn't the one getting his name on the exhibit. It was Martha.

He shook his head. He needed to see her and maybe together they could figure this out. The thought lifted him and he pushed through the iron gate and bounded up the massive porch.

The butler answered his knock and Jacob removed his hat. "Jacob Duncan to see Miss Jankowski."

The older man sniffed and peered down his nose. "One moment." The oak door slammed shut and Jacob sighed. Rocking back on his heels, he sorted through the events again. There had to be something he was missing. Someone. Who would want to sabotage *both* teams?

The door swung open and Martha greeted him. "Jacob!" She scowled. "What are you doing here? Don't you know they're looking for you?"

The anger in her voice caught him off guard. "Looking for me?" He shook his head "I wanted to let you know I was back from—"

She crossed her arms. "Back? *Back?* You left without a word. Left me at that café all alone. You were gone from the dig when it is absolutely critical for all hands to be available and working." But even as she stood there, angry and upset, he noticed the relief in her eyes.

"Wait . . ." He took a step back. "I . . . I left you a note. My cousin telegrammed and said he needed me urgently in Colorado Springs. I wouldn't have just left you like that."

Her face softened. She gripped the knob of the door. "Your cousin? There was no note from you, Jacob. Nothing. They brought me down to the police station and had the foreman of the other dig there. He told me your contract with them was never terminated. He showed it to me. He confessed that they were using you as a spy." Her bottom lip trembled, and her voice lowered. "I can't believe you would do this to me. After I shared my feelings with you."

"Martha—"

"No." Her head shook back and forth. "I'm glad you are okay, but I can't believe anything you say to me anymore. I want you off my porch. Do not contact me anymore. You are off the dig."

"Martha!" He stepped forward, hands spread wide. His heart raced. Why was she reacting like this, like she couldn't even hear a word he was saying. "I'm not lying to you. I'm just as confused as you are. When I got to Colorado Springs, my cousin wasn't even there. It's like someone wants us to be divided. Wants us to lose focus on the dig when such a huge discovery has been made." His hands fell to his sides. His sides still ached from the attack a few weeks ago, and right now, he couldn't breathe. Panic clutched at his lungs, but he forced a deep breath through them. "Please let me finish and help you get your name on this exhibit."

Martha stared at him for a long minute. "No. No. You've charmed me with your sweetness and kindness for the last time. For all your talk about God, you're just as fake as everyone else. You've lied to me from the beginning. Spying, sabotage . . . it's all been one big lie and I can't do it anymore. Go away, Jacob. I don't want to see you again."

He pushed a hand through his hair. "If you would just listen—"

The door slammed shut.

He turned and faced the street. His eyes barely registered the activity of the upscale neighborhood. All he felt was the raging emptiness inside. Where had he gone wrong? Had he not followed the Lord? Why was Martha so angry with him? Is this what love looked like?

Suddenly, he missed his family. The simplicity of their love, kindness, and hope. The wisdom of his mother and the strength of his father. His siblings and their teasing, full of good-natured ribbing. His church family and being fed the Word every week. Being out in Denver had been a trial and a test. Maybe his parents had been right. Maybe he had chosen the wrong path after all.

~~~~~~~

Martha pressed her forehead against the door for a moment then turned toward the parlor.

Gerard emerged from the shadows of the hallway. "Will you be needing anything, miss?"

He'd been their steadfast butler for as long as she could remember, but tonight his tone was softer than she'd ever heard.

"No, thank you, Gerard. I think I will retire early tonight. Can you ask Chef to send a small tray to my room for dinner?"

The old butler bowed and retraced his steps back to the kitchen.

Martha stood in the immaculate foyer, her emotions a mess. Jacob looked awful. Exhausted. She'd never seen him so unkempt. But her heart couldn't take it. Not one more excuse. Not one more story. His cousin? She snorted then clapped her hand over her mouth. His unmannerly ways had rubbed off on her. Mother would be furious at how low-class she was becom—

Oh! Had she always thought of people and class in such a snooty way? That wasn't right. It wasn't fair to classify Jacob as lower than her. A verse she recently read came to mind. "*I came not to call the righteous, but sinners to repentance.*" Martha sighed. She still had so much to learn, but she was coming to understand what Jacob meant when he said he was a sinner.

Through reading the Bible and trying to understand what it meant to be saved, one thing was becoming clear to her. There were many things in her life that were not pleasing to God. It was easy to think she was a good person. That she was kind to those who had less than her, that her money didn't mean anything. But that wasn't true.

Class. Status. Society. Wealth. Those things had been open doors that got her places. But Martha was starting to see that they could also be things that blinded her to what truly mattered. Mercy. Compassion. Humility.

"God, I know I am a little new at talking to You like this. But I need Your help." Her thoughts went back to Jacob. He'd shown her all those things and more. She chewed on the inside of her cheek. She'd been so harsh with him just now. It wasn't right that she didn't give him a chance to explain himself. But could she trust him?

Another thought struck.

Was all of this just some big plan to stop her dig?

Martha sighed and walked toward the staircase. She didn't know what to think anymore. Exhaustion licked at her heels constantly. The tension in her household was too much. Her mother was becoming someone she didn't know anymore. Lily Rose, too, had become a stranger.

Oddly enough, the biggest hole Martha felt was the absence of her father. Though they'd never been close, he'd been warm with her at times. It was strange how cold life could feel when warmth was taken from it.

Martha slid her hand up the polished banister absently. Was that what she was doing with Jacob? Extinguishing his warmth from her life by being unwilling to listen?

She pressed a palm to her forehead. Perhaps with some food and sleep she would know better what to do in the morning.

A loud pounding pulled her from her thoughts. She turned

to see her butler scurrying to the door. He pulled it open, and Martha saw Jacob's outline in the doorway.

"Please, let Miss Jankowski know I'm here. It's urgent."

"Young man, you are not welcome in this household. The young miss has made that clear. Now go." The older man moved to shut the door, but Martha scurried down the stairs.

"It's okay, Gerard." She spoke loud enough for Jacob to hear her and stop his pleading.

"But miss. Your mother will be put out by the disturbance he is creating in the neighborhood." The butler's bushy eyebrows dipped so low it was almost impossible to see his eyes.

She swallowed down her hesitance and shook her head. "She's not in currently. And this will only take a moment. I will see to it." The least she could do was offer Jacob a chance to tell the truth. And to offer him forgiveness. As hard as that might be.

The faithful butler stared at his young mistress for a moment, then bowed and stepped away.

Taking a deep breath, Martha opened the door fully and looked at Jacob, an eyebrow arched in question.

A crumpled piece of paper fluttered between his fingers. "It's the telegram." Jacob's words were hushed. Reverent. "I forgot I had it in my pocket. This will show you I'm not lying, Martha."

She took the paper and read it, noting the date and time stamped in the corner. "August 5, 5:27 p.m." She read the urgent message then looked up at Jacob.

She'd been so wrong. Again. Her shoulders sagged. She should have known better. Despite all that had happened to him, Jacob had always been truthful with her. Even when she'd been so hurt learning he'd worked with the other team, Jacob had still stuck to his word. She *knew* in her heart who he was—why did she have so much trouble accepting that?

Martha handed the telegram back to him, her fingers brushing his. "Jacob, I'm so sorry. I'm sorry I doubted you." But then everything else came back. "Wait . . . oh no. The police said you were spying for the other team—"

"I would never do that. I told you the truth. They let me go. Without telling me what I did wrong. The foreman even told me I was his best worker. . . . I fear there is something sinister happening and I'm worried for you."

"For me? You should be worried about yourself. Someone has gone to great lengths to blame you, and heavens, they tried to kill you!" She covered her mouth with her hand.

"The letter . . ." Jacob released a groan and paced the top of the steps. "I had a letter from my mother in my pocket the day I was fired. In it, she told me about my cousin John taking a mining job up in the mountains." His eyes widened. "That was after I overheard some men scheming to spy on your dig. They must have taken the letter. Planted the telegram." He stepped toward her and grabbed both of her hands. "Somehow, they got the note I left with my landlady. The one that was supposed to be delivered to you at the café."

She stepped back. "But what does this mean? Who could be behind—"

"Stop! Step Back! Is that him, Miss Ducasse?"

Two burly policemen bounded up the small stairs of the Jankowski porch. Truncheons in hand, they grabbed Jacob by his elbows and roughly turned him around.

Martha cried out and pulled at the officer's jacket. "What are you doing? You're hurting him! Be careful. He's recovering from wounds."

"Wounds received while murdering a man, Miss Jankowski," the officer growled. He looked at the figure outside on the planked path. "Are you sure this is him?"

Martha took two steps forward and gasped. "Lily Rose! What are you doing? What is happening?"

But her companion ignored her and nodded at the policemen. "That's him."

Jacob struggled against the massive men, but they remained unfazed. "Jacob Duncan, you are under arrest for murder."

Martha swallowed and took a step back. "No. No!"

Jacob looked at her, panic and fear filling his face. "I have no idea what this is about, Martha. Please believe me. Please . . ." His voice trailed off as the officers removed him from the property.

Lily Rose came up and placed an arm around her. "Don't worry, Martha. That man will never plague your life again."

She wrenched herself from the older woman's grasp and glared at her, angry tears streaming down her face. "What have you done? What is going on?"

Her companion appeared completely unemotional about the entire scene. She merely smiled. "Jacob Duncan has murdered a man on his former team. And there's proof he did it."

twenty-one

"Oh, may God show us what life means."

~Earl Douglass

She swirled the last bit of brandy in the bottom of her glass. The Duncan fellow should be taken care of now. If she had her way, he'd be dead by Monday.

And she *always* got her way.

She grinned. Power was a wonderful thing. When she was younger, she hated her father for how he treated her, but then she grew to love him after she came to appreciate his talents and the money. All the money . . .

When he'd brought her alongside in the business, she'd tripled their profits. Which made her papa proud.

Then she'd killed him.

She really wasn't good at sharing. He should have known that. He'd raised her, after all.

The clock chimed. One more business meeting this evening and she could turn her attention to the next part of her plan.

It was time. Martha wouldn't have anyone else to turn to with Jacob behind bars. So she would come to her.

The girl would probably cry and beg and plead for guidance.

How fortuitous that she was always willing to give it.

———◦———

SATURDAY, AUGUST 10, 1889 • DENVER JAIL

Jacob sat on the filthy cot in the jail cell and rested his head in his hands.

God, I've never been in a situation so dire. I can't see a way out, but I know You can. Help my faith to grow stronger even though I feel weaker than ever. Show Martha Your comfort and love like never before. I'm scared, but please help me to put aside my fears and rest in You.

His prayers had been short but plentiful since his arrest. Every few minutes, he lifted another to his Heavenly Father.

He hadn't slept last night. He'd tried, but his mind kept replaying his last words with Martha. The moment of elation when she heard him out and believed him. The care and concern in her eyes. Then the shock when he was taken away.

How cruel that because of him she'd had to endure all of this.

What would she think now?

A man he'd never even met had been killed. A bloody knife had been found in Jacob's room. There was even a witness who said he'd done it.

They might as well get the hangman's noose ready for him today.

His only hope was for Almighty God to intervene.

To his landlady's credit, she told the police chief he couldn't have done it. But right now, she was the only one who believed in him.

Maybe Martha did too, but he couldn't expect that from her. Not when he'd been taken away right in front of her. He'd seen the look of horror on her face. And Lily Rose was right there, to fill her mind with doubt.

The last few weeks, the ugliness of her hatred had made her appear old and haggard. Her blonde hair appeared grayer each time he saw her.

What had happened to wound her in such a way?

Shuffling sounded down the long hallway.

"I need to see him, right now."

Wait. That was Martha's voice.

Jacob stood and went over to the door. He gripped the bars and held his breath. She'd come to see him!

The sound of footsteps headed in his direction made him smile. *Thank You, Lord.*

"Jacob?" Martha rushed past the guard. "Are you all right?"

It didn't matter that he was behind bars right now. She was here! He couldn't contain his smile. "I'm much better now that you're here."

She reached through the bars and gripped his hand with her gloved one. "I've contacted a lawyer. He's going to come help this afternoon, and I have the word of the police chief that nothing will be done to you before then."

Ah. She'd been worried about his life hanging in the balance as well. "Thank you for doing that. I have been praying all night about what to do, asking God to strengthen my faith during this."

Her eyes shimmered and she stepped closer. "Strengthen your faith? You're the strongest man of faith that I've ever known. Even when others treated you abominably. Including me." She ducked her head. "I'm so sorry, Jacob." Lifting her eyes, she caught his gaze again.

"I meant what I said, Martha. I love you. I do. But I don't

expect you to stand by my side during this. Especially if your mother disapproves."

Her booted foot stamped the floor as she frowned at him. "Oh, that is ridiculous. I can see clearly now, for the first time in a long time. I will do everything in my power to help you." Her lips pinched together. "I've already visited your landlady. She's sworn that she will testify on your behalf in court, if it comes to that. And . . . she also told me about the note you left with her. She was horrified to learn that the delivery boy never brought it to the café." A long exhale left her. "I'm sorry to say that when I spoke with the boy, he said a woman—matching Lily Rose's description—came and took the note from him. Said she was meeting with me as well."

He closed his eyes and groaned. "I knew someone was behind it, but I wouldn't have guessed Lily Rose's contempt would lead her to such behavior."

"I never would have guessed that either. She's been so supportive and encouraging. I admit her attitude changed and I knew something had happened to devastate her, but she hasn't talked about it."

The guard stepped closer. "Your time is almost up, Miss Jankowski. The police chief will be back any moment."

"Thank you, Cliff." Martha gave Jacob a smile and squeezed his hand. "I will return later today with the lawyer."

"Thank you for coming."

She flashed those dimples again and followed Cliff back down the hallway.

Jacob basked in the scent of her perfume, reminding him that she'd really been there.

He hadn't murdered anyone. And she believed him.

Now if only the rest of Denver could know that too.

The last few weeks had finally brought about some results. They weren't conclusive and all the pieces didn't fit together, but Cole was beginning to understand the puzzle.

The police chief in Denver was on someone's payroll, of that he was certain. Whether the rest of his staff were as well was another story. Cole didn't have any leads in that area. But the police chief had been in charge of the investigation into Edwin Gilbert's death.

None of the law enforcement, in or outside of Denver, wanted to believe a woman was behind the murders. It did sound far-fetched, but the gloves were too much of a clue to ignore.

They weren't cheap gloves. They were of the finest quality. Whoever was behind this had money, and lots of it. Or . . .

The suspect had access to someone with money.

He let that idea simmer for a while.

Shaking his head, he focused on the new lead—the competition for the space at the museum.

It was all the buzz about town. And a lot of sketchy things had happened. A young man named Jacob Duncan had been arrested for murder, and yet his landlady was adamant he didn't do it.

Time to talk to him.

As Cole walked toward the police station, he passed a lovely young woman. Obviously of wealth . . . with blonde hair and blue eyes.

He pulled the sketch out of his pocket. Yep. A close enough resemblance to investigate.

He turned and followed at a safe distance.

When she stopped at a stately mansion, he released a low whistle under his breath. Had he just found his murderer?

Turning back around, he headed to the jail. A deputy took him back to the cells. A man sat on the bench in the cell. . . .

Was he praying? There was a Bible in his hands.

"Mr. Duncan?"

The younger man stood. "Yes, sir?"

"My name is Cole Anderson. I'm with the Pinkertons. I'd like to ask you a few questions."

"Sure." A glimmer of hope whisked across Duncan's face. "As long as you can help me."

"My goal is the truth." He pulled out the sketch from his pocket. "Do you know this woman?"

Duncan studied it. "Well . . ."

"Don't lie to me, young man. That won't help you. Is this the woman that I assume was just here visiting you?"

Jacob jerked back. "Martha?" He looked at the picture again. "No. Well, I guess it is similar to her. But if you ask me, it looks more like her companion, Miss Lily Rose Ducasse. Why?"

JANKOWSKI MANSION

Martha walked back and forth in her room. She'd looked everywhere for Lily Rose but couldn't find her.

Out of sheer desperation, she'd gone to her mother. She'd never been denied a request before. She was ready to beg and plead to get her powerful mother behind Jacob's cause too.

But Mother was nowhere to be found.

Again. The past few months, Martha's world had tipped on its side and spun out of control. What was going on?

You're alone. That's what going on. Nobody cares.

That ugly little voice in the back of her head had tried to make its way into her thoughts more and more over the past twenty-four hours.

No. "I'm not alone. God is with me." She spoke it out to the room, banishing all remnants of her doubts.

A knock at her door caused her to spin around. "Come in." Her heart skipped a beat. Mother?

Gerard opened the door and held out a silver platter. "A messenger just delivered this for you. I promised to bring it to you straightaway."

She lifted the envelope from the tray. Hm. No return address. Simply her name in all capital letters. "Thank you." She smiled at her butler, whose compassionate eyes told more than he'd ever spoken in words.

The man knew more secrets in this house than anyone else. And he'd seen everything yesterday. Was he on her side?

It appeared that way, and she would take it.

He bowed and walked away.

Martha took the envelope over to her desk under the window and opened it. Several pages were inside.

Dear Martha,

I know it has been far too long since my last correspondence. I am sorry for that.

I also heard of your father's passing and that is what prompted this letter.

She flipped to the end of the pages and gasped. It was from Phoebe! She turned the pages back to continue reading. Wait. She read back over the opening, her browns drawn together. Phoebe had written to her? But she had never gotten her letters. . . . Martha felt her stomach roll. Mother. She'd bet Father's lucky coin that Mother had keep them from her. But why? She chewed the inside of her cheek and filed the thought away. She'd worry about it later.

Forgive me for not telling you about my arrival before now, but as you will see, I had to be certain only you would see this letter. I am in Denver for a few days and would love to see you, but it must be a secret meeting.

I haven't wanted to invade your privacy, but before I

continue, I must confess that I hired someone to investigate you to know you weren't involved in your mother's business.

Now that that truth is all out on the table, I will continue.

I'm concerned for you, Martha. I don't think you know what your mother is capable of.

All those years ago, I know it was heartbreaking for you when I left. Your tears have stuck with me. But I had to leave because my sweet mama begged me to go. Yes, she was sick and dying, but I found out much later there was more to the story.

After Mama died, I found letters from Victoria—your mother. They began with bribes for calling me away. Then they grew threatening.

Victoria didn't like the bond you and I forged. She also didn't like my faith and the influence I had upon you. At first, my mother didn't back down. She was determined that you would have a good influence—me—and we prayed for you nightly. At that time, I had no idea that your mother had been working behind the scenes to get rid of me. She'd bribed my mother with hefty sums of money and threats to my well-being to keep me in Colorado Springs.

Mama told me the truth of it all as she was dying. She'd taken the money to ensure that I would have a comfortable life after she died. But oh, she felt so guilty for falling into your mother's schemes. I'm convinced it hastened the end of her life faster than even the doctors anticipated.

Please know how much my mama regretted her actions. She loved my stories about you and how dear you were—and still are—to me. We prayed for you every night. That your brand-new faith would take hold and help you through the years.

Martha choked back a sob. Mother had threatened them? Her mother was forceful, to be sure, but why would she threaten such sweet people?

Somehow, Victoria got word that Mama passed away. She came down to Colorado Springs and told me something bad would happen to me if I ever contacted you again. I'll spare you the details of that conversation. Suffice it to say, the threat was believable enough, not only for my own sake, but yours as well.

Now, please, my purpose in this communication isn't to denigrate your family. But I'm concerned about you. Something isn't right in that house. With your father gone . . . I've had this prodding to come see you, but I knew I couldn't do that in person without telling you what I know first. Then I read the articles in the paper about your father, and my investigator discovered your former foreman was arrested for murder. I knew I had to speak up immediately.

More than anything, I want you to know that I love you and have been praying for you every day. You are not alone, sweet Martha.

For my own safety, I cannot disclose where I am staying. But if you can meet me later—perhaps at luncheon?—tell Gerard. He will make arrangements for us.

I long to hear all about your life and catch up on all the years since I left. But please . . . be careful.

> *With all my love,*
> *Phoebe*

Martha laid the sheets down on her desk. None of it made sense. . . .

Or did it . . . ?

She stood from the chair and paced the room. Mother and Father had never been close to her, but to think of them—especially Mother—threatening Phoebe and her mother? Could they have misunderstood?

The Jankowski name was respected and well-known. Martha didn't even know all the businesses they owned, but they owned a lot. They had invested heavily in the city and, from what Martha understood, increased their family fortune.

Perhaps she'd taken her family's wealth and reputation for granted all these years. She'd been so focused on what *she* wanted to do, and her parents let her pursue whatever fancied her at the time.

Still . . .

The more she thought about it, the more she realized how little she knew about her family's business. If anything at all. For that matter . . .

What did she really know about her mother?

"Good morning, Martha."

Martha gasped and spun. "Mother." She put a hand to her chest. "Goodness, you gave me a fright." Her heart threatened to pound out of her chest, but she forced everything within her to portray a calm façade.

"Not my intention, my dear." She took graceful steps into the room. "I'm sorry to hear about Mr. Duncan being in jail, but I *did* warn you."

Yes, she did. Why? Martha's breath left her, and her stomach sank. If Mother had threatened Phoebe, could she be responsible for Jacob's arrest too? Everything inside her shuddered. No. Not her own mother. "Did you : . . ." Her voice cracked and she swallowed. "Did you have anything to do with his arrest?"

Everything stilled for a moment, then Victoria sat next to her daughter, a smirk marring her beautiful face. "Of course I did, dear."

twenty-two

"I am getting where I do not fear, at least as I used to,
to go to the greatest depth one can reach in science."

~Earl Douglass

Oh dear. The color in her daughter's face went from red to ashen. Victoria lifted her chin. "You do realize that I did all this for you?"

Martha's brow scrunched up. "What? I don't understand." She slumped into her chair.

Oh, for heaven's sake. The child had always been weak. "Take some deep breaths, Martha. This isn't a time to wilt."

Watching the emotions play across her daughter's face, Victoria stood still and waited for her daughter to come to the correct conclusion.

She loved her daughter. Of course she did. She'd never loved anyone else. Certainly not Antoni. Not even her own father.

293

But there was something about giving birth to a new life that had sparked a tiny ember inside Victoria's chest.

Everything she'd done had been with Martha in mind.

Oh, the sweet little girl would never have been able to handle what Victoria had as a child. A pity she wasn't as strong as her mother.

There were many times she'd doubted that Martha would make it in her carefully controlled world. It wasn't an easy place. Tough decisions had to be made without caring what anyone thought. Without any emotion. But eventually, her daughter would take over the family business.

Many years from now.

When Victoria was ready to give up the reins.

A spark of hope had risen when she'd been informed of the confrontation at the museum. Her daughter had done her proud.

Of course, she'd never allow Martha to eliminate her. She was too smart for that.

But Martha would inherit it all. Once she was groomed for it and Victoria was no longer entertained by the work. Victoria almost smiled. Spending her later years traveling without a care in the world . . . once all the fun was over . . .

That would be lovely.

It would simply take time to harden her naïve daughter . . . mold her . . . help her learn how to do things right.

Like her mother did them.

"But he didn't do it."

Martha's squeaky voice brought her attention back to her daughter. Where was the spitfire who gave the museum director a piece of her mind?

"Jacob Duncan isn't worthy of you."

Martha bolted from her chair. Ah, good. The fire in her eyes was back. "But he couldn't have killed anyone. He couldn't have!"

Silly child. "Of course he didn't."

A gasp sounded behind her. "What do you mean . . . he didn't? If not Jacob, then *who* killed my William?"

Victoria swirled on Lily Rose. "*You* are not supposed to be here."

Her daughter's companion surged into the room. "Answer the question, Victoria. You told me it was Jacob. That you had proof. That there was a witness. Who. Killed. William?"

With a glance over her shoulder to her daughter, Victoria lifted her chin. She might as well start with Martha's training right now. "I did."

<hr />

"Mother! How *could* you?" The scream left Martha's lips as Lily Rose ran toward Mother, her hands raised to strike.

"Not another step, Lily Rose." The shiny glint of a knife appeared in Mother's hand. "Unless you want to join your beloved William."

Lily Rose looked toward Martha, her eyes pleading for help.

"Mother, don't you dare hurt Lily Rose. She's done nothing to you." Martha moved across the room until she stood in front of her longtime companion. And just like that, everything made sense.

Her friend's reactions to Jacob . . . the foul moods . . . the tears she'd seen Lily Rose shed on so many occasions the past few weeks.

She'd lost someone she loved.

Sobs erupted from Lily Rose behind Martha.

"Why did you kill him? He was a good man. He was building up his mercantile in Castle Rock so we could marry. What could he have possibly done to you?"

"I don't have to explain myself to anyone. I haven't taken over my family's business without a few casualties along the way."

Martha's eyes fixed on the knife in Mother's hand. She held the weapon with too much ease.

"Now . . . Martha, you need to help your friend pack. She's going far away and will not return under any circumstances. Understood? Otherwise, she will have to be eliminated as well."

Eliminated? Is that how she saw Lily Rose . . . as someone to eliminate?

"Did you hear me, young lady?" Mother made her way to the door. "Don't make me say it again."

Lily Rose pushed forward again. "The police chief is on his way, Victoria. You won't get away with this." Tears streaked her face.

The laugh from her mother was . . . hideous. "I own him, Miss Ducasse. Don't think for an instant that you have any power here. Now, if you value your life, you'll leave." And with that, she headed out of the room. "Meet me in my office in an hour, Martha. No arguments." The command echoed through the doorway.

Martha waited several seconds and then ran over to the door and shut it.

"What are we going to do?" Lily Rose's strangled cry about broke her heart.

Her mother was . . . a monster!

Martha shook her head. No, she couldn't allow herself to think about that right now. They had to figure out how to stop Mother and how to save Jacob. And she knew exactly what to do. "We are going to pray."

Lily Rose frowned. "Martha—you know I don't believe—"

She grabbed her friend's hands. "We're going to pray. We need all the help we can get." With a deep breath, she closed her eyes. "God, I don't even know what to say, but You know everything. We need help. Please guide the way. Calm our hearts. Lily Rose needs Your healing after such a loss. And please . . . spare Jacob." A sob clawed its way up her throat. She released Lily Rose.

Her friend stood looking at her. "I'm so sorry, Martha. I shouldn't have listened to her, but after losing William, I was a wreck, and she was so convincing." She gulped. "William and I . . . we were hoping to get married next summer." She sank onto the bed and cried.

Shock rippled through Martha. Lily Rose had been engaged? "Oh, Lily Rose." She sat next to the weeping woman. "Why didn't you tell me?"

Lily Rose dabbed at her eyes. "I've been alone all my life, Martha. I've enjoyed my time with you, but when I met William . . ." She sighed, tears streaming down her cheeks. "He was the only person in my life who was mine. I didn't have to share him with you or the dig or anything else. And now . . ." Her voice trailed off on a sob.

Martha's heart ached for her friend. And for the kind of friend Martha had been. Had she truly been so absorbed in her own life that Lily Rose thought she wouldn't care about her exciting news? Did she truly believe that Martha didn't care about her?

She could never make up for what had been done to Lily Rose through her own selfishness. But it paled in comparison to Mother's horrific behavior. "I'm so, so sorry. Truly I am. Nothing can make up for my own behavior, Lily Rose. I'm sorry I wasn't a good friend. And I can't begin to express my sorrow for what my mother has done, but we have to stop her."

Wait . . . the hair on the back of Martha's neck stood up and she glanced around the room. Could her mother hear her? No. There wasn't any way . . . right? Even so, she went to Lily Rose's side and whispered into her ear. "I will stall as long as possible. Go get the sheriff down in Castle Rock. See if he will come back with you." She glanced at the clock. "Hurry! The train leaves in twenty minutes. I'll pack your things for you and hide them away. Go . . . now."

Inside his cell, Jacob walked from one side to the other. It took all of three steps one way and three steps back. Ever since Martha's visit he'd been praying. The more time that passed, the greater the urgency in his heart grew.

Not for himself.

For her. His whole body was tense. He wasn't sure how he knew it, but he did. To the core of his being . . .

Martha was in danger.

Was it because of him?

He hated the thought.

Lifting up another prayer, he continued his pacing.

He would gladly give up his life if it meant she would be okay.

An hour had passed in her mother's office. The first fifteen minutes, Martha waited for her parent to arrive. When she did, Police Chief Masterson was with her.

So it was true. Mother owned the man.

That didn't bode well for Martha.

But she sat, spine straight, with schooled features and listened to the woman who'd given birth to her describe their family's legacy.

The smuggling of paintings, sculptures, jewels, gold, silver, people, and ancient artifacts had been going on for centuries. The extent of her family's crimes sickened her. Then to hear of the black-market dealings and slave trade . . . it just about put Martha over the edge.

But when Mother dared to talk about her dig as if it were her own, it took everything in her power to remain calm. Even when the woman claimed her *Apatosaurus*.

Martha kept her voice low. "Are you trying to tell me that you own the museum?"

Victoria—even her mother's name irked her now—laughed. "Of course I do, my dear. I also own the other dig."

"What?" That brought Martha out of her chair.

"Sit. Down." The voice brooked no argument. "I've had enough of your dramatics. It's about time you learned how the real world works. It's clear I have sheltered you far too long. Wake up, Martha. This is your legacy."

The firm set of her jaw and the fierce look in her mother's eyes sent a chill up her spine. Did she think Martha *wanted* this?

"Now . . . I have buyers for the bones. They will pay a hefty price. I wanted you to have the joy of excavating your first dinosaur skeleton, and I was even going to let you win the competition."

None of it mattered anymore. Not in light of the lives lost and the pure evil in front of her. "At what cost, Mother?"

"The cost doesn't matter. I always get what I want. You do too. That will continue as long as you know your place." Her mother took a seat in the high-backed leather chair.

That chair had always looked like a throne to Martha when she was a child. Her grandfather's chair—now her mother's. Seemed fitting enough. Inside, her stomach churned, but she kept her back straight and her mouth in a firm line.

Scuffling sounds from the hall snatched her attention.

"Let me go!" A man was being dragged into the room by Simon and Charles. The bodyguards that never seemed to sleep.

"What have we here?" Her mother stood.

Simon's face was grim. "There's a sheriff outside, ma'am. And this fella wanted to see you."

"A sheriff you say?" Victoria lifted her eyebrows at the police chief. "I take it you can handle this sheriff?"

"Certainly." He walked out of the room.

Mother tipped her head to her men. "Guard the door."

They threw the man down and she glided over. "And who might you be?"

The man stood up, straightened his suit, and glared at her. "I've come for my money."

Another laugh. "Oh, you're the sniveling man who thinks he can blackmail me."

"I don't *think*. I can. Don't think for a second that I'm going to allow you to get away with this."

Martha looked from her mother to the man. What else had the woman done? She couldn't take any more—

"You killed your husband."

The man's snarled words left Martha glued to her chair.

"If you don't want the authorities to know that, lady, you'll pay up."

Mother crossed her thin arms over her chest. "And who is going to believe you?"

"I've got a picture. Right here." He tugged it out of his inner coat pocket. "Don't worry, even if you destroy this one, there's more."

Martha jumped up, stomped over to the man, and grabbed the picture.

The old daguerreotype was of her father before he was scarred. And when she stared into the eyes, she sucked in a breath. It was true. The man in the picture *wasn't* the man who'd shown up when she was six. It wasn't the man she'd grown up with. It wasn't the man whose bedside she'd sat . . .

Wait.

No.

It couldn't be.

The picture shook in her hands. She slowly turned to face her mother. "You killed my real father . . . and *replaced* him with the man who's been in this house all these years?"

She took a step closer to the woman she now understood she'd never known. "And what? When *he* got in your way, you shoved him down the stairs?" She pointed a finger at her mother's face. "Am I next?"

The words seemed to slide right off her. "Don't be melodramatic, my dear. You are my flesh and blood. I couldn't kill you. Your father was bringing too much attention to himself. In our line of work, that can be disastrous. It's taken all these years for me to bring my plan to fruition. While Cope and Marsh were obsessed with the competition, they didn't realize there was another power in the paleontological field rising up. *Me.*"

"So you used him? You used me?" She crossed her arms over her chest needing some sort of barrier between the two of them.

"You are very talented, Martha, but it's not time for you to shine yet. You'll have your day, I promise. You can be in charge of every paleontological dig you'd like."

The man pushed his way between them. "I don't have time for your little family spat here. I want my money."

The flash of silver should have warned Martha, but her mother was quick. In the blink of an eye, she was around Martha and had thrust the blade into their visitor.

"No!" Martha willed her frozen feet to move and shoved her mother aside as she lunged for the crumpling man. He might be here to blackmail her mother, but he didn't deserve to die!

Shouting and more scuffling sounded out in the hallway.

Martha placed her hands over the man's wound as blood poured out. She pressed his jacket over it, but she couldn't stop the flow.

"Hold it right there!"

Martha looked up at the voice she didn't recognize.

Gunshots sounded, followed by loud thumps.

"Catch her!"

The sound of footsteps running away . . . then nothing.

"Help! In here! I've got an injured man."

No one came.

Each tick of the clock passed in agonizing silence. The man underneath her hands had ceased all movement. She started to cry.

Another life lost because of her mother.

No. Please, God . . . no!

Jacob stepped outside the jail and drew in a long breath. Fresh air. He glanced up. The last rays of sunlight were fading into a riot of oranges and reds. It had been the longest twenty-two hours of his life.

But now he was free. A smile lifted his lips. Freedom. It was a beautiful thing. *Thank you, Lord.*

Martha gripped his elbow. "I'm sorry it took so long to get you released. They're still searching for Mother. Her body-guards were the only ones who knew all of her hideouts, and they are both in the hospital with wounds from their fight with the sheriff. Once they caught Police Chief Masterson, I knew it would be safe for them to release you. But we still don't know how many more of my mother's accomplices are out there."

"Please don't apologize." He stopped and turned toward her. "I'm thankful to be free and with you."

"Me too." She sidled a bit closer. "But I'm afraid it's all a dream and you'll disappear." Her face fell and tears glistened in her eyes. "I don't deserve you, Jacob. Especially not after what my mother did to you."

Pulling her into his arms was the most natural thing he'd ever done. He pressed his lips into the crown of her hair, her sweet verbena scent filling his senses. "You aren't responsible for your mother's actions, and in my heart, I've already for-given her."

"But how can you?" She sobbed against his chest. "She's a

horrible, horrible person. I can't even begin to fathom all that she—and my family—have done over the generations. Who am I, Jacob?" Lifting her head, she snagged his gaze. "If what they've done is what it means to be a Jankowski, I no longer want to be one."

He ran a finger down her cheek, her tears dampening his skin. He didn't want to overwhelm her when her whole world had turned upside down. But she needed to know his feelings for her hadn't changed. Wouldn't change. "First and foremost, you are a child of God. Second, I'd love for you to be a Duncan one day." The words were out before he could catch them. This was *not* the right time, but he'd blurted out his heart anyway.

She ducked her head and stepped out of his arms, pink filling her cheeks. "Do you want to be associated with me after all this? Truly?" The doubt in her eyes crushed him.

He could throttle Victoria Jankowski for all she'd put her daughter through! "Of course I do. I thought I loved you before, Martha. But the thought of losing you was more than my heart could take. I would willingly lay down my life for you. I never want to take another moment together for granted."

Her blue eyes, puffy from crying but still as radiant as a Colorado summer sky, roamed his face. Slowly, a smile turned her lips upward. "I feel the same."

He cupped her face with his hands. Then lowered his lips to hers. The kiss was soft and sweet, and the passion in his heart threatened to overwhelm him.

When she melted into him, he deepened the kiss and let out a little moan. So this was what he had to look forward to. It was better than . . . well, than anything. He pulled back and grinned. "I have a question for you, Martha Jankowski."

"Oh?" The pink in her cheeks was lovely.

"You don't have to answer right away, but I would like to spend the rest of my life with you. If you are amenable."

She bit her lip and tipped her head to the side, considering his words. "I am more than amenable to that idea, Mr. Duncan."

"Good." He got down on one knee right there in front of the jailhouse. "Martha . . . will you be my dig partner?"

Her giggle shook her frame. "Forever and always. I love you."

"I love you too." This time, he took her in his arms and kissed her with every bit of love within him.

Two days later, Pinkerton agent Cole Anderson sat in the Jankowski mansion's parlor and faced Jacob and Martha. "I'm sorry to tell you that your mother hasn't been caught yet."

Martha sucked in a breath. "What does that mean for us? Are we safe?"

Jacob leaned closer and wrapped an arm around her shoulders.

Cole held up a hand. "I don't think she'll come back here. It's too risky and she likes to be in control. We had a confrontation, so she knows that *I* know who she is and that she's committed numerous murders. From what we've been able to ascertain, she's fled to Europe or possibly South America with a great deal of money. The woman was always prepared for this kind of scenario. Her reach is wide, she's got hired hands everywhere it seems." He rubbed his jaw. "But rest assured, I will find her. Now that we have all the evidence, my boss has promised that we will stop at nothing to find her. Your mother will be brought to justice."

Martha sniffed and lifted a hankie to her eyes. "After all this time, I thought I knew her. But I refuse to live my life afraid of her any longer. We are in God's care."

"That's the best place you can be, miss." Cole stood, hat in his hand. He held out a hand to Duncan.

Jacob shook it. "Thank you, Mr. Anderson. I just hope you can find her before she hurts anyone else."

Cole slapped his hat on his head and smiled. "Victoria Jankowski isn't afraid of me. She's not afraid of anything. And that makes her arrogant. And that"—he smiled—"is why I'll catch her."

EPILOGUE

"There's truly a fascination in discovery and pleasure and
encouragement in success and we certainly have been
successful in uncovering great scientific treasures. What
is still uncovered spurs us on."

~Earl Douglass

Martha stood in front of the brand-new display of her *Apatosaurus* at the museum. She smoothed the fabric of her simple
white gown as she stood next to Jacob, in front of their pastor.

After all they'd been through since they met over a year ago,
today they would become husband and wife.

"This is a little unconventional, but I'm excited for you
both." Pastor Muldoon leaned in and winked. He peered over
his shoulder at the mammoth skeleton and grinned. "Dearly
beloved . . ."

It was a simple ceremony, with only the pastor's wife and
Phoebe present. But it was the most beautiful wedding Martha
had ever attended. Because it was hers. And she was with Jacob.

It had taken her months to sort through the mess of her life.

Her mother hadn't been caught . . . yet. But the smuggling ring and all the other illegal businesses had been shut down. That was a step in the right direction. Martha wanted nothing to do with the empire her family had built.

The few legitimate businesses that were left were reorganized and sold to families who would continue to operate them aboveboard. Martha kept the museum so that—with her husband—they could fill it with fossils and provide education for the next generation. Good had to come out of all that had happened.

Martha sold the mansion in Denver, the three country estates, and all the land her parents had owned. She and Jacob had given away most of the money and set up funds to help the city clean up after the disastrous news came out about their police chief and many of his men.

All Martha wanted was a clean slate for her city—and a fresh start for her and Jacob.

After months of counseling with the pastor, they'd put the past behind them. Though there were days it was still a struggle, Marth was working on forgiving her mother. She knew she could do it with the Lord's help, and the encouragement of her husband. Together they had grown in wisdom and knowledge of the Lord. And in their love for one another.

The most exciting part—well, other than marrying the love of her life—was that they'd found another quarry full of bones. And another one just over the ridge from her first quarry. The locations were all rich with fossils. Jacob and Martha could dig for the rest of their lives in peace and contentment. Learning and growing. Studying fossils. And hopefully using it all to give paleontology a good name again.

"Miss Martha Jankowski, do y—"

"I do." She grinned at the pastor.

Jacob laughed and wiggled his eyebrows at her. He leaned toward Pastor Muldoon. "I think she's a little excited."

The giggles took over and she covered her mouth with her hand. "My apologies, Pastor." But she couldn't keep still.

"I'll save you the time"—Jacob winked at the pastor and, much to her delight, swept Martha into his arms—"I do too."

Sweeter words had never been spoken.

NOTE FROM THE AUTHOR

I hope you have enjoyed the second installment of the TREA-SURES OF THE EARTH series. This book was a labor of love and grief.

My sweet dad fell and went into the hospital while I was writing this book. Then, after several weeks in the hospital, he was able to go home for a couple days. The last thing he saw was his home before his eyes shut, his body began to shut down, and we had to make the difficult decision to place him in a hospice facility for his final hours/days. I wrote an email to my incredible editors—Jessica Sharpe and Karen Ball—to let them know what was happening and turned in the manuscript that day as we headed out to be with my family.

Dad went home to be with the Lord the following week, and some of the toughest months in my life followed.

Let me tell you, the creative juices were hit hard by grief. It was like slogging through mud.

So this book is in your hands because I had some wonderful people working with me and helping me. Karen Ball, Jessica

Sharpe, and Carrie Kintz helped me through my grief and through all the edits.

I thank each one of you for journeying with me. For reading. For encouraging. For praying for our family.

Set in Stone is now very dear to me.

While many lectures like the ones portrayed in *Set in Stone* happened during this time, the names of all involved in the story, along with the events, are fictitious.

This series wouldn't be here without the amazing work of Earl Douglass. His granddaughter—Diane Douglass Iverson—has been supportive and so helpful on this writing journey. If you have been fascinated or intrigued by any of his quotes in the book, please check out *Speak to the Earth and It Will Teach You: The Life and Times of Earl Douglass 1862–1931* (BookSurge Publishing, 2009)—a compilation of his journals and all of his life written by his son Gawin and edited by Diane.

I had a lot of fun researching for this book. Georges Cuvier—whom our character mentions in the story—was an interesting guy. Sometimes referred to as the "founding father of paleontology," I had to give him a little shout-out after reading so much of his writings.

Gregor Johann Mendel—now known as the father of genetics—was a man who truly fascinated me. He was an Augustinian friar (Moravian monk) and abbot of St. Thomas's Abbey in Brünn, as well as a biologist and mathematician. He established the laws of Mendelian inheritance. Though the terms microevolution and macroevolution weren't in use yet, he understood and observed in his studies that genetic change had natural limits. Organisms could only have so much variation. While the law of independent assortment, the law of segregation, and the law of dominance and uniformity are complex, it was engrossing to get into the mind of this incredible man who wrote papers on his research and studies on tens of thousands of pea plants back in the 1860s. If you'd like to read Mendel's paper, *Experiments in Plant Hybridization*, translated into English, check it out here: http://www.esp.org /foundations/genetics/classical/gm-65.pdf.

Bone Wars by Tom Rea is another book that gave life and breath to this story. John Bell Hatcher's letter about the mammal teeth found in ant hills that I used in one of the lectures is true. Since we don't know exactly when he was there, I included it in the story. (It could have been any time between 1889 and 1895.) Sadly, he was never given credit by Marsh in any publications, even though he was the guy doing all the work. In fact, one of Hatcher's letters talks about how Marsh had spent three and a half days total on sites—while the assistants were there for days/weeks/months/years. In 1900, Hatcher was hired by the Carnegie Museum after doing work for Princeton. Because of Hatcher's great work, we understand so much more—even though Marsh took all of the credit.

As you can see, the Bone Wars are still a bit contentious, and the paleontological community still feels the ripples.

For a fun and short video about the Bone Wars, go to: https:// ed.ted.com/lessons/the-bone-wars-the-most-notorious -scientific-feud-in-history-lukas-rieppel.

ACKNOWLEDGMENTS

For this book, I want to give my heartfelt thanks to everyone who helped me through the loss of my dad. *Set in Stone* is here because of you.

Jess and Karen—whew. Where would I be without you? Thank you is not enough, but it's the best I can give through my tears right now.

Carrie—this book literally wouldn't be here without you. You are such a blessing. Thank you.

Jeremy—what a road we've traveled. But I wouldn't do it with anyone else. I love you.

My Lord and Savior—thank You for the gift of story and giving me another chance to share that gift.

My readers—man, you guys are the very best. Thank you. Thank you. Thank you.

Looking forward to next time,
Kimberley

If you enjoyed *Set in Stone*,
read on
for an excerpt from

The

HEART'S CHOICE

BY TRACIE PETERSON
AND KIMBERLEY WOODHOUSE

Rebecca Whitman is the first female court reporter in Montana. During a murder trial, she's convinced that the defendant is innocent, but no one except the handsome new Carnegie librarian, Mark Andrews, will listen to her. In a race against time, will they be able to find the evidence they need—and open their hearts to love—before it's too late?

Available now wherever books are sold.

one

The downright icy air around him burned his lungs as he inhaled, but it couldn't take away the sense of euphoria that filled him. After all these years of hard work, he'd gained the position of a lifetime!

The head of the brand-new Carnegie Library.

He, Mark Andrews, was the head of the Carnegie Library!

Of course, his father probably wouldn't be excited. Or impressed. Angus Andrews wanted Mark to love ranching. Plain and simple. But being a librarian had been Mark's dream. He'd gone after it and obtained it. Not only was he the librarian, but he was in charge of the whole place.

In the darkness of the early morning, he stared up at the large Second Renaissance Revival–style building in front of him. The deep bracketed eaves above the pilastered entry made the dome above stand out.

From the domed, octagonal entry to the gray sandstone from the Columbus quarries making up the base to the deep red of the brick exterior, the structure was beautiful.

"There's the cowboy."

Mark turned at the voice breaking the silence of the morning to hold out a hand to Judge Milton Ashbury. "Good morning, Judge."

No surprise that the man used his childhood nickname. Though he'd left the ranch, people around here would probably always call him Cowboy.

"Ready for the big ceremony? I know you haven't had much time to get settled."

True enough. Mark had arrived four days prior and had spent every waking hour with the books. "I'm looking forward to today, sir. Thank you."

A high-pitched *yip* diverted his attention downward.

"And who's this?" Mark crouched down to pet the white ball of fur.

The older man let out a long sigh. "Marvella's newest passion. His name is Sir Theophilus."

Mark raised his eyebrows, working hard to keep his amusement to himself.

It didn't work. A snicker escaped.

The little thing couldn't weigh more than a few pounds and seemed all fur. It bounced around on its tiny little paws, stabbing at the dirt and snow in the street, and then at the judge's pants.

Mark cleared his throat and gave his best effort to swipe the mirth off his face. "My apologies. It's a gallant name."

"Don't apologize. I think it's ridiculous as well, but you know my wife. Her group of church ladies named him. Apparently they are now working through the book of Luke, and it seemed apropos." The man's bushy white eyebrows, mustache, and beard all wiggled as he rolled his eyes. "And since my loving wife thinks I need more exercise, I've been declared the one to walk him in the mornings instead of 'pacing the halls,' as she puts it." With a shake of his head, he peered down at the little dog. "As long as no one thinks he belongs to me, I don't mind. I have a reputation to uphold, you know."

Mark chuckled. "Well, it *is* barely six a.m., sir. I think you're safe." He glanced around. "There aren't too many folks out at this time of day."

"Which is a godsend." The judge straightened his coat with the hand not holding the leash. "I wouldn't want to be seen with this little fluff ball too often."

And yet despite the man's gruff words, there was no denying the twinkle in Ashbury's eyes. If Mark wasn't mistaken, the good judge liked the little dog but wouldn't ever admit it. "He certainly is cute. How much will he grow?"

One bushy, wild eyebrow shot up. "This is it, young man. He's full grown, or so my wife informs me."

"Oh." Mark grinned. Maybe it was best to change the subject. "How are things with you? I know you were voted in as the district judge while I was in college. Are you enjoying the position?"

"Very much. All except for the travel. It's a large district to cover, and while most of the larger cases are transferred here to Kalispell, I still need to travel out to the other areas." He stuffed his left hand into his coat pocket. "At my age, it's beginning to be wearisome."

"I can imagine." Montana was a rugged land and not always easily accessible. "Can you request that all cases be brought here?"

"As our great state keeps growing and more districts are added, yes, eventually. Until then, I'm afraid I will have to travel, which is much easier when the snow is no longer on the ground." Another yip from Sir Theophilus made the judge check his pocket watch. "I better head back, Marvella will be waiting."

"Please give her my love, sir."

Judge Ashbury laid a hand on Mark's shoulder and stepped

a few inches closer. "We're all proud of you. It's wonderful to have you back home doing what you love—what you were called to do. I know things have been difficult with your father over the years but remember that he loves you. Marvella and I have been praying for the Lord's will to be done. You're family to us, and we're glad you're home." The man's eyes filled with a sheen of tears. He dipped his chin and cleared his throat. "I'll be back for the dedication ceremony later."

"Thank you, sir." Mark struggled to clear his own throat. He blinked several times as he watched the man and his tiny dog walk back toward the Ashbury mansion.

The judge and his wife understood Mark like no one else. They'd been like a doting aunt and uncle, filling the aching hole left in his life when his mother died. Mark had been a mere five years old. The Ashburys had poured into Mark from the time his family arrived in Kalispell to now. They clearly saw the passion in Mark for intellectual pursuits. They'd encouraged him and cheered him on. The judge had even lent Mark book after book from his own prized collection.

Mark straightened. Had he ever let the couple know how much they meant to him? How much he appreciated their belief in him?

The judge's words just now conveyed a lot. Soon Mark would make a point of sharing with them everything that was on his heart and mind, but it would need to wait until the library was up and running.

And after he had a long heart-to-heart with his father. Which was long overdue.

When Mark went out East for college a decade ago, Dad hadn't liked it but let him go. Probably hoped that time away from the ranch would prove Mark wrong—that he would miss the ranch and everything related to it. Instead it solidified Mark's love of words and books, his desire to earn the directorship of a large library, and his passion to share the love of books with people who hadn't had the chance to know the precious gift of reading. What doors reading could open. The dreams it could spark.

And yet . . .

Deep down, Mark sensed he'd failed. Oh, not his dreams or the Ashburys' hopes for him. However . . .

Had he failed his father? Dad's expectations had been high. Still were. And he and his father had let deep rifts develop in their relationship.

He could only pray that coming home and spending time with his father would allow mending to take place.

Enough. He needed to focus on the matters at hand. In the moonlight Mark glanced across Third Street and allowed the thrill of the coming day to take over. With swift strides, he crossed the road and walked up to the library's main entrance.

Andrew Carnegie, one of America's leading philanthropists, had given a generous donation of ten thousand dollars to the city for the library. The only provision was that the city had to provide the land and the funding to keep the library operating. So they purchased two lots here on the northeast corner of Third Street East and Second Avenue East.

Etched into the sandstone above the double doors was *CARNEGIE*, a testament to the wealthy man who didn't want to die rich. And in fact, Mark had heard that libraries were being built across the country thanks to Mr. Carnegie.

What an amazing thing to do.

Mark would be eternally grateful. Not just for the library, but for the opportunity of the job. He had high hopes and dreams for this place. For his home. To educate people. Help kids who, like Mark, wanted a life beyond ranching and farming. To have the opportunity for a college education.

Not that farming and ranching were bad. Not at all. But books and reading opened up doors to entire worlds beyond Kalispell.

It wasn't a bad town. No. In fact, he loved it here. That's one of the reasons he came back. But if he had the chance to impact the next generation, he wanted to take it. Especially with the age of machinery upon them. The world was changing at an alarming rate and their best option was to keep up with it the best they could.

They weren't living in the nineteenth century anymore.

Standing at the foot of the stairs, Mark smiled again. The entry was angled to the northeast corner of the block with the dome rising high in the pre-dawn sky. The tall wood doors welcomed him.

As he took the nine cement steps up to the front, his smile grew. Today was the day.

The dedication.

He slipped his key into the door, unlocked it, and opened it to the eight-sided entryway. The smell of lemon oil—which he'd used to detail and polish all the wood in the building—filled his nose.

The new construction was full of rich wood trim. From the hand-carved banisters on the multi-angled staircase that led to the daylight basement, to every window and door in the place, the craftsmanship was of the highest quality.

As he closed the door, he took a long slow breath and let the true aroma of the library take over.

The unmistakable smell of books.

Lots of books.

More than four thousand tomes filled the shelves. He'd cataloged, placed, and *knew* each one of them.

Breathing deep of the scents he loved and the satisfaction of a job well done, he filled his lungs and let his chest puff out. Just a bit. This moment was worth it. No one was around to see him anyway.

In a few hours, they would open the doors and hold the dedication ceremony. And in a couple weeks, the library would be open to the public. There were still furnishings and decorations to bring in and many little projects to do. Thankfully, he wasn't in charge of all that. The women of the Ladies Library Association were handling that side of things.

He strode toward the front circulation desk, where he would make his place every day. He turned on the light, then made a circle under the dome of the entry. Each window and door in the place had a beautiful, butted head casing with a hand-carved rope pattern in it. They drew the eye upward to the dome and high ceilings—the visualization of knowledge and higher learning. The oak floors shone in the light. He could imagine hearing footsteps throughout the library of those eager to read and learn.

He made his way to his desk, shed his coat and hat, and hesitated.

Kate.

Would his sister come today? He'd sent a note out to the ranch, but he hadn't heard back. It had been quite a surprise to come home and find Kate married. To a fellow Mark had never heard of. The man wasn't even from Kalispell.

But Harvey Monroe must be a decent guy if Dad had agreed to the wedding.

Dad . . .

Mark let out a deep sigh. Things hadn't been great between them lately. If he was honest, things hadn't been all that good since Mark left for college. Especially since he hadn't come home to the ranch after his schooling. But he was back now. He could make amends. Spend time with his family. And hopefully prove to his father that what he did was important.

A knock on the front door drew his gaze. He checked his watch. Wasn't even seven yet. Who could that be?

Mark strode to the door and unlocked it, then opened it a few inches.

"Mr. Andrews." The gangly kid handed him an envelope through the space. "Your father asked me to bring this by."

Mark took the envelope. "Thank you."

But it was no use, the kid was already loping down the stairs.

With a tear to the envelope, Mark then pulled out a piece of his dad's ranch stationery.

Mark,

I am calling a family meeting this evening. It is imperative that you be in attendance. 6:00 p.m. sharp.

Dad

Mark walked back to his desk and set the missive down. Just like Dad to demand an audience. So much for hoping that his family would come to the dedication today. He hadn't seen them since he returned—even though he'd sent several messages out to the ranch. Perhaps Kate would come. Clearly, he wouldn't see his father there.

Shaking his head against the negative thoughts, he refocused his attention on the excitement of the day.

He could deal with his father later.

~~~

RIVER VIEW RANCH • ANDREWS FAMILY RANCH • TEN MILES NORTH OF KALISPELL

"I've come to a decision."

Angus Andrews placed his hands on the arms of his favorite leather wingback chair and narrowed his eyes. Even though they were clear and full of fire—as always—they couldn't hide the fact that Dad was aging. A lot.

More than Mark could have imagined.

He sent a glance to his sister. When Kate had answered

the door, she'd hugged him tight and introduced him to her husband, but Dad hadn't given him as much as a how-are-you before insisting they all sit for the family meeting.

The man hadn't changed a bit. Whatever he said was law.

Kate took her seat next to Harvey and sent Mark a sympathetic look.

"This is how things will go. Kate and Harvey will continue running the ranch like they have been. All the day-to-day, hands-on work. Mark will take over the books and the management side of things. With all his college education, he must have some good insight into how we can grow. Kate and Mark will be equals in this endeavor. This is your ranch now. I'm getting too old and haven't been feeling all that great. I need to hand everything over to you two." Dad thrummed his fingers on his knee.

Mark had been expecting this from his father in the years to come, but not so soon. He'd hoped for some time to settle in and have a chance to prove himself. How was he supposed to answer his father honestly and honor him at the same time? "I'm not sure I will have time for all that, Dad. My work at the library will keep me busy."

His father grimaced. He waved off Mark's words. "After a time, I'm sure you'll be back here permanently, otherwise you wouldn't have come home. Get the library going, and then come back where you belong."

The man never listened. Never. As much as Mark hated the temper he'd inherited from his Scottish father, he let it seep to the surface. "I came back home, yes, but my job is the director of the library." There. At least he didn't allow it to boil over.

"Your *job* is to do what your father says." Dad's right hand pointed out the window. "I built all this for you. Don't be ungrateful."

Mark did a silent count to ten. "Kate is more than capable of running the business end and the physical end now that she has Harvey. You have plenty of hired ranch hands. She lives for this place. You know that."

"This ranch is for *both* of you. Now stop arguing with me." Red infused his father's face.

Enough. The ordering had to stop. "Dad, I'm the director of the library." Was he wrong to—in essence—tell his father no? Was he dishonoring the only parent he had left?

"Don't be so contrary, young man." His father pushed to his feet and shoved a finger at him.

Mark stood as well but kept his tone low. Forceful, but low. "You never listen. I thought after all these years things would be different." He stepped toward his sister and leaned down to give her a hug. "Come see me soon?"

"Of course." Unshed tears glistened in her eyes.

He turned his gaze to his new brother-in-law. "It was nice to meet you. I'm sorry for the circumstances, but perhaps we could chat at the library sometime?"

Harvey gave him a sympathetic smile. "Nice to meet you too. Next time I'm in town, I'll look you up."

Mark headed toward the door without another glance at his father. It was for the best.

"Don't you walk out on me, Cowboy!"

The words halted his feet. He couldn't—wouldn't—look back. His face toward the door, he kept his words calm. "I'm not walking out, Dad. I'm giving us both some space so I don't lose my temper and say things I will regret. My mind is made up. I never wanted to run the ranch. I appreciate all you put into this place, I do. But you know I don't love it like Kate does."

"Always choosing books over your family, aren't you?"

As silly as the words were, they still stung. Mark spun around. "I'm not choosing *anything* over you, Dad. I thought you would be happy and *proud*. I've worked hard for this. I've been given an incredible opportunity. And I'm back home where I can spend time with all of you." As his gaze spanned the room, from Dad's fury to Kate's anguish to Harvey's discomfort, his heart twinged.

Dad fisted his hands. "Proud? When you've wasted ten years gallivanting around doing whatever you pleased. I allowed it, but now it's time to come home and do your duty. I didn't raise a quitter."

No. He would not let the words that sprang to mind have their entrance to his heart. Dad didn't mean it. The heat of the moment always brought out the worst in him and he said things for dramatic effect. How often had he and Kate joked about their father's bluster?

Kate held up a hand toward each of them. "I think we all need to sit back down. Perhaps have some dinner and cool our tempers."

Dad shook his head. "No. I'm not sitting down to dinner with him. Is that still your answer, Mark? You gonna tell me no again?"

Mark took a long breath and then exhaled. "I'm sorry, Dad. But my answer is no."

"Fine!" His father's roar echoed off the walls of the room. "Do whatever you want. Kate will inherit the ranch. From this day forward, you're disowned. You hear me?"

"I heard you. I'm guessing all of Kalispell heard you." As much as Mark tried to keep his voice under control, the words burst out of his mouth in equal volume to his father's. He stomped out of the room.

Why had he ever come home?

He couldn't sleep. He kept getting up to pace the room while the events of the evening replayed in his mind. Why couldn't Dad see Kate's passion for the ranch and be grateful?

Especially now that she was married to a husband who seemed to love the ranch too.

Mark pulled back the drapes and gazed out into the darkness. There was so little sunlight these days. Winter had brought its long, dark nights. At least the dedication ceremony had gone well. The people of Kalispell seemed more than pleased to have the new library in place. A crowd had waited outside in the cold, they'd been so excited. Two schoolteachers from the local high school even made arrangements to bring their classes over to learn about the Dewey decimal system.

He let the curtains fall into place and went back to the bed. Sat on the edge. Mark prayed. For wisdom. For healing. He didn't want to hurt his dad or dishonor him, but he'd made a commitment to the town—and to God—regarding the library.

"Lord, I need wisdom to deal with this matter. I love my father, but I love my work at the library as well. Since Dad paid for me to go to college, I thought he understood my passion and the plans I had for the future. Plans I feel certain are ones that You have ordained for me. If I'm in the wrong, please help me to see that and be willing to acknowledge it. Please show me what to do."

Every last bit of anger he'd held onto from the evening dissipated. The whole ride home, he'd muttered under his breath about his father's outburst and how the older man was clearly in the wrong. What a waste of time and energy.

And what irony to accuse his father when he'd been equally wrong in his response.

"God, I'm ashamed of my behavior toward my dad, but he brings out the worst in me. Help me to bite my tongue when I need to. Which is probably a lot more than I think." He blew out his breath between his lips.

Why was his relationship with his father so full of conflict?

Why couldn't they understand and accept each other? Was the only way to rectify that to give up everything he'd worked for—his hopes and dreams . . . ?

Mark's throat tightened. Could it be? He bowed his head, but his heart hurt as he prayed, "Is that what You want me to do, God?"

Kimberley Woodhouse (KimberleyWoodhouse.com) is an award-winning, bestselling author of more than thirty fiction and nonfiction books. Kim and her incredible husband of thirty-plus years live in Colorado, where they play golf together, spend time with their kids and grandbaby, and research all the history around them.

Sign Up for Kimberley's Newsletter

Keep up to date with Kimberley's latest
news on book releases and events by signing up for her email list at the link below.

KimberleyWoodhouse.com.

FOLLOW KIMBERLEY ON SOCIAL MEDIA

Kimberley Woodhouse @KimberleyWoodhouse @KimWoodhouse

More from Kimberley Woodhouse

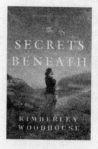

Anna Lakeman has spent her life working alongside her paleontologist father. When they find dinosaur bones, a rich investor tries to take over their dig. As Anna fights for recognition of her work and reconnects with an old beau, tensions mount and secrets are unburied. How can they keep the perils of the past from threatening their renewed affection?

The Secrets Beneath
TREASURES OF THE EARTH #1

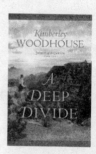  

Kimberley Woodhouse presents a dramatic historical romance series set at the El Tovar Hotel, which overlooks the majesty of the Grand Canyon. Seamlessly combining adventure, romance, and faith in the Gilded Age era, you will be turning the pages until the very end.

SECRETS OF THE CANYON:
A Deep Divide, A Gem of Truth, A Mark of Grace

✦ BETHANYHOUSE